M000199838

PRAISE FOR KATIE MacALISTER'S MATCHMAKER IN WONDERLAND ROMANCES

"Gut-wrenchingly funny! . . . If you want romance, some hilarious sex scenes, a bit of a mystery, and to have a goofy grin . . . then by all means read this book!"—*Open Book Society*

"Charming, sexy, and laugh-out-loud funny."—*Fresh Fiction*

"As entertaining as the romance, comedy of dialogue and action, and amusing cast of characters prove to be . . . the intriguing underlying setting and mystery provide something extra for the reader to enjoy."—*Heroes and Heartbreakers*

"Witty, charming, and erotically tender . . . [a] sparkling romance."—*Publishers Weekly*

"Hilarious and seductive in all the right places . . . a funny, adventurous, sensuous romance with something for everyone."—*Fresh Fiction*

"Mutual attraction, madcap adventures, and sexy fun ensue. This delightfully fluffy romance . . . is the perfect antidote to the blues."—*Booklist*

ALSO BY KATIE MACALISTER

Dark Ones Series
A GIRL'S GUIDE TO VAMPIRES
SEX AND THE SINGLE VAMPIRE
SEX, LIES, AND VAMPIRES
EVEN VAMPIRES GET THE BLUES
BRING OUT YOUR DEAD (NOVELLA)
THE LAST OF THE RED-HOT VAMPIRES
CROUCHING VAMPIRE, HIDDEN FANG
UNLEASHED (NOVELLA)
IN THE COMPANY OF VAMPIRES
CONFESSIONS OF A VAMPIRE'S GIRLFRIEND
MUCH ADO ABOUT VAMPIRES
A TALE OF TWO VAMPIRES
THE UNDEAD IN MY BED (NOVELLA)
THE VAMPIRE ALWAYS RISES

DRAGON SEPT SERIES
YOU SLAY ME
FIRE ME UP
LIGHT MY FIRE
HOLY SMOKES
DEATH'S EXCELLENT VACATION (SHORT STORY)
PLAYING WITH FIRE
UP IN SMOKE
ME AND MY SHADOW
LOVE IN THE TIME OF DRAGONS
THE UNBEARABLE LIGHTNESS OF DRAGONS
SPARKS FLY
DRAGON FALL
DRAGON STORM
DRAGON SOUL
DRAGON UNBOUND

DRAGON HUNTER SERIES
MEMOIRS OF A DRAGON HUNER
DAY OF THE DRAGON

BORN PROPHECY SERIES
FIREBORN
STARBORN
SHADOWBORN

Time Thief Series
TIME THIEF
TIME CROSSED (SHORT STORY)
THE ART OF STEALING TIME

Matchmaker in Wonderland Series
THE IMPORTANCE OF BEING ALICE
A MIDSUMMER NIGHT'S ROMP
DARING IN A BLUE DRESS
PERILS OF PAULIE

Papaioannou Series
IT'S ALL GREEK TO ME
EVER FALLEN IN LOVE
A TALE OF TWO COUSINS

Contemporary Single Titles
IMPROPER ENGLISH
BIRD OF PARADISE (NOVELLA)
MEN IN KILTS
THE CORSET DIARIES
A HARD DAY'S KNIGHT
BLOW ME DOWN
YOU AUTO-COMPLETE ME

Noble Historical Series
NOBLE INTENTIONS
NOBLE DESTINY
THE TROUBLE WITH HARRY
THE TRUTH ABOUT LEO

Paranormal Single Titles
AIN'T MYTH-BEHAVING

Mysteries
GHOST OF A CHANCE

Steampunk Romance
STEAMED

DARING IN A BLUE DRESS

A MATCHMAKER IN WONDERLAND NOVEL

Katie MacAlister

FAT CAT BOOKS

Teri Robinson is a wonderful woman who saves animals, cherishes her family, and has a wicked sense of humor. It's with much appreciation for her fine llama sensibilities, her maker talents, and her love of mustaches that I dedicate this book to her.

ONE

"If there is anything worse than a sister-in-law afflicted by pregnancy hormones," Emanuel Alden Ainslie commented to his brother, "it's a sister-in-law afflicted by pregnancy hormones while planning to marry off every available male within a five-kilometer range."

"Don't be ridiculous," Elliott Ainslie, eighth Baron Ainslie, scoffed, watching with a smile as Alice sat chatting with the dowager baroness on the newly rebuilt stone verandah.

Alden was a bit jealous of the emotion behind that smile, although he certainly wouldn't mention that. Not now. Not when Alice had decided that matchmaking was her new hobby.

"She's not trying to pair off every unattached male," Elliott continued. "Just you lot. She said, and I believe I'm paraphrasing her accurately, that there was no sense in Mum and Dad's adopting ten children if she—Alice—couldn't find her many brothers-in-law women to make them all as happy as she made Gunner and me."

Alden looked from his eldest brother, Elliott, to the second eldest, Gunner. The three men had climbed to the top of the restored tower in order to verify the recent repair work had been done according to Elliott's expectations. "I must have missed the part where Alice found Lorina for you, Gun. I thought she was part of that archaeology show that filmed here last year."

"She was," Gunner answered, smiling when his wife of six months strolled out to join the other two ladies as they sipped lemonade, ate a copious amount of seedcake—the current focus of Alice's food cravings—and made plans for god only knew what. "Alice is stretching it a bit to claim our meeting as one of her triumphs, but Lorina had met her some years ago, so we don't mind if she adds us to her matchmaking curriculum vitae."

Alden peered over the edge of the tower and looked down at the three women on the verandah. Although Alice had been installed at the castle as its chatelaine for more than a year, he'd met her only half a dozen times. She was pleasant enough, as was Gunner's bride, but of late . . . He sighed. "I could do without her turning her sights on me."

"Who? Alice?" Elliott stopped smiling at his wife and glanced at Alden. "I thought you liked her."

Alden sensed the undercurrent of warning in Elliott's voice. "I do like her. She's funny. I like a sense of humor in a woman. But . . . it's just . . . you know me. I'm not very comfortable around women."

"You're shy, that's all," Gunner said, glancing at his mobile phone. "It's nothing you can't overcome with a little work. Try one of those speed-dating setups. That will force you to meet a large number of women, so many you will have to be extroverted by sheer act of preservation."

Alden grimaced. There was nothing worse than speed dating that he could think of short of gelding or global nuclear war, and frankly, he'd question the war's being as bad as the idea of meeting a bunch of strangers, especially female strangers. "Can't Alice pick on one of our other brothers? Surely some of them aren't dating anyone."

"She could, and she no doubt will at some point, but for now, she's insisting that it's time you settle down."

"You're over thirty, Alden," Gunner said with a nod. "You're not getting any younger."

"Exactly. And more to the point, Alice is pregnant," Elliott said as if everyone in the immediate area didn't already know that. "She has . . . fancies. And if one of those fancies is to find a woman for the next brother, chronologically speaking, then, by god, you are going to humor her."

"Josiah is older than me," Alden protested. "She should be focusing on him, and letting me get on with life."

"He's only a few days older than you, and since he's out of the country, Alice decided it was time you were made deliriously happy."

Alden made a face. "But I don't want to be deliriously happy! I just want to be left alone."

"To do what?" Gunner asked him, the men slowly making their way down the stone spiral staircase to the ground floor. "Go back to university? You've already earned more degrees than all the rest of us put together."

"I like learning new things," Alden said stubbornly. "There's nothing wrong with having curiosity, and wanting to learn more about life, you know."

"There is when you are part of the drain on the already stressed estate income," Elliott said firmly. "We've had this out already, Alden—I simply can't support you any longer."

"Which is why I'm flipping Bestwood Hall. I should make a packet off of it."

"Bestwood," Gunner said with an obvious roll of his eyes. "That monstrosity. Whatever possessed you to take every last pound you had and invest it in a decaying old house out on the edge of nowhere?"

"And more importantly, why do you think you can sell it at profit?" Elliott, the more practical brother, asked as they emerged into the sunshine of the early-summer day. "If no one but you was willing to buy it, why do you think slapping a bit of paint around will increase the value?"

"The solicitor said that Lady Sybilla sold the house to me because she liked my name," Alden said with as much dignity as he could muster. "I'm sure there were any number of other interested parties. In fact, I know there were— the estate agent who put the deal together for me said that someone had asked if I was willing to part with it. And that was less than a week after I closed on the sale. So, you see, you annoying brothers of mine, I'm not the fool you think I am."

"Is that so?" Elliott paused and tipped his head to the side. "How much was the offer?"

"Well . . . as to that . . ." Alden gave a little cough.

"As I thought. Less than what you paid for it?" Elliott asked.

"Perhaps." Alden tried to look down his nose at his eldest brother, but unfortunately, at that moment they'd emerged onto the verandah, and both Elliott and Gunner had all their attention focused on their respective women.

Once again, Alden was aware of a little pang of jealousy. No, not jealousy, he decided as he strolled over to the table and accepted a glass of lemonade. Envy. Perhaps it wouldn't be so bad if Alice was to find a woman for him. Perhaps the hellish nightmare of meeting someone new wouldn't be quite so terrible if Alice prepared the ground for him. Perhaps . . .

"Alden!" Alice said brightly, pushing a white metal chair at him. "Just the man I wanted to see. Now, I promised you I'd find a woman for you, and I've done it."

Perhaps he was out of his mind.

Panic swamped him at the thought of a woman expecting him to be romantic. To court her. Hell, even the thought of dinner with a woman made his palms sweat. He gulped down the lemonade, thrust the glass onto the table, and said hurriedly, "No time to chat. Must dash. Have to be at Bestwood first thing in the morning, and I have to pack."

"But—you haven't heard anything about the woman I found for you," Alice said, a frown on her brow.

"Later," he said loudly over his shoulder, bolting for the nearest door.

"I'll send her down to Bestwood Hall to meet you," Alice called after him. "She'd probably like to help—"

The slam of the library door thankfully cut off the rest of her comments. Alden hurried up the stairs to the small room at the back of the castle that had traditionally been his when he was in residence.

"Stupid, stupid, stupid," he said aloud, thrusting various pieces of clothing into a couple of suitcases. "You're a grown man. It's just stupid that the thought of meeting women puts you in such a panic. Gunner's right—you need to just get a grip, go to a bar, and start talking to the nearest woman."

A little shudder ran through him at that thought. He swept through the room, dumping books, photos of family, and his collection of antique astronomical equipment into his two bags, all the while lecturing himself on the futility of being such an idiot. The lecture did little good—he'd been over it all so many times before—but the familiarity of it provided an odd sort of comfort, at least enough that his heart was no longer racing, nor were his hands shaking by the time he got his bags loaded into the Mini Cooper that he'd bought from a former university roommate.

"You're not leaving now, are you?" Elliott asked a few minutes later when Alden ran him to earth in the room that Elliott used as his office. He was seated at a laptop, and was no doubt writing away on his latest book. "I thought you were leaving in the morning. Surely you can stay to dinner."

"It's better if I'm off now. It'll take me almost eight hours to drive to Bestwood, and if I get in late tonight, I'll be ready to start the renovations first thing in the morning."

Elliott rose from his desk and came around it, embracing Alden in a bear hug. "You don't have to date this woman, you know."

"What woman?" Alden asked, a spike of panic shooting through him. Dear god, had Alice brought the woman to Ainslie Castle during the time he'd been packing?

"Alice's old college friend. The one she thought would be perfect for you. I know the last thing in the world you want to do right now is think about dating, but I'd appreciate it if you were polite to her when she shows up at your eyesore."

Alden made a face. "That's what I need, a woman hanging around expecting me to entertain her when I will have loads of work ahead of me. Couldn't Alice—"

"No. Trust me, this is the best way. If you don't like her—and love Alice as I do, I have to admit that she's not necessarily the great matchmaker she thinks she is—then you can simply cry off by telling the woman you have work to do. Just show her around the house—that's all I ask. You can do that for us, can't you?"

"I suppose," Alden replied, aware he sounded ungracious. "It's not that I have anything against your wife. It's just . . ."

Elliott gave him another hug, then clapped a hand on his shoulder, and walked out to the back drive with him. "I know. It's not easy for you. Just don't try so hard to be a scintillating conversationalist."

Alden laughed. "I'd settle for being able to talk without my tongue twisting around itself."

"You're a smart man. You have the Ainslie charm, when you let people see it. Stop worrying so much about what others think and just be yourself."

"I try, El," he said, his shoulders slumping in defeat. "But it just doesn't come to me the way it does to the rest of you."

"Think of it as a game," Elliott said, stopping at the door to the car. "And, Alden?"

Alden opened the door and tossed in a small backpack. "Yes?"

Elliott smiled. "Stay out of trouble, all right? I'm tied up with this book, and the baby coming in a few months, and I really don't want to have to rescue you like I did Gunner."

"I have absolutely no intention in getting myself locked into the bowels of Bestwood Hall," Alden replied with much dignity.

"See that you don't."

Alden waved as he fired up the car, and, with a little spray of gravel that had Elliott shouting abuse, zoomed down the drive and off to his new life. Despite the threat of Alice's friend hanging over his head like a particularly depressing cloud, his spirits rose at the thought of what lay ahead of him.

"Bestwood," he said aloud, enjoying the way the word sounded. "Bestwood Hall. Not a manor, not an abbey, but a hall. Why, hello, how do you do? This? Yes, that's Bestwood Hall. I own it. I am the master of Bestwood Hall. Heh. That sounds like a Victorian melodrama: The Mystery of Bestwood Hall. The Ghost of Bestwood Hall. Big Bouncing Baby Bustles of Bestwood Hall."

He amused himself for a while with titles; then his mind drifted over the work that was before him. Buying the house wasn't difficult—he'd heard about it from Toby, one of his many former university roommates, who was now a solicitor dealing with complex wills and estates.

"You're looking for a house, right?" Toby had said some three months earlier, when Alden had run out of funds and been forced to take a job working under the table for a less-than-scrupulous builder. "Something you can fix up and sell for a profit?"

"I am," Alden said, a little flare of hope burning inside him. "But I don't have much capital. One of my biological relations left me a small amount in an antiquated trust, and my brother Elliott convinced the trustee to release the funds if they were used to purchase a property."

"Your biological . . . oh, that's right, you're adopted. I forgot that your family was . . ."

"Multicultural," Alden said, coming to Toby's rescue. "That's the politically correct term for Mum and Dad adopting kids from whatever country took their fancy. A few of my brothers are from Africa, a couple from what used to be the Eastern bloc, and the rest of us from assorted locations elsewhere. My biological family was from Scotland, and Mum kept in contact with them on my behalf until I was old enough to decide if I wanted to know them or not."

"And do you?" Toby asked, clearly intrigued.

"I would have if they hadn't all died off." Alden shrugged. "I didn't get to meet any of them, but that didn't stop a distant cousin from leaving me the little trust, albeit a frustrating one."

"I hate those trusts," Toby said in an acid tone. "The kind that are tied with the most annoying red tape that you can imagine. Just last week our senior partner dropped a heinous case on me involving not one but two entailments . . . but I digress."

"Do you have a house for me to look at?" Alden asked, hoping against hope that the property would be within his means, both monetarily and with regard to renovation. "Where is it? More importantly, how much is it?"

"It's an old house—Tudor, I think—although I don't know that you'd want it. It's barely habitable. The old man who owned it was not only a miser but a recluse. He lived there for more than eighty years, along with his wife and a couple of crusty servants, leaving behind a mountain of debts that his widow couldn't possibly pay in her lifetime. A local bank took charge of the house last year due to the debts, and I've just heard from an old friend at the bank that they're looking for a buyer."

"There's bound to be lots of people interested in a historical property," Alden protested, his hopes dashed. He rather liked the idea of restoring a Tudor house. It appealed to his fascination with history.

"Normally, I'd agree. But according to Tom Scott, my friend at the bank, the managers are trying to handle the sale for Lady Sybilla in such a way as to not upset her."

"That seems a bit odd. A bank caring about someone who's lost possession of their house, that is."

"Ah, but you aren't factoring in the element of ye old family retainer," Toby told him. "Tom says the bank managers insist on handling the situation with kid gloves. There's an old family connection, or something of that sort, I gather. So rather than putting the place on the market and fetching the highest price, they're looking for someone to agree to their terms so they can avoid the publicity that would go along with a public sale."

"The managers must really like the old lady," Alden said thoughtfully, wondering if he dared hope that his meager trust would cover the sale of a historic house and land.

"Well, there are conditions that go with the sale, of course," Toby said.

Alden nodded, even though his friend wouldn't see the gesture. "I had no doubt there would be. Something prohibitive, no doubt."

"Not horribly so, actually. Tom told me the gist of the restrictions. . . . I know I wrote it down, just in case you'd be interested. . . . Ah, here it is. The buyer must grant Lady Sybilla the right to stay on the estate in the gatehouse for the duration of her life. Also, the house can't be demolished with the purpose of rebuilding, and any restorations must be done in a manner appropriate to the style of the existing structures. All pretty benign restrictions, if you ask me."

"And how much are they asking for the house?"

Alden's eyes widened when Toby went into specifics. Buying the house would wipe out not only his trust, but also the carefully nurtured nest egg he'd built up over the past eighteen years. It wouldn't leave him with any funds to hire people to do restoration work, which meant he'd have to do it all himself.

"That's an awful lot of money," he said at last.

"Too much for you?"

"No." He thought for a few minutes more. "Is there . . . this is going to sound very crass, but are there any restrictions about selling the house once it's legally mine?"

"No," Toby said slowly, the rustle of papers evident. "No, I don't see anything about selling it. There's the stipulation that Lady Sybilla be allowed residence in the gatehouse for her lifetime, but other than that, I don't see anything that would keep you from selling. Do you plan on selling soon?"

"Not right away. What I thought I'd do is get the place fixed up. You know, renovate it, and maybe update a few things like the plumbing and heating, and then sell it."

"Ah. What the Americans call 'flipping a house.' Very smart, if you ask me. Although you'd have to take into account Lady Sybilla's presence on the estate."

"Yes, well, without intending to be either heartless or crass, in all likelihood, it'll take me a year or two to fix the house up if I have to do it by myself, and by then . . ."

"By then Lady Sybilla would have gone to her just reward," Toby finished for him. "A very valid point, Alden. Very valid indeed, and I can't see anyone taking issue with you for selling the place once she's gone."

And thus it had come about that the bank invited him to tour the house and grounds, and after a whirlwind tour through both—without catching sight of Lady Sybilla, who evidently rested in the afternoon—his offer was approved.

"Today it's all mine," he said to himself as he drove west, the sun dipping low until a rich, velvety navy blue began to claim the sky. "I'm a homeowner. A hall owner. I'm Alden Ainslie of Bestwood Hall. . . . At least I am for the present. No telling where I'll be once I fix the house up. After all, this could be the start of a brand-new career. People make millions doing this sort of thing—why can't I? It's just a matter of fixing things up to look nice, and then capitalizing on the market. Yes, this is going to be good. It's going to be very good."

The optimism stayed with him for three hours, until his transmission decided it had enough and failed completely, stranding him for the night in a small town. He left a message with the solicitor's office, where he was to have picked up the keys to Bestwood, and settled down as best he could in a dingy hotel located across the street from the car repair shop.

"Not an auspicious start," he told himself as he eyed the sagging bed. "But that's not a bad thing. Things can only go up from here."

There were times when he was astounded with just how unprescient he could be.

TWO

"Hallelujah, you're leaving! Oh dear, I didn't mean it that way, Mercy. I just meant hallelujah. You know, kind of a lesser hallelujah. Hallelujah minus a few points of exclamation, if you will. Erm. You know?"

I smiled and stuffed the last of my clothing into the duffel bag that had gone through many years with me. It was faded in spots, was torn on the end flaps, and had many stains acquired from various roommates and the inevitable accidents that come with living in confined spaces with numerous people. In other words, it was a good visual representation of myself: a bit worn, having seen a lot of life, and definitely not stylishly attractive. "It's OK, Kim. I know what you mean. You've been nothing but accommodating, letting me stay with you and Rafe when I know you'd rather be by yourselves."

"It's not that we don't love having you here—lord knows, you do the bulk of the housework, and it's going to be a nightmare having to do all that again—but I'm thinking of you, I really am. You need to find yourself, really find yourself. Find what makes you happy, and what you want to do with your life."

"Well, that's the big question, isn't it?" I smiled at my friend. I'd met her a year ago, when we both were attending a criminal justice class at a London university.

She made a face. "You have been to enough universities. . . . Couldn't you pick a degree and find a job doing that?"

"Doing what?"

"Whatever your degree is. Would be." She sighed, and made a frustrated gesture. "Whatever job would be pertinent to the degree that you don't yet have, but would have if you stuck it through to the end."

"It's never quite that easy," I said, cramming the few precious books I had left into the bag, grunting a little as I forced the zipper up its pregnant, bulging length. "Technically, I have a lot of credits in a number of subjects, everything from English to medieval history, phys ed, and of course criminal justice. But that doesn't mean I'm qualified to get a job that pays more than minimum wage."

Kim raised an eyebrow and looked doubtful.

"OK, OK, I could probably get a job, but not one I'd like," I said in response, hating the fact that people didn't understand my need to learn everything there was to be learned. "If only I could get your universities to give me more financial aid, everything would be groovy."

"Groovy?" Kim snorted. "Your liberal arts are showing. And do you really think that more time at uni is what you need? Look at this temporary tutoring job you found."

"I didn't actually find it—an old friend did," I interrupted. "She knew I was desperate, and I didn't like the other option she found for me."

"Regardless, it serves to illustrate my point—you could become a teacher, a proper teacher, not just a summer tutor."

I shuddered. "Those kids . . . oh, Kim, those kids! Their mother was bad enough at the interview with her pretentious sneering, and trying her best to impress me with all the money her husband has, but her kids! They were hell spawn."

"I'm quite certain they're not that bad," Kim said with gentle chiding.

"You didn't see them. Natalia, the seven-year-old, spent the entire time her mother and I were chatting racing around on her Rollerblades, screaming at everyone in the park. And not shrieks of laughter—the kid has a worse potty mouth than my father does. And the nine-year-old Jocelyn was even worse. He actually threw a tantrum, an honest-to-god tantrum, when some other child dared to do a skateboard flip or twist or whatever that Jocelyn couldn't duplicate. The child needs desperately to be in therapy. Both of them do, and those are the little monsters I'm supposed to spend three months tutoring. You know why they need tutoring? Because they're so out of control not even their expensive private school can cram learning into their thick heads."

"Ouch," Kim said, flinching, but I wasn't sure if it was in response to my attack on the kids I'd agreed to teach or to my situation. I hoped it was the latter. "Still, it's a job, and you never know what doors it may open. If the parents are as rich as you say—"

"The car that picked her and the monsters up had its own driver."

"—if they are that well-off, then perhaps they can help you find a job that you will enjoy more. I agree that the children don't sound pleasant, but perhaps they just need a firm hand. A sort of Mary Poppins figure to come into their lives and turn them into pleasant little people."

"Mary Poppins I am not, but thanks for the pep talk." I checked around the small spare room that I'd been occupying for the last three months—much to Kim's boyfriend Rafe's growing unhappiness—and hefted my bag. "And thank you for letting me stay with you while I tried to get my feet under me. It was a nightmare having that bastard scammer wipe out my bank account, feeble as it was, and you made all the difference."

She gave me a knowing look. "Next time, don't fall for a hard-luck story and let someone have access to your personal information so he can steal money out of your account."

"Oh, trust me, lesson learned," I said, giving her a hug made awkward by the approximately fifty pounds of bag slung across my back.

"Although it certainly would have been easier for you to simply call home—"

I lifted a hand in acknowledgment, and staggered out of the room, down the stairs to the exit of the building, Kim accompanying me as far as the street. "That is not an option. Happy two's-companying, Kim. Be sure to thank Rafe for me—I appreciate you guys putting up with me more than you'll know."

"You're very welcome. Now go turn those poor children's lives around, and enjoy not trying to force more facts into your head." She smiled, giving me a little wave as I started down the street toward the nearest tube stop. "And network with your new bosses. Maybe they can help you find the perfect job. You need to do something more with your life than just go to school!"

Her words stuck with me for the next hour as I took the train that would carry me off to the coast of Cornwall, where my much-dreaded summer job awaited.

"The problem is," I said aloud, staring blindly out the window of the train, where it sat in the bustling station, the noises of thousands of people passing through the confined spaces thankfully muffled by the windows, "I like learning."

"Oh, sorry, is this taken?" A woman paused at the open doorway to the compartment in which I sat.

I glanced around the empty plush maroon seats, three of which faced another bank of three, and said, "No, not at all. I was just talking to myself."

"I do that a lot, too," the woman said, hefting a couple of suitcases onto the white metal racks arranged above the seats. She gave a quick look around the compartment, adding, "I haven't seen a train like this since I was small."

"From what the ticket person said, I gather they had some mechanical issues, and had to pull a few old compartments out of retirement. I think it's kind of fun, actually. It's very Agatha Christie, don't you think? I half expected to find a body under the seat, and a box of stolen jewels hidden in the luggage rack."

She gave a tight, brief smile and took the seat opposite me, pulling out her phone and moodily tapping at it before setting it on the seat next to her. Distantly, a metallic voice droned some instruction or information, wholly incomprehensible. "They are different, aren't they? I suppose these old compartments let people talk more than the row seats we normally get."

"Exactly. I'm Mercy, by the way. Mercedes, actually, but everyone calls me Mercy." I didn't offer my hand, not because I felt she'd spurn it, but because she was tapping at her phone again, clearly preoccupied.

"Janna," she said abruptly, then looked up, a frown pulling her brows together. "Sorry, that's my name. Are you Canadian or American?"

"Both, actually. My mother was from British Columbia, but my dad is a Californian. I was studying history of law here in London, but ran out of funds, so now I'm heading to Cornwall to start a new job." I stopped, realizing I was doing the oversharing thing that caused so many Americans to be the butts of jokes by folks less willing to blab out every little nuance of their life to strangers.

"Oh?" She looked up from her phone. Her face was tight with some worry or concern. "Sorry, I'm scattered today. Geoff, my partner—well, ex-partner, I guess you could say—he's gone off to Ibiza to work at a resort, and now he's telling me that he made a mistake leaving me, and I should go out there with him."

I settled back into the well-worn (but still oddly comfortable) seat, prepared to enjoy the human drama that never failed to intrigue. "Goodness. Ibiza sounds exotic and sunny."

"It is." She glanced out of the window, her lips a thin line. The train gave a lurch and then started forward, rolling us past the mass of humanity that filled the station. "I wish I knew what to do. We were together for four years, and one day it all fell apart...." She stopped and gave me a chagrined look. "Sorry. I'm babbling."

"No, not at all. I don't mind if you want to talk. I'm told I have a very sympathetic manner, probably due to the two years of psychology I took back at the University of Calgary."

She looked a bit doubtful, but evidently the promise of a sympathetic ear was too much, because within five minutes, she was telling me about her life, her hopes, and especially her plans of life with Geoff, which had been dashed when he ran away from her growing demands of commitment. "And now," she finished up some twenty minutes later, "now he says he can't live without me, and wants me to throw away everything and go to Ibiza with him."

"That's a tough situation," I said slowly, not wanting to give advice that wasn't desired (or needed). "I suppose there's pros and cons to consider."

"Not so many cons, that's the problem," she said miserably, glancing at her phone. "I really have nothing keeping me here. My roommates will replace me without any trouble. I haven't even started the job I'm on the way to, and it's only for the summer. And the resort where Geoff works sounds like heaven. He said I won't have any problem getting a job there."

"Sounds like your mind is already made up," I said.

She bit her lip. "I hate to leave Vandal in a lurch. That's the only bad part."

"Vandal?"

"The man who hired me for the summer. He's nice, if a bit of a flirt, and I hate to run off and leave them without the help they need." She eyed me for a minute. "You said you were going to Cornwall for a job, also?"

I made a face. "Unfortunately, yes. A friend set me up as tutor for a couple of spoiled kids with an impossible mother, and you're not thinking what I think you're thinking, because if you are, I'm quite likely to take you up on it."

She laughed. "Those must be some really spoiled children."

"You have no idea. What exactly is the job you're talking about?"

"General dogsbody, really. Taking tickets at a summer attraction, helping with costumes, fetching and carrying, that sort of thing. It doesn't pay much, but you do get room and board, and can keep any tips that float your way."

"How much is 'doesn't pay much,' if you don't mind my asking?"

Her phone chirruped again, instantly drawing her attention. She read the incoming text, and smiled. "He's so sweet now that he realizes what an idiot he'd been to leave."

I gave her a benevolent smile of my own. "Sounds like he's seen the error of his ways."

"He has." She looked up, her expression solidifying into one of determination. "I can't miss this opportunity. He's absolutely right in that we only have one life, and to dally in might-have-beens is just a waste. Here, let me give you Vandal's mobile number. I'll text him that I've had a change of plans, but that I've found a replacement."

"Hang on," I said, panicking when she started tapping on her phone. "Much as I'd like to dump my job, I can't do that without giving my employer a warning. She might be annoying, but I'd feel like a heel if I quit without giving notice."

Janna made a face. "That's terribly noble of you."

"Not really. I'm just a firm believer in karma and treating people how I want to be treated."

She thought for a moment, then scribbled out a phone number onto a torn bit of envelope that she extracted from her purse. "I'm going to give you Vandal's info anyway, just in case you can't stomach the family." She looked up. "Where are you going?"

"Treacher," I said, naming a small town on the coast.

"That's not far at all from Bestford, just a kilometer or two." She finished writing and handed me the paper. "Vandal and company are at a big old house. It's supposed to be very scenic, even if the house has seen better days."

I tucked away the paper, shaking my head a little as I did so. "I'm sure it's charming, but like I said, I can't quit a job when the woman hiring me is expecting me to show up. But I'll keep it in case everything goes pear-shaped."

"You do that." She looked up as the train slowed as it pulled into a suburb station, and tapped quickly on her phone. "If you don't mind, I'll text Vandal about you. What's your phone number?"

"I don't have one."

"Ah. Do you have any way to be contacted?"

I thought for a moment. "I suppose via my employer." I gave her the name and phone number.

"Excellent." She jumped up and grabbed her luggage, her purse, and the magazine she'd had with her. "I'll text Vandal that you're a possibility, but that you have to see how your other job goes first."

"You're really going to Ibiza?" I asked, following her to the aisle.

"I am." She hurried down the worn aisle, stopping to look back at me, her face alight. "Sometimes, you just have to do what feels right. Good luck, Mercy."

"Have a happy life with Geoff," I answered, waving when she dashed down the stairs to the platform.

I reclaimed my seat, smiling when a gaggle of school-girls filled my compartment, chattering inanely about some pop star or other. I bit my lip during the ride to Cornwall, wondering, as the miles slipped past us, whether I couldn't just call Mrs. Innes from the station and tell her I'd had a change of mind.

No, I told myself. You don't want to be that person. Give the job a chance. It might lead to other things, better things, and make everything worthwhile.

I didn't really believe the job would do anything but get me through the summer with enough money to return home to California, where I'd be in exactly the same straits I was in England, but that was the future, and if there was one thing I'd mastered, it was not to worry about what might be.

Mrs. Innes wasn't waiting for me at the station. I stood watching the handful of people toddle off to their houses, wondering if this was a portent of things to come, or just a matter of Mrs. Innes being delayed.

After half an hour of sitting around the tiny station by myself, I went into the town, and begged a lady at a small grocery shop to let me use her phone, calling my employer to find out what I should be doing.

A woman with a distinct Eastern European accent answered. "Hallo?"

"Hi, this is Mercy Starling. Mrs. Innes was supposed to pick me up at the train station a little bit ago, but I haven't seen any sign of her. Can you tell me if she's on her way?"

"Mrs. Ince no here. She in Greece."

"She's what?" I shook my head. "She can't be. She hired me to take care of her kids."

"Mrs. Ince in Greece," the woman insisted.

"But . . . what about the children? Jocelyn and Natalia? Are they there?" I had a wild thought that Mrs. Innes had run off to have a vacation and left her kids behind—she struck me as exactly that type of person. "I'm supposed to be tutoring them this summer."

"Oh. Tutor." There was a rustling of paper. "Have message for tutor. Message say no needed for three weeks. Come back then. Childrens in Greece with mama and papa."

Anger filled me then, anger at being so unimportant to Mrs. Innes when I had just talked myself out of dumping her because she didn't deserve to be treated that way. "Well, that solves that little dilemma," I said aloud. I'd just drop Mrs. Innes a note saying that I appreciated the job, but couldn't wait three weeks.

"Eh?" the shop woman said, turning from where she was helping a customer.

"Sorry, just talking aloud." I dug out a few more coins, and laid them on the counter. "Would you mind terribly if I made another call?"

"Not at all, luv." She scooped the coins up with a deft hand, and turned back to gossip with the lady who was waiting.

It took me a minute to dig out of my bag the scrap of paper with the number that Janna had written on it, but I dialed the number with only a minimum of grumbling under my breath.

"—to think I went to all the trouble, not to mention expense, of coming all the way to Cornwall—oh, hello. Is this Vandal?"

The voice that answered me was muffled, drowned out by the fuzzy white noise familiar to people on a busy motorway. "It is indeed. And you are?"

"My name is Mercy Starling. A woman named Janna—"

"Ah, you're Janna's friend who's going to take her place. Excellent. Can you get yourself to Bestford? I'm coming up from Dover with a load of equipment, but I won't be there until early evening."

I figured there had to be a train going that way, or at least a bus. If nothing else, Janna said it was only a couple of miles away—dragging my bag wasn't ideal, but given my present state of mind, it was better than staying here and fuming. "Sure. I'm at the town next to Bestford, so I should be able to make it there on my own."

"Great. Just ask the locals how to get to Bestwood Hall. There's a private road leading to the house itself, but if you have the bus drop you at the end of it, I'll pick you up on my way in."

"Sounds good. Um. I'm not super-clear on what the job is, other than kind of a general gofer situation. What exactly do you guys do? Janna didn't tell me other than saying something about performance."

Vandal's voice cut out as he started to speak, but I could have sworn he said something about medieval knights before the connection went dead. I stared at the phone for a moment, then spun around and marched over to the shop window, which held a variety of posters and advertisements. Sure enough, located right in the middle of notices of parish meetings, pony club summer parties, and house-cleaners looking for work was a colorful poster showing a man in full fourteenth-century plate armor, wielding a big-ass sword.

Join the Hard Day's Knights, read the headline. *Learn to fight the medieval way! Britain's premiere medieval combat full-contact troupe comes to Cornwall for a summer session of swordplay, archery, and medieval combat. Join us at Bestwood Hall for the day, or a week! Classes run hourly and weekly, with personalized instruction available.*

There was more, but I didn't stop to read it. I simply thanked the shop lady, grabbed my duffel bag and slung it over my back, and headed out to find a bus that would take me to the summer job to end all summer jobs.

It wasn't until about four that I finished navigating the convoluted network of buses that inexplicably took me to three different towns before dropping me off at my destination. I had a two-and-a-half-mile hike out to where Bestwood Hall was located, and by the time I turned off the paved road, and onto a graveled one bearing a sign that announced Bestwood Hall was a mere mile ahead, I was sweaty, my shoulder hurt where the duffel strap dug into it, and my legs felt like they were made of marshmallows.

"Screw it," I said, dropping the bag and plopping myself down onto it in a graceless heap. I stared balefully at large black wrought iron gates, one of which hung askew, like a bird with a broken wing. "I'm taking a rest. Hopefully Vandal will find me before I have to drag myself another mile."

Around me, sounds of wildlife could be heard; sitting quietly, I could hear at least ten different birdcalls and songs. A gentle lowing sound from the distance reminded me of the rurality of the area, and the fluffy little white blobs seen on a faraway hill bespoke the presence of more than just cows grazing the lush pastureland. Behind me, the grasses rustled mysteriously, and at one point, a sharp-eyed little brown face peered out at me.

"Ferret?" I asked the face. "Weasel? Stoat? I wish I knew the difference, but I haven't taken the zoology courses that I wanted, so I'm afraid I don't know what you are."

A low rumbling sound grew louder as I spoke, a car appearing down the road. The face considered me for another few seconds; then with a twitch of his whiskers, he was gone. I shifted my attention from the tall tangled grasses to the car, wondering if it was Vandal. When the car slowed down at the dirt road, I got to my feet, relief swamping me. I grabbed my bag and stepped out into the road, smiling gratefully when the car pulled to a stop in front of me.

"You have the best timing ever," I told him, crossing in front of the car to get to the passenger side, and shoving my bag into the backseat before taking my place. "I can't tell you how grateful I am to see you. I really was not looking forward to that mile walk, and I was getting to the point where I was explaining to the weasel or stoat about the zoology classes."

Vandal stared at me for a minute. "Er . . . you're a zoologist?"

"No, but I'd like to be one."

"Ah. A noble pursuit, I believe."

"It's interesting, that's for sure. But like I said, you have excellent timing. My feet hurt bad enough without having to do another mile."

"Another mile?"

I pointed to the sign. "It wouldn't be bad, except my bag weighs a ton."

He turned around in his seat to take a good look at my bag. "What's in it?"

"Just my stuff." I settled back in the seat with a sigh of comfort. "Things I need for the summer."

His eyes narrowed at me, and I had to admit, I was probably more aware of him than an employee should be of her employer. He looked like he was in his early thirties, with a slight case of stubble that made my knees feel a bit wobbly, a square chin, and a couple of dents on his cheeks that warned he might be the possessor of dimples. I sincerely hoped not—I had low enough tolerance to men with square chins and manly stubble, but if Vandal threw in dimples on top of it, then I'd have a hell of time keeping my libido under control.

Especially since it had been two years since I'd had a boyfriend.

Two long years.

"Things you need for the summer?" Vandal looked confused as he repeated what I'd said, his face suddenly clearing as he nodded. "Ah. You're here to . . . er . . . help me, yes?"

"That's right." I slid him a curious glance when he put the car into gear and began to bump his way down the somewhat rutted dirt road. Had he forgotten our conversation already? "I hope you don't mind about the substitution."

"Eh?" He risked a glance at me for a few seconds, then returned his attention to the road.

"You know, Janna. Since she was supposed to be here, but I'm here to do the job, instead. I appreciate you letting me come in her place."

"Ah. I didn't realize there were two of you. She's very resourceful."

"Who is, Janna?"

"No, my . . ." He waved a hand, the car bouncing hard when we hit a pothole, and then clutched the steering wheel with both hands. "My sister-in-law."

"Ah. That must be nice," I said agreeably, wondering what that had to do with the price of tea in China.

Vandal was silent for a few seconds, then gestured awkwardly, his voice growing more hesitant and stilted as he said, "I suppose if you're going to stay for a bit that I should warn you that the house is bound to be fairly uncomfortable. It needs a lot of work."

"That's OK. I'm used to roughing it." I slid a look at him out of the corner of my eyes. Had I said something to offend him? All of a sudden, he sounded . . . off. Like he didn't want me there. "My folks sent me to camp every summer, and you learn fast how to cope with a camp bed and a tent."

"Just so. I . . ." He coughed, and inadvertently jerked the car, slamming the brakes on, then muttering an apology before gripping the steering wheel so tight his knuckles were white. The car lurched forward again as he said, "I'm afraid I didn't catch your name."

"Mercedes Starling, but everyone but my dad calls me Mercy. Wow." I leaned forward when the road curved to the left, suddenly revealing the house where it sat surrounded by rather wild green lawns and hedges. "That's . . . that's impressive. Much more than I was expecting."

"It is pretty, isn't it?" Vandal said, his voice warming as he pulled to a (smooth, this time) stop so we could admire the view. He gazed at it, his attention wholly focused on the sight before us, and I couldn't blame him for staring. The house was old, as I'd expected, made of a lovely soft gray stone, with lots of recessed, narrow arched windows. The main entrance was set under a tower bedecked with a gorgeous series of stained-glass windows. To the right, a wing had been added—probably at a later date, since the windows didn't match that of the main house, but it, too, was of the same gray stone. Tall chimneys dotted the roofline, and I counted six pillars that seemed to be an afterthought of the designer (or, more likely, a later owner).

"It's lovely, just lovely," I agreed. We sat in companionable silence for a few minutes. "How old is it?"

"Mid–fifteen hundreds, for the main house. The front wing and the block to the north were added a century later. Evidently there was a south block that housed a power generator, but that blew up more than thirty years ago, so now the house is a bit off-balance, architecturally speaking. But still very nice, don't you think?" Vandal suddenly seemed to recall himself, for he shot me an unreadable look, cleared his throat, and, with a grinding of gears that had us both wincing, drove forward. I clutched the dashboard when we came to an abrupt stop at the entrance to the house. He looked like he wanted to say something, his Adam's apple bobbling up and down a couple of times, but after making an inarticulate noise of frustration, he simply got out of the car.

Great, I thought to myself. *Now he's back to being annoyed with me, and I don't have the slightest clue why.*

Vandal stared up at the house, his hands on his hips, as I got out of the car and hesitantly took a few steps toward him. I half expected him to say something brusque, but the look on his face was one of sheer pleasure. No, not pleasure—contentment, a quiet, soul-deep contentment. I had no idea why he was so happy all of a sudden. . . . Perhaps he had mercurial mood swings? Or maybe he liked houses? Or it could be that he was simply tired of being in the car, and was glad to be at his destination.

"There's a lot to be done to bring it up to a point where it can be lived in," he said, his eyes still on the house. I had a feeling he was talking more to himself than to me. "But to be honest, I'm looking forward to the work."

"You're going to work on the house?" I asked, pulling my duffel bag out of the car, and moving around the end of it to join him at the bottom of five shallow steps that led up to the double-door entrance. "Why?"

He shot me an irritated look. "Because it needs it. Evidently the previous owner did little with it other than have it wired for electricity, and installed bathrooms at the insistence of his wife. It's quite a daunting prospect, isn't it? Not the sort of thing that the casual person might wish to take on as a holiday."

I blinked at him for a second before turning back to consider the house. "Oh, I don't know. I've always felt that places like this have a presence of their own, a soul if you will. Something this old doesn't witness the parade of humanity going through it without absorbing a certain amount of it, don't you think? I imagine restoring it to its glory would be very satisfying." I reached out and patted the mossy stone balustrade that lined the steps. "I think the place would like to be done up. It has an air of genteel decay about it, doesn't it?"

"It's not decayed," he said, bristling, leaving me to momentarily mull over what I'd said to offend him now. "It just needs some work. And I'm not afraid of getting my hands dirty."

What a very odd man he was. "OK," I said slowly, wondering what I'd gotten myself into. Why hadn't I checked up on this Hard Day's Knights organization before I offered myself for the job? "I see your point, but I guess I just don't understand why you are so interested in working here. Is it some arrangement you made with the owner so you could hold your medieval fair here?"

"Medieval fair?" He turned to face me, his expression showing his confusion. "What are you talking about?"

"The medieval fair," I said slowly, beginning to have serious doubts about this job. "You know, the one you hired me for."

He blinked a couple of times, then ran a hand through his curly brown hair. "I didn't hire anyone, and I don't have a fair, medieval or otherwise."

"You're not Vandal?" I asked, taking a firm grip on my purse, prepared to snatch the container of pepper spray should the man go completely bonkers.

"No. I'm Alden Ainslie. I own this place." He frowned. "I take it that you were not sent here to be ... er ... be my ..."

To my surprise, a faint dusky pink darkened his cheeks when his words frittered away to nothing. I couldn't remember the last time I'd seen a man blush. I was amused by that, but my mind was focused on more important facts.

So this was Alden Ainslie, the owner of Bestwood Hall. How very interesting. "I don't know what you think I was sent here to do, Alden Ainslie, but I can assure you that I do not have any immoral or illegal intentions."

His cheeks darkened as he stammered, "No, I ... that's not what I ... I wouldn't presume ..."

"It's OK," I interrupted, feeling a man who could blush like that was not someone who was trying to pass off innuendos as commonplace conversation. "Forget it. What I'd like to know is where Vandal is."

"Who is Vandal?"

"The guy running the medieval fair that's taking place here."

"What?" His embarrassment clearly faded, because he added in a testy tone, "There is a medieval fair being operated on the grounds of Bestwood?"

"It's my first day, so I don't know a lot about it, but Janna—she's the woman I met on the train who told me about this job—she said that the fair had paid the owner money to let them use the garden area for their medieval camp. People come here to learn how to fight with swords, and basic archery, and other medieval-lite sort of stuff. I'm going to be the ticket taker, face painter, and general dogsbody."

"The owner rented out the grounds. . . ." He paused, his eyes suddenly opening wide as he spun on his heel. "She wouldn't dare!"

"Who wouldn't—" My words were cut off when Alden took off without a backward glance, loping across the drive and around the part of the house that jutted out toward us. He disappeared around the back.

I had a feeling the summer was going to be interesting. Especially if Alden was going to be around.

"Mmrowr," I said to myself, then smiled, hoisted my bag, and followed after him at a much more sober pace.

THREE

The back of the house opened onto a vista that was almost as impressive as the front. I'd seen many formal gardens in my time in England, but the expanse of green that lay before me wasn't anywhere near the word "formal."

"More like wild," I said to myself as I dropped my bag at the steps leading up to a stone verandah, and stood considering the expanse of green, unevenly mowed lawn that stretched to the left to two small outbuildings, and what looked like a stable. To the right, the lawn led to a wall of dark green, probably a hedge marking a smaller garden, and a large red and white striped marquee tent. A small marquee sat in front, with a wooden sign reading REGISTRATION leaning haphazardly against a card table. Over the top of the hedge, I could see another marquee, this one yellow and white.

The garden proper had no fountains, but did contain two flower beds that were messy with weeds, daisies, and several choked rosebushes. A stack of metal folding chairs lay next to them, along with several boxes, a couple of ice coolers, and a small round table at which sat a very old lady and a small woman with pink hair and her arm in a sling. Alden stood next to them.

I approached, the weed-bedecked gravel crunching underfoot as I walked across a drive that curved around one side of the house, swooped across the back, then swung toward the largest of the outbuildings.

"—have absolutely no right to do that, which I'm sure you know." Alden's voice was an amusing mix of sexy British-tinged bass, and irritation. "I'm sure my solicitor will agree."

"Young man," the old lady said in a rich, plummy voice of the generation born between world wars. I swear she enunciated each letter with exacting precision, her voice reeking of privilege and blue blood. "I do not know who you are, but I must ask you to stop berating me. It is unseemly in a gentleman, and not something I will tolerate in my own garden."

"It's not your garden any longer, Lady Sybilla," Alden said firmly, although he did drop the volume of his voice. "I know your solicitor contacted you last week to tell you when I would be arriving."

"I have no knowledge of what you speak," the old lady said, sniffing and looking away.

Pink Hair patted the old woman's arm while turning a frown on Alden. "That's OK, Lady Syb. Don't let him browbeat you."

"And just who are you?" Alden asked. I stopped beside him and offered a pleasant smile to everyone.

"Fenice Carson, not that it's any of your business," Pink Hair snapped. "I don't know who you are, but I don't think it's nice of you to accost Lady Sybilla like that."

"My name is Alden Ainslie, and I'm the owner of Bestwood Hall," Alden said tersely.

"Owner?" Fenice's eyes narrowed. "What do you mean, owner?"

"I mean that as of last week, I purchased Bestwood Hall from Lady Sybilla." He gave the old woman a look that included a raised eyebrow. "The terms of the sale included the proviso that she move from the main house to the gatekeeper's cottage, where I am obliged to provide housing for her until such time as she no longer needs it. She is not, however, still to be in residence in the house, nor is she supposed—

without my express permission—to make legal arrangements with vendors who wish to use the house or grounds."

"You talk like a solicitor," Fenice said in a voice that was fairly accusatory. "Are you one?"

"No, although I did two years of law. I decided it wasn't for me," Alden said, then turned to me. "What was the name of the man who you said hired you? Renegade? Rogue?"

"Vandal," I said.

"That's the fellow. Do you have his number? I'd like to tell him that any agreement he made with Lady Sybilla has been made null and void by the sale of the property to me, and that he needs to clear out his equipment immediately."

Fenice pursed her lips, then cleared her throat and forced a smile. "We've had an awkward introduction, haven't we? Shall we begin again? I'm Fenice Carson, co-owner and archery instructor for Hard Day's Knights, a medieval full-contact combat unit that my brother, Patrick, and I started a year ago. Would you like some tea?" She held up the teapot that sat before her and the elderly Lady Sybilla. "I don't believe I've met your friend?"

"Who? Oh." Alden looked oddly embarrassed when Fenice nodded toward me. I didn't know whether I should be amused or offended by such a reaction, and was just mulling that over when Fenice handed both Alden and me cups of tea. "This is . . ." He coughed, gestured toward me, and started again. "Her name is Mercy Starling. She said she works for the man named Scoundrel."

"Vandal," I corrected, and gave both ladies another smile.

"Really?" Fenice examined me with obvious doubt. "He didn't tell me about this. Patrick is Vandal, by the way. He has some silly notion that the nickname makes him irresistible to women, so don't feel like you have to use it. Mercy, you say?"

"Janna was supposed to have the job, but she went away to Ibiza, and my own summer job fell through with a seriously depressing crash, so I approached Vandal, and he said I could have the job."

"I see. That explains it, then, doesn't it?" She passed a plate of cookies to me.

"It explains nothing," Alden said, spurning the offer of cookies, and setting down his cup with enough firmness that it splashed tea onto the saucer. "It doesn't explain why I arrived to take ownership of my house—a house that is supposed to be depleted of humans—and instead I find not only Lady Sybilla clearly still in residence, but my back garden infested with medieval reenactors."

"We're not reenactors," Fenice said quickly. "Not in the sense you mean. We are a combat troupe. We put on shows sometimes, yes, but we also compete in a sport that is very real." She nodded toward her sling with her free hand. "And can be quite dangerous. I broke my collarbone two days ago at a training session with another group we help out from time to time. They had a bunch of stockbrokers from London learning how to use swords, and one of them didn't listen to the instructions, and I ended up with a cracked bone. I haven't told Patrick yet—he'll have a fit when he finds out, since it will leave us without an archery instructor—but I assure you that we are not simply a group who dresses up and pretends we live in the past. As for us packing up the equipment, I think you misunderstand the situation. We paid to be here, and I don't see that the sale of the house itself has anything to do with that agreement. Patrick has a contract with Lady Sybilla."

"Ouch," I said sympathetically. "You're an archer? At one point in time, I thought about getting a degree in physical education—"

"I'm sorry," Alden interrupted, putting a hand on my arm. "My apologies for cutting you off, Mercy, but am I to understand that you are refusing to take your things and leave?" The last was directed at Fenice.

"That's right." Fenice tipped her chin up. "We have an agreement, signed by the owner of Bestwood, that says we have rented this area for three weeks to use for our combat training school."

"I am the owner of Bestwood," Alden repeated, looking frustrated. His hair, full of dark chocolate brown curls that were shot through with dark honey strands, looked like it was standing on end.

"Now you are, but you weren't when we made the agreement."

Alden took a deep breath, and turned to Lady Sybilla. "Do you have anything to say about the situation?"

The old lady looked him over like he was a bit of undercooked dinner being offered for her inspection. She gave the impression that she was using one of those quizzing glasses the Regency folk loved so much. "I remember you. You're the lad who wants me to leave my family home."

"It was your husband's family home, not yours," Alden pointed out. "And I—"

"You want me to leave my adopted family home." Lady Sybilla gave another sniff. "You wish to throw me out onto the road where any vagabond could abuse me with his ruffian ways."

"Wow," I said, looking at Alden. "That's harsh, dude."

"Oh, for the love of . . . I don't want to toss her out into the road!" Alden gestured past what I assumed was the old stable block. "She has a home! A very nice home. I should know, because I had to pay for the house to be updated with fresh paint, and a herd of cleaning ladies that were in there for three days straight, and, of course, furniture moving, not to mention having the roof repaired."

"Oh." I looked at the elderly woman. "That seems pretty nice of Alden. Hi, I don't think we've been introduced. I'm Mercy."

"Lady Sybilla Baskerville, youngest daughter of the Earl of Glamgoran, and relic of the late Sir James Baskerville of Bestwood Hall," she replied in her stiff, very upper-crust voice. She offered me her fingers for a brief ladylike shake. "You have an air about you similar to that of my late sister Pamela."

"I do? Uh . . ."

"I always found Pamela very comforting. You will tell your young man that I do not wish to leave the home that has been mine since I was a young gel of twenty."

"Oh, he's not mine. I just found him on the drive," I said, correcting her.

"Lady Sybilla," Alden said, spreading his hands in an attempt to reason with her. "You act like I'm a villain who wants to wash his hands of you, when the truth is far from that. You, yourself, set the terms of the sale. As it is, I am providing you with a home rent free for the rest of your life. All I ask is that you honor those terms, and move to the gatekeeper's house so that I can renovate the empty house."

"But it's not empty," Fenice said, leaning back in the chair and smiling at us.

It didn't reach her eyes. I thought that was somehow significant.

Alden shot her an annoyed glance. "I know it's not empty now, but once Lady Sybilla moves to the gatehouse—"

"No, that's not what I meant." Fenice's smile became distinctly more cat-who-ate-the-cream. "Lady Sybilla told us that Patrick and I could stay in the house. And now that Mercy is here, she'll need a place to stay as well, so that makes three of us, although Patrick said something about dossing down in the barn to guard the equipment. Even so, that's three of us, not counting Adams."

"Who is Adams?" Alden asked, somewhat wildly, I thought. I eyed him, wondering if I should pat him soothingly on the arm. He certainly did not seem to be taking well the news about Lady Sybilla's refusal to vacate her old home.

"Adams is with me," Lady Sybilla said in her rich voice. "She used to work for Lord Baskerville in an agricultural advisory position, but after his passing some twenty-two years ago, she has become my companion and maidservant. I do not intend to have her sent away from me, if that is what you plan to do, you beastly man."

"I am not beastly," Alden said, his voice rife with frustration. "I don't wish to send anyone away—I simply want you to move into the gatekeeper's lodge as you agreed to do. You can take your maid with you. Hell, for that matter, you can take everyone with you," he said, jerking his head toward me. "The more the merrier and all that. But no one—I repeat, no one—is going to be staying in the house but me. I have a lot of renovation plans, and none of them can be achieved if people are getting underfoot."

I had to admit, I had been in the process of feeling sympathy toward him. He seemed nice enough, having agreed to give the old lady a home when he probably could have insisted she clear out for good, and he even went to what had to be a substantial expense making sure her new digs were comfortable. But then he went and ruined that impression by more or less dumping me with the others into the lodge with poor Lady Sybilla.

I turned and squinted at the house. It didn't look in its prime, but it also didn't look like it was about to fall down about our ears. "You know," I said amiably, "I bet Fenice and I could find two bedrooms in a house that size where we wouldn't be underfoot. I mean, you can't renovate the entire house at once, can you?"

"That's not the point," Alden said, running a hand through his hair. He looked at the end of his tether. "The house is supposed to be empty, and now I find that not only has Lady Sybilla let out the grounds without my permission, but now others have joined her in the house. My house. The one I've sunk every last pound into."

"We aren't any trouble," Fenice said quickly. "Patrick and I spend most of our time out here getting the equipment ready, and of course, once the classes begin tomorrow, we'll be outside for the entire day."

"See? No one will get in your way. I'm bound to be with Vandal and Fenice all day, too," I said, giving him a little nudge with my elbow. I was momentarily startled at my familiarity, but after a moment in which I was braced for a negative reaction from him in response, I relaxed. He didn't seem to notice the nudge.

"That's not the point," Alden repeated stubbornly.

I smiled to myself, feeling an odd sort of irritated kinship with the man. I knew all about stubbornly clinging to one's beliefs despite an easier path. "I know, but look at it this way—Lady Sybilla has to know oodles about the house, so she can help you."

"I will not help anyone who wishes to turn me out from my rightful place," Lady Sybilla said with utmost dignity.

"You want to restore it to its original state, right?" I asked quickly, just as Alden was about to answer Lady Sybilla's latest shot. "Well, here's someone who knew what the house looked like some sixty years ago. You can pick her brain for what the house was like then."

"That's hardly restoring it to its original state," Alden said, his gaze suddenly on me.

He had lovely eyes. They were a pale blue with a thick black ring around the outer edge of the iris, surrounded by eyelashes that on a woman I would have sworn were fake.

"No," I said, telling myself to stop being so shallow as to be swayed by a pair of pretty eyes. "But it's better than nothing. She might know how it used to look. You won't know until you ask her, and just think of the time you'll save if she's right on hand, rather than you having constantly to run to the gatekeeper's lodge."

He was silent for a moment, his eyes not leaving my face. "Why, if you do not mind me inquiring, have you taken it upon yourself to become a part of this situation?"

"That was quite rude, you know. I thought you Brits were supposed to have impeccable manners." I straightened my shoulders, about to tell him it was none of his business what I did or said, but my inner self admitted that he had a point—I was butting in. Instead, I gave him a half-apologetic, half-wry smile. "Sorry, I shouldn't have snapped at you like that. It's because I'm a middle child."

Both of his eyebrows rose. "As am I. What does that have to do with the current situation?"

"Middle kids are almost always peacemakers. In my

case, that's my character to a tee. Well, that and the fact that I love to learn things, but I'm told curiosity is another middle-child trait, so that's not too surprising. Are you a curious person, too?"

"Yes, but that's not—"

"Then it's all settled," I said brightly, and gave him another elbow nudge. This one he noticed. "You can do your work, and we'll stay out of your way, and Lady Sybilla will help you put the house to rights, and in return, you won't boot her out to the gatekeeper's lodge until you absolutely have to. I like it when things work out. It makes my shui happy."

"People don't have shui," he said with a little frown.

"Really? How do you know?"

"Because like you, I enjoy learning things, and have studied the five arts of Chinese metaphysics; thus, I understand exactly what qi is supposed to be—what you have confused with shui—and it has nothing to do with your personal sense of satisfaction."

"Huh," I said, making a mental note to look up the five arts of Chinese metaphysics. "Interesting. I'll have to Google that later." I smiled at him. "My Google-fu is very strong, you know."

He came perilously close to an eye roll, but stopped himself in time. "Regardless, I don't have need of Lady Sybilla's presence to successfully complete a restoration of the house—"

"No, but it's nice to have her on hand, isn't it? I bet her husband had a library with all sorts of papers and documents on the house that would be useful." I turned to Lady Sybilla. "You have old house documents, don't you?"

"Quite a number, yes," she allowed, and for a second, I saw a glint of amusement in her faded eyes. "I own that should I be ripped from the very bosom of my home—if you will pardon the salty language—then I should feel obligated to take with me those things that are most precious, including all of my husband's papers, and his entire library."

"Most of the library was sold off years ago," Alden said, sliding her a look out of the corners of his eyes. "Or so says your legal representative."

"Sir James's books, yes, but not his personal effects." Lady Sybilla brushed a crumb from the table. "Those are most precious to me."

"So it's all settled," I said happily, feeling I'd done my good deed for the day in making peace in an unpleasant situation despite the sometimes-annoying Alden. "I'm sure you'll find lots of good historical info in Lady Sybilla's papers. I'm certainly envious of you having the chance to go through them. There's nothing I love more than primary historical documents, especially those of the Georgian and Victorian periods."

"Then you can look through them," Alden said somewhat snappishly. "I won't have time. I will be renovating a house despite it being inhabited by an army of people who refuse to leave the premises."

"Oooh, would you mind if I had a peek?" I asked Lady Sybilla. "I almost have a degree in British history, so I know what I'm doing. Mostly. I do have an abiding love of history, though."

"You may catalog his papers if you like," Lady Sybilla said graciously, and, with no little amount of creaking, got to her feet. She clutched an ebony-and-silver-handled cane in one hand, looking down her nose at Alden (not an easy feat when he was at least ten inches taller than she was), and added, "Very well, young man. I will allow you to conduct work on the house, but I must insist that you leave my rooms unmolested. Adams and I have them exactly to my taste."

Alden started to protest, but checked himself, his shoulders slumping as he said morosely, "You're not going to leave the house until you're ready, are you?"

"Most certainly not."

He sighed. "I could have you thrown out, you know. Legally, I have that right."

"But you shan't." Lady Sybilla creaked past him without even pausing. "Because you are a gentleman, or so says my solicitor. Do not disappoint me, young man."

She sailed off with stately dignity. Alden watched her for a few seconds, then turned back to us, his face a picture of resignation mingled with frustration.

"Oh, it won't be that bad," I said in an attempt to comfort him. "She's too old to get in your way much. I mean, you have that whole house to fix up."

"I suppose it wouldn't hurt to leave her rooms until later, but when I get to them, she must move to the gatekeeper's lodge. And I won't add her board to my expenses, which are strained enough as is. Nor for you lot," he added, his brows pulling together when his gaze shifted from me to Fenice.

"We wouldn't dream of imposing on you in that way," she said with exaggerated courtesy, and, with a cheeky grin at me, grabbed my arm and hauled me in the opposite direction to that of Lady Sybilla, taking me out into the depths of the garden. "Come along, I'll show you what's what."

"Sounds good. I did want to tell you something about the archery—"

"Ugh, don't mention that. Patrick is going to be furious when he sees me. Speaking of that wastrel, did he say when he was going to be here? He was supposed to fetch the equipment two days ago and be back by noon, and it's long past that now."

"He just said sometime in early evening."

"That rotter. I'll rip a few strips off of him if he left me to face the irate owner on my own...."

I looked over my shoulder as I followed Fenice.

Alden stood watching us, an oddly puzzled look on his face, but when my gaze met his, he immediately turned and, with his hands stuffed into his pockets, walked quickly toward the stone verandah.

My spirits dropped at such an obvious rejection. I didn't even know why I was being so spurned, but I knew I didn't like it. A little spike of pride had me telling myself that I didn't care what he thought, that he probably didn't like women anyway, and that I had more important things to do than be concerned over the opinion of such a misanthropic, annoying man.

"I don't give a flying fig what he thinks," I said under my breath as ahead of me, Fenice pointed at the small cluster of outbuildings, and explained what they were being used to store. "Besides, I probably won't see him again. He'll be inside, and I'll be outside, and never the twain shall meet."

I sighed at that thought, inexplicably depressed.

He really did have nice eyes.

FOUR

"Yes, I arrived with the car intact, although just barely. And it cost a fortune to fix the starter, which I can ill afford." Alden took a deep breath, and opened the door to what he remembered was a formal dining room. He half expected to find ghostly, sheet-covered furniture lurking in the darkness, but the room, like so many others he'd surveyed in the last half hour, was empty.

"So long as you're safe. Alice wants to know when we can see the place," Elliott said, the faint clicking of keys reaching Alden's ears. No doubt Elliott was anxious to get back to work, and had called only to make sure Alden had arrived at last. "Not that we're pressuring you. I know from hard experience just how long it can take for repairs to be made."

"Given the amount of work I'm seeing, next year wouldn't be a bad guess."

He entered the room, intending on opening the dusty, grime-bedecked olive green velvet curtains, but paused when one end of the mantel over a particularly ugly fireplace suddenly gave up the will to live, and released its hold on the wall, falling to the ground with an appalling wooden screech and a substantial thud. A gentle tinkle of plaster followed.

Alden gave the mantel a warning look, and added, "Maybe 2020 would be a better estimate."

"What was that noise? It sounded like a banshee scream-ing."

"It was the mantel. I believe it just tried to commit sui-cide."

Alden grasped the curtain, and gave it a sideways tug.

The curtain came loose in his hand, and slithered to the floor with a dejected fwooping noise, a small mushroom cloud of dust rising around him, immediately settling on his shoes, and trouser legs.

Alden pursed his lips.

"Don't be ridiculous. Inanimate objects like mantels don't get depressed and suicidal."

"You haven't seen this place," Alden countered, squint-ing out of the flyspecked window. He thought it looked out onto the garden at the side of the house, but it was difficult to see through what must be decades of grime and neglect. "It's like the whole house has gone emo. If it was a person, I'd expect it to be clothed in black, drinking absinthe, and writing depressing poetry about the futility of life and the existential being of nothingness."

"Now you're being dramatic. A house is a house is a house. As you should well know, having grown up here. If any house had the right to mope around and write sad poet-ry, it would be Ainslie Castle."

The second curtain, with a little whisper of hopeless-ness, rippled and fell to the floor next to its partner. Alden coughed and waved away the eruption of dust.

His shoes were now almost gray. "I repeat, you haven't seen this place. And that's not the worst of it."

"Oh? What's happened other than your car having is-sues?"

Alden told Elliott about Lady Sybilla, and the frustra-tion of having to deal not only with her, but with what was apparently going to be some sort of medieval fair in his back garden. "And don't tell me to throw Lady Sybilla out, El. I can't do it, I just can't. I tried, but she just looked at me with those faded eyes, and shaky hands, and all I could picture was the poor old thing being stuffed into a nursing home."

"But she has a home in the gatekeeper's lodge that you agreed to let her use until her demise."

"You know that, and I know that, but Lady Sybilla seems to feel otherwise." Alden ran a hand through his hair before remembering it was covered in dust and cobwebs. "I just have to face the fact that I'm stuck with her until I absolutely have to move her out of her rooms. Fortunately, there's a lot I can do in other parts of the house where she won't be in the way. It's the other group I really want rid of. Surely I can't be expected to honor any agreement made by a former owner? What's the legality of that?"

"Hmm." Elliott was quiet for a minute. "It doesn't sound like you should be responsible for letting those people have your garden, but on the other hand, this is English civil law we're talking about—I wouldn't be surprised if the whole thing was considered a debt on the estate, and thus it transfers to the new owner."

"Great." Alden nudged aside the pools of fallen curtains to sit down on the window seat below the now-denuded window. Across the room, a lightbulb in the wall sconce fizzled, then went out with a soft pop. "So I'm stuck with them?"

"I don't know. Talk to the solicitor who handled the sale and see what he has to say."

"I will, although he seems to be more on Lady Sybilla's side than mine. Old family retainers, I think."

Elliott snorted. "If you like, I can ask around."

"I don't know." Alden got to his feet and wandered over to the fireplace to see just how bad the mantel was. He didn't even flinch when, placing his hand on it, the end still attached released its hold on the wall and fell to his feet. Dust swirled up into the fireplace in an intricate design. "Legal opinion takes time. The group is here now, so what good will it be to find out a month from now that I was in the right?"

"It would help if you wanted to get some money out of them for using your land without your knowledge or consent."

As Elliott spoke, Alden leaned down and reached up into the fireplace. The way the dust had dissipated had left him believing the damper was open. The last thing he needed was to leave an open passage for birds or rodents.

"Getting a judgment against them would take even longer," Alden said a bit diffidently, his hand scrabbling for the metal handle. He caught it, and gave it a tug. A dead bat fell to the floor, rolled out, and came to rest against his shoe. "I think I'm stuck with them, just as I am Sybilla."

"It's your call, Alden. If you want them gone, make a stand," Elliott said.

Alden looked at the rusty brown bat, then reached out to pick it up. "I was wrong," he said aloud.

"About what?"

"The bat isn't dead." He hurriedly set it back onto the floor of the fireplace, looking around for something with which to capture it.

"What bat? Are you all right? You didn't eat or drink anything with a funny taste, did you?"

"No. Well, yes, but that was because I bought a sandwich at a petrol station on the way up here. My chimney has bats."

"Truer words were never spoken, but I've never judged you for the path you've taken in life."

"I wasn't speaking euphemistically. There's a bat here. A real bat. But it doesn't seem too well, so I suppose I should get it to someone who knows about them. I wonder if Mercy could help it."

"Probably. Merciful dealings with animals has always been my byword."

"Not that sort of mercy. This one is a woman."

"Oh?"

"Don't say it like that. I thought she was Alice's protégée at first until she—Mercy—informed me she was just hired to work with the dog and pony show taking place in my garden. She mentioned something about zoology. I'll ask her what she thinks of the bat."

"You certainly know how to woo the ladies," Elliott said with gentle humor.

Alden made a face at nothing. "I'm not trying to woo her. I'm not trying to woo anyone. Didn't you listen? She's not part of Alice's matchmaking project. She's just . . ." Interesting. Somewhat maddening. But with a curiosity that he suspected matched his own. ". . . just a woman. One who I'd rather was elsewhere."

"That's what we all think at first, and then one day, you realize they have seemingly infinite powers that they use to keep us utterly besotted." Elliott sighed. "Tell me more about this group that is blighting your existence."

Alden relayed everything he knew while he scooped up a rattan basket that had been lying on its side, forgotten in a dismal corner of the room, and placed it gently over the bat, making sure the gaps within the woven pattern of the basket let air in.

He opened the door to leave. The now-empty curtain rod fell to the ground with a muffled clang.

"You know . . . I hate to say it, but it sounds more and more like you're going to have to let these medieval people stay out the term of their agreement," Elliott said once he'd finished. "Consider it from their point of view—they paid to have access to the garden, and had no idea Lady Sybilla was going to sell out from under them."

Alden emerged from the house to the pleasant heat of a summer afternoon, breathing deeply of air that smelled like baked earth, freshly mowed grass, and salt air that had swept in from the coast a scant quarter mile away. "I agree, but that doesn't help me."

"Well, as you said, there's a lot to keep you occupied in the house itself. It shouldn't be too bad having them doing a little fake medieval combat in the back garden."

"If they were confined to that location, I might be able to ignore them, but Lady Sybilla told them they could stay in the house. Which means they'll be occupying part of a wing, and then there will be tourists and whatnot roaming around. In other words, everyone will be in my way, getting underfoot when I'm trying to renovate."

"I think you're anticipating problems where there are none," Elliott counseled, but at that moment, a small group of people emerged from a bank of rhododendrons. The leader was a large man with ginger hair, a red face, and intimidatingly bushy eyebrows. Behind him followed two women and one man, all of whom wore binoculars strung around their necks and clutched small notebooks.

"Now, to the west, we've spotted three Dartford warbler nests. And of course, the cormorants have their main breeding ground beyond the copse, down on the shore." The man nodded at Alden. "Good afternoon to you, sir."

"Hello." Alden watched in surprise as the man and his group passed by, apparently not intending on stopping. Alden stepped forward and blocked their path. "And just who might you be?"

"I might be the Pied Piper," the ginger man said with a genial smile. "As it happens, I'm Barry Butcher." He stuck out his hand.

Alden shook it automatically. "What exactly are you doing here?"

The man's bristly eyebrows rose in surprise. "I might ask you the same, mate. But let's start with your name, first."

"Alden Ainslie." He cast his eye over the other three people. They seemed to fade in comparison with the boisterous man leading them. They clutched their notebooks, identical wary expressions on all three of their faces. "I own Bestwood Hall."

"The new owner!" Barry clapped him on the shoulder, sending Alden staggering a few steps to the side. "Can't tell you how much I've been wanting to talk to you. Expect you're wondering why we're traipsing through your land, eh? Well, I'll tell you—it's our Hairy Tits."

Alden stared at him, convinced he had misheard.

"We're with the Hairy Tit Conservancy Trust, you know," Barry added, just as if that were common knowledge.

"Our tits like your land. Specifically, the area between the north copse and the western edge where the cliffs lead down to the beach. We've had a record number of tits spotted this year, and we have high hopes that if they're left undisturbed, they'll make a full recovery."

"Their numbers are very low," one of the women said earnestly, her fingers white on her notebook. "They were put on the endangered list two years ago."

"That's right. Only three breeding places in the whole of England, and the biggest is on your land." Barry waggled his massive eyebrows. "Which brings me to the subject I wanted to speak to you about—that piece of land you have."

"What piece of land?" Alden asked, mentally pulling up a map of the estate.

"The bit with our tits, of course. The stretch that runs from the copse of oak trees to the cliffs. It's about ten acres, wouldn't you say, Poppet?"

The woman evidently named Poppet nodded vigorously. "We've looked it up on the county maps. It's almost exactly ten acres, a mere fraction of your one hundred and twenty acres."

"We in the Hairy Tit Conservancy Trust would like to purchase that land. To preserve and protect the habitat of the endangered tit." Barry beamed like he was giving Alden a present.

"That's . . . I'm . . ." Alden tried hard to pull himself out of his verbal stumbling fit. "I couldn't think of selling any of the land. The estate was cut down to just seventy-two acres, not one hundred and twenty, and almost all of that is leased out to farmers. The house itself stands on less than twenty acres, your bird area included."

"We'll offer a fair price, mind you. We don't intend for this to be a hardship on you," Barry said, then clapped his hand on Alden's arm and walked him a few steps away from the others. "Just between you and me, that bit of land isn't worth half of what the trust is prepared to offer you. It would be a folly to turn up your nose to that sort of money, especially if you're intending on renovating the old place. I know what sort of money that can run to, and I'm sure you'd be grateful for an influx of cash."

"I'm sorry," Alden said firmly. "The land isn't for sale."

"You haven't heard the figure we're offering yet," Barry said, and named a sum that had Alden mentally raising his eyebrows. "Tell me that isn't generous!"

"It's very generous, but the land simply is not for sale."

"Now, then," Barry said, giving him another shoulder punch. "Don't be hasty in thinking it over. I'll come back another day when you're not so busy and we'll have a natter about it. In the meantime, you think of what you could do with that money."

"I really don't need to think about it—"

"We'll get out of your hair," Barry said loudly, and waved the others forward. "We'll continue on to the cliffs, and walk up to the tit sanctuary before turning to the west to check out the cormorants. Nice meeting you at last, Ainslie."

"A pleasure," the woman named Poppet said with a little bob before she hurried after the others.

Alden watched in exasperation, partly with himself for not being able to articulate in a manner that made his feelings clear, but mostly for what he could tell was going to be a man who refused to accept no as an answer. "What is it with people feeling they can do whatever they want on my land?"

"Still going on about that, are you?"

Mercy emerged from the back of the house, tipping her head to the side as she considered him. "Boy, you really do like to hold on to grudges, don't you? You shouldn't, though. It's bad for the digestion."

"I'm not holding on to a grudge," he told her, so annoyed he wasn't above arguing. And yet, at the same time, he was oddly pleased to see her. There was something about her, a sense of warmth and comfort, that was strangely enticing. "If you had people tramping through your land looking for rare, quasi-obscenely named birds, not to mention having your plans altered by a batty old woman—speaking of that, what do you know of bats?—then you'd feel the same way as I do."

"Oh, I don't know." She struck a thoughtful pose, and Alden was instantly aware that he was standing there, in the hot summer sunshine, chatting with a woman. His palms pricked with sudden perspiration. "I think I'd welcome the change. I try to do that, you know—embrace change. I mean, life is change, isn't it? What's the use in trying to force everything into little cubbyholes when it all comes bursting out the next minute?"

"What bursts out?" he asked, mildly confused. A faint sheen of sweat started on his back, not just from the effect of wearing a dark shirt on a hot day. He fought the urge to stammer, and forced himself to speak slowly and calmly. "And I'm not forcing life into cubbyholes. I couldn't if I wanted, since your friends refuse to cooperate."

"Employers," she corrected gently, giving him another considering look.

Alden wanted to bolt, and had to physically force himself to stand still, damp palms, sweating back, and trembling legs notwithstanding. "Just so."

"Life bursts out of cubbyholes is what I meant. If I were you . . ." She leaned in, dropping her voice to an intimate level that seemed to go straight to Alden's groin. He was horrified at such a reaction to a woman he'd just met. He was even more horrified at the thought that she might notice he was having a physical reaction to her. "I'd stop fighting what life hands you, and instead make the best of the situation. You never know. Some good may come out of it."

"Erm . . . if you'll excuse me. I believe . . . er . . . something . . . er . . . needs me."

"Something needs you?"

"Yes. Something is . . . it's on fire."

"What?" she asked, and he had a fleeting glimpse of disbelief on her face before he hurried past her, running down the gravel path that curved around the side of the house and led toward the front expanse.

He knew he was being insufferably rude, but he couldn't

stand there in the sun with Mercy that close to him, so close her breath softly caressed his cheek, the scent of a sun-warmed woman seemingly wrapping invisible tendrils of sexual awareness around him tighter and tighter until he felt he couldn't breathe.

"Bloody hell," he swore to himself, stopping to lean against a sheltered wall. "Bloody, buggery hell. You're a fool. A big fool. A colossal fool. All she wanted to do was talk, and you start babbling and run away. . . ." He suddenly remembered the phone, now gripped tightly in his hand, and lifted it to his ear. "You still there, El?"

"Yeees," Elliot drawled. "That was quite a scene. Almost as good as the Hairy Tit man, but not quite. I agree that you were a colossal fool. Is something on fire?"

"No," Alden answered miserably, and slumped to the ground. Rocks poked painfully at his legs, but he felt it was just penance for treating Mercy to such rudeness. "But any hopes I had of trying to speak to a woman without making a complete ass of myself have gone up in flames."

"Possibly, but I don't think it's quite as dire as that. What was she doing that made your voice go up an octave and sound like you were choking?"

"She leaned in to say something." He gave a little shudder at the way he'd run off. "The look on her face when I bolted . . . El, I'm doomed, I'm just doomed."

"Don't be maudlin. You just need practice talking to women. Once you realize they're just as scared of you as you are of them, you'll be fine."

Alden uttered a strangled little laugh.

"There, now, you see? You're laughing. All is not quite as lost as you imagine. What did you think about the offer on your north acres?"

"I don't think anything of it. I'm not going to sell."

"It's a nice chunk of money," Elliott said thoughtfully. "It could come in handy with your remodeling."

"I'm sure it would, but I'm not going to sell something I just went through hell to buy."

"Well, it's your decision. If you intend on selling the house once you've fixed it up, you'll likely be happy you kept the land."

"That's assuming I can do everything I need to do with a medieval fair running in the garden."

"Ignore them, and focus on your work. Their lease on the garden will be over with before you know it."

"You're right," Alden said, getting back to his feet and brushing off his trousers. "The house is what's important. Everything else is just distraction. Especially Mercy. I can tell she's going to be pestering me a lot."

"Oh?"

"Yes. She says she's a middle-child peacemaker." Alden snorted. "She clearly is one of those bossy women who likes to take charge of things and run them. Well, she's not going to run me. I don't need her or her interfering ways."

Elliott audibly choked.

"And the sooner she realizes that, the happier we'll all be. Not that I'll see her much. She'll be with the others out in the garden, and I'll be focusing on the house," Alden said over the sound of Elliott coughing and wheezing. "'Focus on the house' is my new motto in life. I will focus like the wind. I will be the most focused man who ever lived. I will focus like, as the Americans say—did I tell you that Mercy is American?—as she would say, I will focus like no one's business."

A spate of coughing was the answer to his declaration.

"Are you all right?" he asked solicitously.

"No," Elliott wheezed, his voice hoarse and gritty. "But at least I didn't run away from Alice when I met her."

"You're supposed to be supportive. That sort of comment is not supportive. That is judgmental and petty. I will leave you to your judgmental, petty coughing fit that you wholly deserve, and go attend to my house." A dull grating sound started overhead, growing sharper until he looked up in time to see three tiles and an ancient bird's nest fall to the ground in front of him. "It is, after all, what's important."

"You're protesting too much," came the hoarse reply.

"I'm not doing any such thing. I'm simply telling you where my priorities lie, and that I really don't want a woman munging up my plans. If you could find a way to have Alice call off her protégée, I'd be grateful. There are enough people clogging up the house now without having another one."

"Too late, I believe," Elliott wheezed. "Alice said something about the woman being on her way."

"Dammit." Alden straightened his shoulders, stepped over the slates and the bird's nest, and set out again on the gravel path. "Well, I'll just deal with the woman when she arrives. Perhaps I can leave her a note, and I won't even have to see her. Oh, hell, I forgot to ask Mercy about the bat. Er . . . I don't suppose . . ."

"No," Elliot said, his voice still rough around the edges, although he had stopped coughing. "I will not call her up and ask her for you."

"That's a fine sort of supportiveness you practice," Alden said pointedly, and, after a few more remarks of that nature, hung up the phone. He waffled for a minute, trying to rally enough inner strength to hunt down Mercy so he could apologize for his brusqueness, followed by an inquiry into her experience with possibly ill bats, but decided in the end that he'd put off that task until later. Instead, he toured the remainder of the estate, checked the condition of the outbuildings, and took photos of various spots around the exterior of the house about which he'd seek professional opinions.

An hour had passed when his stomach reminded him that he'd had a meager lunch at best, and perhaps a little food might be in order. The thought that Mercy might be in the kitchen was almost enough to send him running (again), but in the end, he persuaded himself that she wasn't likely to be present.

She had other things to do, no doubt. There was that Vandal character—he sounded like a right bloke with the ladies. He just bet Mercy would fall for that sort of a man. Not that he cared. Not that it mattered whom she fell for, so long as she didn't expect to stand around chatting with him, and leaning in to the point where he could smell that delicious scent that seemed to wrap around her, or feel the nearness of her body. No, he didn't need that in his life, and certainly not after his experience of the afternoon.

"I've had enough emotional trauma for the day," he said aloud, letting himself in through a pair of French doors into what he knew was the long, narrow room that used to be a library.

"Really? What's traumatized you now?"

He froze at the door. Mercy was seated at a card table that had been set up to the right of the doors, a massive mound of books, journals, loose papers, and what looked to be sheet music spilling off the table onto stacks on the floor.

"Or should I say who?"

"Who has done what?" he asked, confused by the fact that she was there in his formerly empty library, that she had set up a desk so quickly with what were clearly Lady Sybilla's papers and assorted documents, and that he felt a spurt of pleasure at seeing her. He wasn't happy to see her, he reminded himself. She terrified him, just as every other woman had ever since puberty.

"Caused trauma." She watched him with interesting hazel eyes that appeared now to be a stormy gray tinged with green.

"You," his mouth answered without his brain giving the all clear to do so. The second the word left his mouth, he was mortified. Shame heated his cheeks, which in turn made him feel even more uncomfortable. Men didn't blush— women did.

"Me?" Her brows, straight slashes of chocolate brown, pulled together in consternation. "What have I done to traumatize you?"

"I . . . you . . ." His tongue seemed to stumble over the words as he gestured hopelessly. "It's not really you, per se. . . ."

"You're blushing," she said, disbelief rampant in her voice.

He couldn't be more mortified if he had set out to achieve that goal. With an inarticulate noise of self-loathing, he turned stiffly toward the French doors, intending to retreat to an unoccupied room where he could chastise himself in private, but a warm hand on his arm stopped him.

"Hey, I'm sorry. That was rude of me. You're obviously upset with me about something, but I don't know what it is, so I don't know how to fix it. I don't suppose you'd like to start over? Pretend we're meeting for the first time?"

The look in her (now darker gray with more brown than green) eyes kept him from running away again. There was sympathy there, yes, but no pity. Just concern and worry. "No! That would be infinitely worse."

"Really? Why?"

He closed his eyes for a moment and tried to focus on breathing calmly, as a therapist had once counseled him to do when faced with stressful social situations. "Because then I'd have to meet you all over again."

"And that's . . . unpleasant?"

He opened his eyes to find her in front of him, a puzzled expression on her face. But there was a hint of pain in her interesting, changeable eyes. Pain that he had caused.

"Yes."

She took a deep breath and he felt her withdraw. She didn't move physically, but he knew he had insulted her deeply, and yet his tongue felt like it was tied in knots, unable to explain the hellish nightmare of his intentions. "I see. I'm sorry if you don't like me, but—"

"No, it's not that." He gestured awkwardly, tried to think of words that would make everything right, make her understand, but they all tumbled around in his brain and refused to form sentences. He tottered over to her chair and slumped down in it, elbows on knees, and his head in his hands. "It's not you, it's me. It's . . . women."

"You don't like women? You're gay?"

"Not gay. It's just . . . hard."

Air swirled gently around him, the faint spicy aroma of exotic scents teasing his nose. Whatever perfume she wore went straight to his head. "If I ask 'What's hard?' you're not going to make a dick joke, are you?"

"No," he said, braving a little smile as he looked up. "I'm the least likely person to do that."

"Why?" she asked, kneeling on the ground next to him. She tsked, and pulled a packet of papers out from under her knee. "Lady Sybilla's private journal. She swears it'll make a best seller if I type it up for her. Why are you not likely to make a dick joke, not that I want you to, mind, but still, why the least likely business?"

He sat up straight, his hands on his knees, unable to look her in the eye when he bared his soul. He didn't even wonder over the fact that he suddenly was driven to explain the truth to her—he just knew he had to. He owed it to her. He didn't want her hurt simply because he was socially inept. "I'm . . . I have anxieties. Social anxieties. With women."

"You're . . . shy?" she asked, her nose wrinkling a little.

He thought it was a wholly charming expression, one that perfectly suited her open, honest face. He considered that face for a few moments. She wasn't what would have been described as classically beautiful, with a round face, straight eyebrows, and a little nose that drifted toward the upturned category. Her hair was the color of dark honey, straight and cut in a shoulder-length bob that rippled like silk curtains when she tipped her head to the side, as she was doing now. No, she wasn't strictly beautiful, but he found her all the more appealing because of that.

"'Shy' is a good word for it. I don't communicate well with women." He made another awkward gesture. "I try, but . . . it all gets tangled up, and . . . and then . . ."

"And then you just want to escape." She nodded. "I know exactly what that feels like. One time, when I was in Edinburgh taking some classes in criminology, I was wearing my favorite pair of capris. They were light blue. Really pale baby blue. And my period came, but I didn't know, because I'm not always crampy, and I spent a good chunk of the day running around with a huge old stain that no one told me about, and when I found out, I could have died. I just wanted to hole up in my room and never face all those people in all those classes who must have seen me, but instead, I told myself that there was nothing to be ashamed about a perfectly natural occurrence, and I wasn't going to let societal reaction to women's bodies and their functions ruin my life. So I went to my classes the next day with my head held high."

"That must have been truly horrific," he said, empathy making him flinch at her story.

"Oh, it was. It was hard as hell to do it, and you know what? It's hard to tell you, an almost stranger, about something so intimate, but here we are both surviving the incident and, I hope, finding a little common ground because of it." She smiled, and patted his knee in an impersonal manner. "I know you can't help anxiety, and being shy around women, but the next time things get all tangled up around me, just think about me going to classes the day after Stainageddon, and remember that I've been in embarrassing situations and survived."

"Thank you," he said, smiling back at her, and even placing his hand on hers in order to give her fingers a friendly squeeze.

"Good lord!" she said, staring down at their hands. "Look at you touching a woman! Of your own accord! Let me alert the newspapers—wait, do we have a camera? Maybe I should post this online!"

He made a face and pinched the back of her hand. "Are you going to make fun of me every time I manage to speak to you?"

"Of course I am," she said, laughing and getting to her feet. She held out her hands for him, and he allowed her to pull him up. "I wanted to be a psychologist for a while, and one of the things I learned in two years of psych classes is that you need to desensitize whatever you're afraid of. If I make a big deal about you talking to me, and touching my hand, and staring at my boobs, then soon you won't even think twice about those things."

He felt the color rushing to his face again. Dear god, had she noticed his reaction to her earlier? He'd kept careful control of his libido since walking into the library, but perhaps she knew the way her scent sank into his blood. Horrified, he pulled his hands from hers, and stammered, "I wasn't ogling your breasts!"

"No, you weren't, and that makes me wonder why." She puffed out her chest and peered downward at her breasts. "Is there something wrong with them? Do you not like them? Would a push-up bra help?"

He stared first at her face, then at her chest (since she seemed to expect him to do so), then back to her face. "Are you . . . is this more desensitization?"

"No. That was ribbing. This is desensitization." She put both her hands on his chest, and leaned forward, kissing his cheek. "There, now you've been kissed by a woman you just met, and you got to look at her boobs with her full permission. And we both survived with no ill effects."

He was speechless for a few seconds, wishing she'd stay standing so close to him, but she immediately backed up. "Thank you," he finally got out. "I . . . thank you. For everything. For understanding."

"You're welcome." Her head tipped again, the hair sliding in a way that made his fingers itch to touch it. "Maybe tomorrow we can throw caution to the wind and hold hands."

That sounded like a very fine idea to Alden, but he couldn't possibly tell her that. Instead, his mouth blurted out the very worst thing it could. "There's a woman coming here, to the house."

"Oh," Mercy said, and once again, he felt a slight withdrawal of her personality. It was as if a cloud had rolled in front of the sun. "Gotcha. You're in a relationship."

"No, I'm not," he said quickly, shaking his head. "It's . . . someone I might like, is all."

"I understand. I wasn't trying to push myself on you, just in case that's what you were thinking. I mean, you're nice, and I like you now that I know you don't loathe me, but I wasn't chasing you. The hand-holding thing was just a joke. If you'd rather I not get touchy-feely, I won't."

What the hell? How had it gotten to this point? He wanted badly to tell her that he had no intention of liking whomever Alice sent out to him, but couldn't think of a way to say that without sounding horribly churlish. Instead, he addressed the more important issue. "No, I don't mind. You touching me, that is. Christ, that sounds risqué." He took a couple of deep breaths, adding, "Well, that just made it worse. Maybe you're right. Maybe we should start over."

"Can't do that." She glanced at her watch, made a tsking noise, and collected up all the papers that had spilled onto the floor. "Ack, it's been an hour already. Fenice is expecting me."

"Why can't we start over?" Alden asked, more because he wanted to see what Mercy would say than because he really wished to erase the last few minutes.

"Because I've already kissed you, and once you kiss someone, there's no going back. Would you mind moving your left foot? Thank you."

"I don't . . ." He moved aside, bending to help her collect the papers and books. "I'm not . . . this woman who is coming isn't someone I'm involved with."

"Gotcha." She tidied up the now teeming stacks of papers and books on the rickety card table. "I know how it is when you just meet someone, and it takes time for things to warm up. Gotta run. Fenice had to deal with a guy who brought a bunch of bales of hay, and we didn't get to finish having our talk about archery."

"Hay?" he asked, rubbing his chin as she hurried around him and opened the French doors. "Archery? Wait, do you mean she's having hay delivered to my garden? My nice, orderly garden?"

His voice echoed slightly in the empty room. Mercy was gone, jogging down the gravel path toward the back of the house, waving good-bye as she did so.

He sighed and sat back down in the chair, absently rubbing the spot on his cheek she had kissed, and wondering if the day would ever come when he could talk to a woman like a normal man. A piece of paper fluttered to the floor, and he picked it up, absently smoothing it out. It was a letter from the late baron to Sybilla.

A little smile curled Alden's lips.

FIVE

"Oh, there she is. Mercy, come meet Patrick." Fenice waved me over as soon as she saw me trot down the stairs into the garden. "He's late, which surprises no one, I'm sure, but at least he made it here."

"In one piece, which is more than I can say for you," her brother replied, poking at her arm before he turned and flashed a megawatt smile at me. He even executed a fancy bow, saying, "The name is Vandal, and the pleasure is all mine, milady Mercedes. Welcome to Hard Day's Knights."

"Hi," I said, wanting to giggle at his Renaissance Faire roguish persona, but decided that might be rude. So instead, I bobbed a little curtsy. "It's nice to meet you in person."

"It is, indeed." His eyebrows waggled, but he turned back to Fenice when she whapped him with her good arm. "What for are you beating me, sister mine?"

"We were having a discussion about what to do with the new owner. Stop flirting with Mercy and focus."

I had to admit, Vandal wasn't hard on the eyes in any way. He was of a medium build—wiry, but not hipster thin—and tall, taller than Alden, who was just a few inches above my height. He had long hair midway down his back, which was tied back with a leather thong, and narrow, high cheekbones that made me think of Vikings.

"I told you that there was nothing to worry about," Vandal said while I was giving him the visual once-over. "We have a contract, signed and sealed, and nothing this new bloke can do will break it. Stop fussing about that and tell me what the hell we're going to do for an archery instructor since you've gone and broken your collarbone."

"Actually, I was going to talk to you about that, Fenice," I said quickly, before she could reply. "If all you need is someone to teach kids how to use a bow and arrow, I can do that."

They both turned to me, surprise etched on their faces. "You can?" Fenice asked, frowning a little. "You're an archer?"

"Well . . . I did do two and a half years of a phys ed degree at a university in Oregon, and spent a year on the longbow archery team. I can use a crossbow, too, although I'm not as good with it as I am the longbow."

"What draw weight?" Fenice asked.

"Oh, I can do seventy, but I'm more accurate at forty-five."

"She's an archer," Fenice said to Vandal, relief filling her voice. "Bless the goddess, she's a real archer."

"A longbow archer yet, none of that modern compound-bow business. It does seem most propitious," Vandal answered, giving me a thoughtful look. "Why don't we try you out on Fen's bow and see how you do?"

I murmured something about not wanting to use a valuable bow, but Fenice waved it away, and the three of us moved over to the far side of the garden where a couple of archery butts had been placed. There were also three large plastic bins containing what I imagined were the bows and arrows intended for instructional use. Fenice reached behind the pyramid of bins and pulled out a beautifully embossed leather quiver and a canvas case that obviously held a bow.

"I won't let you use Eloise—she's my competition bow, and was custom-made for me by one of the best bow makers in Europe—but you can use Tarantella." Fenice pulled out a lovely hickory bow about six feet long, and handed it to me.

I balanced it on my palm for a second, then firmly grasped the jute cording that had been wrapped around the center of the bow as a grip, and extended my arm. With my right hand, I used my middle three fingers, and pulled the string back to my cheek, holding it for a few seconds before letting my fingers relax. The string slipped past them, twanging a sharp, high note.

"Nice bow," I told Fenice, accepting the quiver she held out to me. I slipped one of the arrows out, and locked it on the bow, feeling more than a little cocky. I silently recited my shooting mantra (Turn arm down; turn palm up), grasped the string, and, with the traditional swooping move upward, brought the string back to the far corner of my mouth while slowly lowering the bow until I had the target in sight. "Now let's see if I can hit a bull's-eye right off the ... ow!"

I had let my fingers relax before I finished my sentence, causing the arrow to sail off, and unfortunately getting a nasty case of string slap on the arm holding the bow.

The arrow landed a good six feet away from the butt.

Fenice pursed her lips while I rubbed the stinging spot on my forearm.

"Hurt yourself?" Vandal asked, displaying what I felt was obnoxiously faux innocence.

"Just a little string slap," I growled, locking another arrow onto the bow.

"Comes from hyperextending your arm, doesn't it? I don't believe I've ever seen Fenice do that."

"Oh, shut it," I snapped, then realized I was being rude to my boss. "Sorry, I shouldn't have said that. Yes, it was an amateur move, and yes, I know better than to swing my arm around so that the string smacks it. I was just being a smarty-pants, but I've learned my lesson."

Vandal grinned at me. "And I apologize as well. I shouldn't rag you the way I do Fen."

I took a deep breath, pulled the string back to my cheek, sighted the target, then held my breath for the count of three before releasing the arrow.

"Now, that's what I'm talking about," I said, doing a little fist pump when the arrow (just barely) hit the bull's-eye.

"That's not dead center," Fenice said critically.

"No, but surely it's good enough to teach tourists how to shoot," I argued.

"It is, but there's a little matter of Fight Knight at the end of our three weeks," Vandal said.

"What's that?" I asked.

Fenice turned to him, her eyes wide. "You didn't!"

He nodded, smiling. "I did."

"You got approval to hold it? It's sanctioned and everything?"

"I did, and it is. That's why I was late coming back today—I met with the council and got their approval."

Fenice whooped and flung her good arm around her brother, giving him a loud kiss on the cheek. "I forgive you everything but that time when I was five and you locked me in a cupboard and wouldn't let me out until I ate the horse's mash."

"To answer your question, dear lady," Vandal said when Fenice released him, "Fight Knight is a competition held every year. Medieval combat troupes take turns hosting it, and this year, the club who was supposed to be doing so had to give it up when they imploded with political drama over the embezzlement of club funds. Since it's at short notice, the overseeing council said that we could have it here at Bestwood. It's quite the feather in our cap, since Hard Day's Knights is a new venture."

"I wish Walker and Pepper were here. They'd be so proud," Fenice said, then explained to me, "We're also part of a jousting troupe called Three Dog Knights. The leader of the group and his wife are in Australia to do a bunch of tourneys there. We would have gone with them, but we wanted to start up the melee combat troupe to supplement the jousting team, so we stayed here, and now my brilliant brother has gotten us the plum to end all plums!" She kissed him again and did a little jig of happiness.

"That's very cool, but I don't see—oh, you do not think I'm going to compete, do you?" I gestured with the bow to the arrow sticking out of the ground. "I told you I wasn't competition level. Teaching tourists is about as far as I could go."

"You have three weeks to practice," Fenice said, grimacing when she moved her shoulder. "And if you can't do it, then you can't do it. It won't be the end of the world if we don't have someone competing. I wish my shoulder would be ready by then, but I wouldn't be able to draw properly, not with Eloise."

"Isn't it like a conflict of interest to be competing when you're hosting as well?" I asked.

"Only if we supplied the judging team, but they have already been booked and paid for by the group who crashed and burned. So Fenice, Alec, and I are all free to compete."

"Alec?" I glanced around, but didn't see anyone else.

"He's our armorer," Fenice said, taking back her bow and the quiver. "He doesn't actually create armor for our students, but he makes whatever adjustments he can so that the collection of armor Patrick brought back from France will work with various body sizes."

"Alec comes in tomorrow morning," Vandal added, waving at the stable as we headed toward the drive, where a battered white van was parked. "You'll meet him then. But in the meantime, we have a bunch of armor to unload, ladies, and little time to do it. I want everything set up so that we'll be ready for the first students in the morning."

"About that . . . I was supposed to be taking registrations and helping ladies dress up—"

Fenice stopped me before I could finish my question. "We'll switch jobs. Or what would have been my job if I hadn't cocked up my arm. You can do the archery groups, and I'll handle the women who want to playact they're medieval damsels in distress."

"You don't sound very approving of that aspect of your business," I said carefully, not wanting to be judgmental.

Vandal laughed when Fenice snorted, and said in a disgusted tone of voice, "I'm not. A bigger waste of time I can't think of, but Patrick insists that we give the wives and girl-friends something to do while the men are out learning how to wield a disemboweling ax and long sword."

We reached the van at the last of her words. Vandal opened up the double doors at the back, and started pulling out large blue plastic bins that had lumpy armor shapes visible. "I'm not trying to jump on you for being sexist, because I'm sure you're not, but . . . well . . ."

"It sounds sexist?" Fenice asked.

"Yeah. Don't any women participate in the fighting bit?"

"Some," she said with a one-shouldered twitch that I took to be a shrug. "More and more each year, but it's nowhere near equal numbers. Until that time, I'm going to have little patience for women who don't think they can fight as well as men. Or throw knives, or shoot a bow, or any of the other skills we hope to feature in future sessions."

"Amen to that, sister. More women need to realize they can do anything a man can do except pee while standing up, and there are devices that let us do that," I said.

"You are preaching, as you Yanks say, to the choir. I'm a police officer eleven months out of the year, and I know all about women having to struggle for everything handed to men. Whereas Patrick . . ." She looked sourly at her brother.

Vandal doffed a pretend hat. "There are no such glass ceilings in the world of accountancy."

I giggled a little at the thought of the roguish Vandal being an accountant by day. "So for one month, you guys get to be"—I waved my hand—"this?"

"That's right. Plus weekends. Most weekends we work at this or the jousting," Fenice said.

"Enough chatter, ladies! More moving." Vandal shoved a bin at me, and instructed me where to haul it. The following hour was spent lugging bins to the stable, and unpacking them into stacks arranged by type. I learned all about plate helms, gauntlets, bazubands, greaves, and brigs.

"This stuff weighs a ton," I complained at one point, while lugging a bin of the rounded knee protectors known as cops. "How much does it add up to?"

"About a hundred pounds for the armor. More with the protective padding worn underneath," Fenice answered.

"It's worth it when you've got a six-foot-four man bashing at you with a mace," Vandal commented as he staggered past with a plastic tub of thick, padded cotton arming tunics.

I made a face at that thought. While it looked interesting, I decided I'd stick to archery.

We were just putting away the last bin of helms when a voice spoke from outside the stable. "What in god's name do you need all those bales of hay for? It's drifting out all over my nice, tidy garden!"

"That," Fenice said, looking meaningfully at Vandal as he straightened a rack of pauldrons, "is the new lord and master."

"Ah." His shoulders twitched as he tugged down his shirt, and he marched out of the stable with purpose in every stride. Fenice and I exchanged glances, and hurried after him.

"You must be the new Lord Baskerville," Vandal said, stopping in front of Alden. "I'm Vandal. My sister, Fenice, tells me you have said some harsh things to her about our medieval training camp."

"I'm not Lord Baskerville. There is no Lord Baskerville. The previous owner was a baronet, and thus was Sir James Baskerville. Nor did I say harsh things to anyone, unless you consider the things I muttered under my breath as rude, and I was careful that no one should overhear those."

I smiled at Alden. He'd evidently been running his hands through his hair again, because it stood on end in a distractingly cute manner. My entire body was happy to see him again, but I told it to cool its jets—Alden had a girlfriend coming to visit him.

"We have a contract with Lady Sybilla," Vandal continued. "It's perfectly legal. I had my solicitor go over it in order to get the insurance we needed for the event. So whatever you think you're going to do to intimidate us won't work. We have the right to be here running our classes for three weeks, and that's exactly what we're going to do."

I frowned at Vandal. He was being awfully aggressive toward Alden when the poor man hadn't done anything other than inquire about the bales of hay.

"Is that so?" Alden asked, clearly getting irate.

"Now, now," Fenice said, a worried look on her face. "There's no need for anyone to get upset. I told you that we'd worked things out with the new owner, Patrick."

"Yes, Patrick," Alden said with emphasis on the name. I gave him a point for that, since it was obvious that Vandal preferred his character name. "We have worked things out, so I don't need you getting in my face."

Vandal puffed up like he was going to explode. Fenice grabbed one of his arms, saying something about needing to finish the sorting before it got too dark to see.

Ever the peacemaker, I moved in front of Vandal and smiled at Alden. "Hey, maybe you could show me where the kitchen is? Fenice says that although you are kindly letting us stay in the house, we need to cook for ourselves, and I'm famished. I thought I'd whip up an omelet or something easy like that. Would you like to join us?"

"I don't like omelets," Alden said stiffly, leaving me unsure if he was suddenly feeling awkward again, or if he was still ruffled by Vandal's aggression.

"Oddly enough, neither do I," I said, taking his arm and turning him so we could stroll to the house. "But I bet we could find something to make that everyone would like."

"I was going to eat at a pub—" he protested, but came along willingly enough.

"Bah. What you need after your day is a home-cooked meal. Something that'll give you the oomph to get up tomorrow morning and start renovating. Which way?"

We'd reached the doors to the library where I had set up the temporary table as my desk.

"To the left," he said, moving ahead of me.

It would take a stronger woman than me to not eyeball his behind as he marched over to a door and held it open for me.

"I know what you're doing, you know," he said as I exited the library.

"Walking? I've been doing it for about thirty-three years now, so I feel like I have a pretty good handle on it."

Naturally, at that moment, I tripped over something invisible, probably an atom of oxygen. Alden's arm shot out to grab me and keep me from careening into the wall.

"You were saying?"

I made a face at him. "I'm also fairly clumsy, but I prefer to ignore that facet of my life and focus on the times when I move with lithe, swanlike grace. Would you like to see me do the Queen Elizabeth wave? I have it down pat, and it's one of my most elegant moves."

"Perhaps later, when you're taking the air in your carriage." He slid me a look as we walked down a darkly paneled hallway, shadowed squares and rectangles marking where paintings once graced the walls. The air of abandonment hung heavily over this section of the house, making me speak in a hushed tone.

"By the way, in case you didn't notice, you've been bantering with me a good five minutes. So see? It does get easier with time."

"No, it doesn't," he disagreed as he strode onward down the long, dark, empty hallway.

"You certainly aren't looking uncomfortable to be talking to me," I pointed out, almost trotting to keep up with him. "Which is good! I'm not complaining or anything, I'm just saying that you're clearly feeling much more comfy with me."

"I'm angry, that's all. My discomfort speaking to women has always been lessened by strong emotions, and right now, I'm angry at that Patrick fellow for thinking he can dictate to me. In my own garden!"

"Interesting," I said, mulling over this latest insight into Alden's character. "Change-of-subject time lest you go back out and get into a fight with Vandal. What are you going to do to the house first? As far as renovation goes."

"I'm not sure. The roof needs repair, but it's such a big job, I'll need help with it. I thought of starting with the bedrooms first, but now since some of them will be occupied, I guess I'll start on the ground floor and work through the rooms there."

"I'm sorry we're occupying your bedrooms, but you know, there's something to be said with starting work on the lowest common denominator, and that's the stuff on the ground floor."

"How do you figure that?"

I gave a one-shouldered shrug. "Well . . . you don't have to climb any stairs to get there."

He said nothing, but I could feel him thinking rude things. I couldn't entirely blame him since I'd been speaking nonsense, but there was something inside me that wanted to keep him talking.

Maybe it was his pretty eyes.

Or the way he frowned. He had a sexy frown.

Most likely, though, it was a sense of neediness about him that made me feel protective. One of the personality classes I'd taken had revealed that I had highly empathetic tendencies, making me a sucker for homeless dogs, lost kids, and evidently men with crippling social anxieties.

We turned down a small side passage that was cast into deep shadows despite the long fingers of the setting sun creeping in through the small, high window.

"Damn," he muttered. "Wrong turn."

"It is kind of like a maze in here, isn't it?" I said conversationally as he retraced his steps, then made a left where we'd previously gone right. "Kinda gloomy inside, in a gothically spooky way. I could see one of those atmospheric horror video games being filmed here. I half expect an ax-wielding deranged clown to leap out of a doorway."

"Everything was sold at auction before I bought the house," Alden said. "Including the ax-wielding clowns."

I laughed, delighted that he could make a joke, and was about to point out to him the fact that his attempt at humor signified his growing confidence, but at that moment he made a happy little noise when he opened a door and we emerged into a kitchen that could have been at home in Downton Abbey.

Dominating the room was a turquoise blue enamel range that was approximately as big as a medium-sized sedan, whitewashed glass-fronted cupboards, and vast expanses of counter that were mostly empty. There was also a huge table in the center of the room, around which were scattered five chairs, and one three-legged stool.

"The kitchen," he said, gesturing toward the blue monstrosity that lurked in the shadows.

"You're not going to leave, are you?" I asked when it became obvious he was about to do just that.

"I told you I was going to the pub."

"I know, but if I make something for dinner, wouldn't you rather eat with us?" I flapped a hand helplessly toward the antiquated kitchen appliances. "Assuming, that is, this stuff still works, which I figure it must, because Lady Sybilla has to get food from somewhere, and she doesn't look like the sort of person who pops off to the pub to get a bite to eat."

Alden made a vague gesture, and opened his mouth a couple of times, but didn't actually say anything. He did look extremely uncomfortable, however.

"Uh-oh. Someone stopped being angry," I told him. I bit my lip for a minute while I considered what to do. Obviously, I could leave the poor man be, and let him go off to the pub, where he'd probably spend a perfectly contented evening not talking to pushy Canadian-American women who had a few semesters of psychology classes under their belt.

But where was the fun in that?

"Would you rather I kissed your cheek again, or should

I say something outrageously un-PC so that you get irate at me?"

He stared at me, his brows pulling together in a puzzled frown.

"No, scratch that last one. All I can think of that's outrageously un-PC is kittens clubbing baby seals, and that just is impossible to conceive of. OK, cheek kiss it is."

I laid one hand on his arm and leaned in, about to plant a kiss on his slightly stubbly cheek, when his head turned, and my lips brushed his.

I froze, horribly embarrassed, thinking for a moment that I must have miscalculated my aim, and instead of giving him a platonic (if distracting) smooch, I gave him one straight on the kisser.

"Oh," I said, freezing, which of course meant my mouth didn't move one smidgen from his mouth. "I'm sorry, I was aiming for your cheek. Oh, man, now my lips are touching yours again. Sorry about that, too. And, uh, for that. Crap, the more I talk, the more I touch you. I should move, shouldn't I?"

"Yes," he said, then leaned forward just a smidgen, a tiny little bit, and that was all it seemed to take. One minute I was standing there babbling into his mouth, and the next, it was full-frontal snogging, with my hands tangled in his hair, his arms tight around my back, and all our front parts smooshed together in that time-honored erotic dance that proves so very well the differences between the male and female bodies.

His tongue teased my lips, and without even thinking about whether I should be enjoying kissing a man I'd just met so much, I dabbed at his tongue in a welcoming gesture that urged his tongue to feel right at home in my mouth.

And he did. He tasted, he teased, he tormented my mouth in ways that sent delicious waves of pleasure rolling through me, all of which made me wiggle my hips against him in a wholly shameless way, which I couldn't for the life of me seem to stop.

He made a groaning noise deep in his chest, one that seemed to light little fires throughout my body, and just as I was seriously thinking about releasing his hair and sliding my hands under his shirt, the door behind him opened, whacking Alden on the back.

"—am just going to help Mercy with dinner, and then—oh!"

Fenice stopped in the doorway, gawking.

Immediately, Alden and I parted, with him blushing and moving to the side a couple of steps, and me stammering, "Uh . . . hi. I was just . . . uh . . . I was just . . ."

"It's pretty obvious what you were just doing," Fenice said with a tight little smile. Behind her, Vandal gave her a shove, and pushed his way into the room behind her.

"What were they doing?" he asked with a frown as he looked around the kitchen. "Where's the food? I thought you were going to make an omelet."

I cleared my throat, not meeting Alden's eyes as I said with as much composure as I could manage, "I was just distracting Alden from the argument in the garden. There is no omelet. Alden doesn't care for it, so I thought we could do something else. I'm not sure what food you guys have in stock, though. Come to think of it, I don't even see a fridge here. Surely you must have a refrigerator?"

I asked the last question of Alden, who, although his color was high, appeared to have taken our little wander down the pathways of smuttiness with aplomb.

"There is. It's in the pantry. In there." He nodded toward a narrow door at the far end of the kitchen.

Fenice bustled forward. "We have bacon and sausages—my meat-eating brother demanded that. I'm a vegetarian, so I'll make the omelet if no one else wants to. You all can do bangers and mash if you like."

"I try to limit the amount of red meat I eat, but I think this qualifies as a time when I can go full-banger," I said, heading into the pantry to rummage amongst the goods.

To my mild surprise, Alden followed, saying once we were in the small room, "Erm ... about that kiss—"

Once again the door opened and bumped against his back. Fenice clicked her tongue in dismay, edged around Alden, and said with a bit of acid, "Are you two going at it again? I thought you just met."

"We did just meet," I said at the same time that Alden sputtered, "We were not going at it."

"Indeed. Well, if you can keep your hands off each other long enough for me to get some eggs and veggies, then you can have all the privacy you need to do ..." She waved a hand around vaguely. "Whatever it is you do."

"We don't do anything," I protested. "I told you, I was just distracting him from the argument."

"Right. You did say that." She gathered up a bowl of eggs, a couple of colorful peppers, and a small red onion. "It's none of my business, regardless."

I sighed heavily when she left, turning my gaze back to Alden. I handed him two of the packages of sausage, and a head of garlic. "Great. Now she thinks we have a thing going on."

He blinked at me.

"We don't," I told him. "I was just distracting you. You know, so you wouldn't feel awkward around me."

He stiffened up a bit, and dropped the garlic, and when we both bent down to pick it up, we smacked our foreheads together.

"Ow!" I said, stepping back while rubbing my head.

"Bloody hell," he said at the same time, dropping first one package of sausage, then the other.

I edged forward carefully, holding out my hands as I bent down. "And this has now turned into a scene from a Three Stooges movie. No, don't get them—I will. You just stand there and I'll hand them up, OK?"

"I'm sorry," he said as I handed him the items before turning back to the ancient refrigerator to get some salad makings. "I'm a clumsy oaf ... when things get ... it's ..."

"Hard, I know." I closed the fridge and turned back to smile at him. "Want me to pretend I'm Vandal so you can be mad and articulate again?"

"I'd rather you kissed me again," he said, and then looked both appalled and surprised by that.

I couldn't help it; I laughed out loud. "I suppose that makes sense—if it's a strong emotion that helps you over the hurdle of feeling awkward in situations, then why not lust rather than anger? Although . . . I feel obligated to point out that we don't have a thing going on. I mean, you have this woman coming to see you, and we did just meet, and although I'm a pretty good judge of people, I have never had a relationship with a guy I just met."

"Nor have I," he said hastily, an odd look of embarrassment mixed with stiffness crossing his face. "I didn't mean I wanted to start something with you. I simply thought the kiss was a preferable experience to being angered by Vandal."

"Well, there I agree with you," I said, then leaned forward and brushed my mouth ever so lightly against his. "Kiss accomplished. Now you can be as erudite as you like."

"That wasn't a kiss," he said, a little simmer of heat in his eyes distracting me from my better intentions.

I knew I should walk out of there. I knew it, and yet my mouth said, "Oh? Did you have something else in mind?"

"Yes." He stepped forward one step. Without being aware of it, I moved the remaining distance until our mouths were almost touching. Our bodies certainly were, the cold of the food pressed against my upper stomach doing nothing to detract from the wonderful feeling of his body, all hard lines and heat.

"Like what?" I teased, doing a little shimmy against him, ignoring the slight tickle of arugula where it poked out of its bag and rested between my breasts.

He didn't answer, not with words, anyway. His mouth was just as hot and sweet and wonderful as I remembered, and the second his lips met mine, I knew that I was dangerously close to throwing all caution to the wind and pouncing on him.

He kissed with not just his mouth, but his whole body, his arms and chest and legs pressed against me, leaving me wanting to feel his embrace without the irritation of clothing. I wiggled against him again, causing him to moan into my mouth. With the salad items squashed between our chests, I clutched his shoulders, pulling him closer to me.

And just when I was thinking very seriously about proposing we put dinner on hold for a bit while we romped upstairs into the nearest furnished bedroom, he pulled his mouth from mine and said, "You're squashing my sausage."

I wiggled again, enjoying greatly the way his eyes momentarily crossed. "Sorry about that. I didn't mean to hurt .. . oh. You meant actual sausage, not your ... er ..."

He had backed up and held out, with a rueful glance, two packages of now flattened sausage. I touched one of the squashed sausages with a finger. "Well, that's just ..."

"Awkward?" he offered.

I glanced quickly at him, but he was smiling, his eyes now warm and simmering with the heat generated by our kiss. "Only if we tell Vandal how it is his dinner came to be flat instead of round."

"I won't tell if you don't," he said with a jaunty wink, and turned to go back to the kitchen.

I sighed to myself as I watched him go, reminding myself that he was not available. Oh, sure, he might not mind kissing me, but he was clearly waiting for someone else to arrive. I didn't like that thought at all, not just because of the obvious, but because it meant Alden had no qualms kissing one woman while waiting for another.

"Right," I told myself as I plucked a piece of red lettuce from my cleavage. "Arm's length, that's the key. Just keep him at arm's length and all will be well."

Sometimes, it amazes me at just how naive I can be.

SIX

Dearest Mercy.

Alden stopped and glared at the paper sitting on the small desk in the bedroom he had claimed for his own. Dearest sounded dreadfully intimate. Far too intimate for people who'd just met.

And had kissed twice.

"None of that, now," he told himself, shifting in the chair nonetheless. The memory of those kisses would remain uppermost in his mind for a very long time.

Mercy, it has come to my attention . . .

"Now I sound like a supervisor about to fire her." Alden leaned back in the chair and tapped the pen on his chin as he thought. He'd come up with the idea to write Mercy a note because his therapist had once told him that if he couldn't say something in person, writing it was the next best thing. "There has to be a happy medium. Dear Mercy? Ugh. Hi, Mercy! Oh, lord no. Hmm."

Outside the window, a tree limb tapped on the glass. He glanced at the window, making a mental note to have the willow trimmed. The moon was just starting to come up, its silvery orb barely visible, and Alden, with a mind to airing out a room that evidently hadn't been used since Lady Sybilla's husband died some years before, went to the window to let in a little fresh air.

He struggled with the sash for a few minutes, finally managing to get it raised, the cool air swirling in around him, bringing with it the scent of the ocean, and grass, and the indefinable smell of dirt.

"That's better. Ah, what about a simple *Greetings, Mercy.* Yes. I like that." He returned to his chair, bending over the sheet of notepaper he'd discovered in the small desk that inhabited a corner of the room.

Greetings, Mercy. I hope this note finds you well. I felt obligated to write to explain the circumstances behind the kiss today. The second one, not the first. I think we both know the first was a pure accident, with no intentions behind it other than the simple acknowledgment of assistance received.

He paused, tapping pen to chin again. Was he sounding too businesslike again? He didn't want to give her the impression that he was a bloodless man who wasn't affected to the tips of his toes by the kisses they'd shared. And yet, when he read over the letter, that's exactly the impression he had.

"Pompous ass," he said to himself, and wadded up the sheet, tossing it into a nearby wicker trash bin.

Greetings, Mercy. That second kiss—I wanted to apologize for it at the same time I wish we could do it again and again....

"Oh, hell no," he said, crumpling the paper and tossing it with its brother. "Right. You're making this harder than it needs to be. Just write the damned words."

His hand wavered over the paper while phrases danced around in his head, leaving him as muddled as he was when faced with a woman in person. His frustration ramped into high gear, filling him with anger at his own inability to function, as well as desperation to express himself.

"Just do it!" he snarled at himself, his hand still held impotently over the paper. He wanted to swear at his failure, but couldn't get the words through the tangled emotions, and in the end, driven by a mad need to get something down, dashed off a few words, and leaped up from the desk, the force of his movement sending the chair toppling over backward.

The window sash dropped suddenly, the glass in the lower three panes breaking and tinkling to the carpet.

Alden snarled something rude to the house, and ran out of the room, pausing at the door next to his. He cast a furtive glance around the hall, then slipped the note under the door before returning to his room to clean up the glass.

Your eyes hold more shades of color than I've ever seen. Your smile could brighten the blackest of places. You bring joy where there was none.

He swept the glass into the trash, absently wondering what on earth he had done, but feeling nonetheless that it was the right thing to do. He was truly grateful to Mercy for trying to help him, even if at times she left him feeling more foot-in-mouth than ever before. Not many people other than his brothers and therapist had ever spent time trying to urge him over the awkwardness that seemed to be bred into his bones, but with Mercy, he felt a genuine interest in his well-being.

"Yes," he said aloud, drawing the curtains over the broken window. "It was only right that I should let her know how much I appreciate what she's done. Politeness doesn't cost anything."

The light next to his bed popped and went out.

He wondered, while he took a shower in the small bathroom attached to his bedroom, if Mercy had enough blankets. He'd checked out the room situation earlier in the day, acquiescing to Lady Sybilla's suggestion that he take over the lord's suite, which left three other bedrooms on that particular wing.

"My former room is available should you marry," she had told him with an air of grandiose benevolence. She was retiring for the night into her suite of rooms on the ground floor, which had formerly been a parlor, lady's sitting room, smoking room, and bathroom, all of which had been renovated to suit Lady Sybilla's current needs. Peeking into the rooms earlier in the day, Alden had noticed all the creature comforts, everything from a flat-screen television to a kitchenette complete with minute refrigerator, range, and microwave.

"I don't foresee needing the lady's suite any time in the future," Alden had told Lady Sybilla, and yet, that statement had been negated less than an hour later when, upon his showing Mercy the rooms, she cooed when entering the room nearest his.

"Oooh, periwinkle," she said, looking around the room with delight. It was decorated in various shades of lavender and periwinkle, very feminine and cloying, Alden thought, but admitted it hadn't been created to suit his tastes.

"I'll have this one if you don't mind," she said.

"Ugh. The purple room," Fenice said, pausing by the open doorway. She gestured farther down the hall. "My least favorite of all the colors. I'm in the red room on the other side of the bathroom, which we share. Just be sure to lock the doors when you want privacy, OK? Patrick is sleeping over the stable, he says in order to guard our equipment, but really, I think it's so he can slip out and meet up with the ladies."

"What ladies?" Mercy asked, looking confused.

"Whoever gives him the time of day." Fenice made a face. "Randy little sod. I'm glad you and Alden have hooked up. Otherwise, Patrick would be sure to hit on you. You're just his type."

"I am?" Mercy asked, obviously startled.

Alden was irritated on her behalf. If he heard that Patrick had bothered her the least little bit, he'd be forced to take action. Just the idea of Mercy being annoyed that way had him thinking dark thoughts.

"Just know he's out at the stable if you need him for anything," Fenice finished.

"That doesn't sound very comfortable," Mercy said, turning slowly in a circle to examine what furnishings remained (a bed, a massive wardrobe, which would probably have to be dismantled to remove it from the room, two chairs before an unlit fireplace, and a faded periwinkle and white striped fainting couch).

"Don't you believe it. I saw what he did with the groom's room there—he's got a gas ring for tea, cooler full of beer, and a massive air mattress. He's as happy as he can be. Right, I'm to bed. Good night, you two."

"She definitely thinks we have something going on," Mercy told him when Fenice left.

Alden cleared his throat, relieved that Fenice had gone. "She can think whatever she likes. We know the truth."

"That we don't have anything going on," Mercy said, nodding.

"That's right, we don't."

They stared at each other for a few seconds; then Alden remembered he was in her bedroom, and he wished her a good night.

"You don't think there are any rodents here?" she asked as he was leaving. He paused at the door. "Mice, rats, that sort of thing. I have a phobia about them. I don't see any signs of mouse droppings, or anything that's been gnawed, but I don't suppose you know for sure that there aren't any here?"

He had been on the verge of telling her he had no doubt whatsoever that the house was inhabited by mice, since it was of an age that allowed such things—not to mention having been neglected for decades—but the words stopped before he could get them out.

Mercy hefted one of the chairs and peered into the corner before lifting up the edge of a faded blue and rose rug. "Nope, no signs of poop."

"I think you are safe," he said, making a mental note to call an exterminator and have him assess how much it would cost to have the house mouse-proofed. Or at least their living quarters. "If it would make you feel better, I could put a few traps out."

"Ugh," she said, shivering and rubbing her arms. "That would be even worse. I'd be forever holding my breath waiting for the trap to go off. And once it did, then there would be dead mice all over the place. Horribly dead mice. Ugh, ugh, ugh. Wait—are you saying I need to have traps?"

"Not at all. I simply was offering to put some out to make you feel more secure."

"Oh, OK." She relaxed, and gave him a little smile. "If you say there aren't any mice here, then that's good enough for me. Night."

"Good night."

He'd walked back to his room after that, and spent some time in contemplation of what he wanted to say to her. Then he'd hit upon the brilliant idea of writing the note, and now here he was, lying in bed, glad both that he'd written the note to express his gratitude, and also that he'd had the foresight to bring with him bed linens, pillows, and a couple of duvets.

He ignored the rustling in the wall (he really would have to get an exterminator in) as well as the tap of the tree on the window frame around the now glassless windowpanes, and listened instead to the distant rumble of the surf, allowing it to lull him gently, inevitably to sleep.

It was late, the darkest part of night, when a noise filtered through his sleeping brain to wake him. It wasn't a noise that he expected to hear—the tree tapping, or a night bird calling—but one that instead had a stealthy quality that sent him from sleeping to groggy awareness.

Someone was in his room.

He fumbled for the lamp next to his bed before remembering that the bulb had gone out earlier in what he was coming to think of as the house's attempt to let him know it did not appreciate his presence. "Whosit?" he said inarticulately.

"Alden? It's me." The voice was breathy and soft, and with it, the bed dipped down on the side nearest the door. "You were wrong! There was a mouse in my room! A horrible, vicious, beastly thing."

"Hrn?" he asked, rubbing his face and peering at the barely visible black form that was silhouetted against the darkness of the room.

"A mouse. Were you asleep? You're awake now, right? I said that I have a mouse!"

"Don't bring it in the bed," he said sleepily. "I'm not afraid of them like you are, but I won't have one in my bed."

"Oh my god, don't even joke about me touching it." The bed shook a little as she shifted. "It was huge, Alden. A massive brute of a beast."

"Rat?" he asked without thinking.

"EEK!"

He sighed, and rubbed his face again. "Would you turn on the overhead lights? The bedside lamp committed suicide earlier."

"Sure." The mattress moved again as she rose. "Next to the door?"

"Yes. Argh." He blinked at the sudden glare of lights, squinting at the sight of Mercy standing at the door in what had to be the single most erotic-looking piece of nightwear ever created. It appeared to be made of spider's webs that revealed more than they hid, long, flowing sweeps of it caressing her curves in a way that had his tongue cleaving to the roof of his mouth.

"Sorry. That is bright." Mercy rubbed her bare arms, the movement doing wonderful things to her (nearly bare) breasts. "This is going to sound really weird, but would you mind if I spent the night in here?"

She wanted to spend the night with him? Had his letter been taken in a way he hadn't anticipated?

"Assuming you don't have mice, that is," she added.

He blinked at her a couple of times, thought about telling her the rustling in the walls warned that his room might not be as barren of rodents as she would like, but decided he would be downright certifiable to do so. "I don't mind, no."

"Oh, good." Her shoulders slumped a little in relief. She glanced around the room, taking in the scarce amount of furnishings. "Um. You don't have a big chair or anything I could curl up in?"

"Just the one at the desk, and I took that from the kitchen." He wondered if her almost-gown would tear if she breathed deeply. He fervently hoped so.

"Oh." She looked doubtfully at him where he lay propped up on one elbow.

"I believe this is the point where, if we were in a romantic comedy film, you would join me in bed and you'd barricade your side of the bed with a line of pillows."

She smiled, warming him in ways that would become embarrassing if he didn't have a thick duvet covering him. "And if we were in a romantic novel, we'd wake up to have 'accidental' sex because I would somehow manage to roll myself on top of you while asleep, and we would then both wake up to find ourselves in a compromising position, and so would decide, what the heck? Since we're lying in woman-on-top position already, why not go ahead and have sex?"

He looked at her, aroused to the point where it was going to be not just embarrassing but painful, and wondered if she was hinting at what he thought she was hinting. He tried to form the words to ask her, but the thought of what she'd say if he misinterpreted kept his tongue tied in verbal knots.

"Well?" she said, tipping her head to the side.

Of course she wasn't hinting that she wanted to sleep with him. She had just been kind earlier in kissing him, the act meant as a form of therapy. Highly erotic, enjoyable therapy. Nothing more.

"Alden?"

"Hmm?" No, what he needed to do was turn his room over to her, so she could spend the night in mouse-free comfort. He'd offer to take her room, instead, and thus would martyr himself on the altar of chivalry. Dammit, his dressing gown was all the way across the room next to the door to the bathroom. He supposed that if he rose while clutching the duvet to him, he could manage to scuttle crablike to the door, snagging his dressing gown en route.

"Are you going to ask me to join you? Or do you expect me to try to sleep on that kitchen chair?"

He gawked at her, a flat-out gawk. She didn't just say

what he thought he heard. She couldn't. Could she? He'd better ask, just to be sure. "Erm?"

Her nose wrinkled in puzzlement. "Was that an 'erm, I'd love for you to climb into this bed in my lovely mouseless room,' or was that more of a 'erm, I'm saving myself for the woman who is coming and about whom I've been terribly mysterious, and she would not understand if she heard that you spent the night in my bed even though we didn't do anything naughty' sort of situation?"

"I don't . . . I'm not . . ." He stammered to a stop, then chastised himself and added immediately, "My brain has apparently ceased working for the night."

"OK, now I'm really starting to feel vulnerable," she said, rubbing her arms again, a look of hesitancy replacing her amused teasing expression. "Should I go try to bunk with Fenice? I will do so if you can't stomach the thought of me sleeping in your bed."

"No." He flipped back the duvet, careful to keep it draped over his groin, which at this point was hard and needy and telling him to stop talking and get with the action already. "You don't need to go sleep with Fenice. I just . . . I never thought . . . that is, you don't seem like . . ." He stopped, wanting to bang his head on the wall. Why was it he could never say things without them coming out all wrong?

She had hurried over to the bed at his invitation, but paused in the act of crawling between the covers. "I don't seem like what?"

He stared at her, unable to put into words the thoughts that were rolling around in his beleaguered brain.

She stiffened. "You wouldn't by any chance have been about to say that I don't seem like the sort of woman who jumps into bed with a man she's just met?" She took a deep breath, her eyes burning with an intensity that both aroused and worried him. "There's a name for women—and men—like that. Tell me you did not just stop yourself from using it."

"I didn't. I wouldn't. I was just trying to say that no woman has ever wanted to . . . not on first meeting . . . oh, hell."

She crossed her arms, her expression black. "I see."

"Bloody, bloody, hell. Mercy—"

"No, no need to explain." She took a deep breath, which he was too distressed by his own ineptitude to appreciate. "It's quite clear what you think of me. I will just point out that you, as a man who just met a woman, were clearly thinking about doing exactly what you're damning me for. Not that I was offering to have sex with you; I simply wanted a respite from the mice. But you might want to think about that when you're tarring me with your brush of morality. Since we are at such odds, I will return to my room and remove my unwelcome self from your presence."

She swung around on her heel and marched to the door, slamming it loudly as she exited.

He winced at the noise, then sighed and punched the pillow next to him. How the hell could he have screwed up something so wonderful? Christ, there was no hope for him if Mercy—patient, thoughtful Mercy—couldn't be around without him making a complete ass of himself.

The door was flung open again. Mercy bolted through it and closed the door quickly, leaning against it and panting slightly. "That beast is still in my room. It charged me—so help me god, it charged me!"

He looked at her, unwilling to say anything lest it come out wrong and he insult her again.

"Here's the deal. I get into bed with you, and spend the night. There will be no touching. No kissing. Nothing that could even remotely be interpreted as actions belonging to a woman with no morals."

"I never meant—"

She climbed onto the bed, covering herself with the duvet before using the edge of her hand to tuck it down between them. "And in the morning, once we're both in full possession of our faculties, you can apologize for hurting my feelings. And I will accept your apology because I know that sometimes you say things that you don't mean to say. Until then, a state of frosty détente occurs between us. Nothing more."

She rolled onto her side, giving him her back. There was enough room on the massive bed for her to lie completely separate from him, no part of their bodies touching. His penis sang a mournful dirge over that fact. Alden, with a look at the back of her head, said softly, "You don't have to wait until morning for an apology. I in no way meant to besmirch your character by implying you had low moral values. I was trying to say that . . . that . . . ."

She rolled over and cocked an eyebrow. "Well?"

"No woman has ever wanted me that way before," he said in a rush. "Not where they wanted to go to bed on the first date. I was rather flattered when I thought that you wanted to, but now I know better."

"But we haven't even had a date," she pointed out.

"At first meeting, then," he said, aware that his cheeks were unusually warm. "I'm not like Vandal. Women don't seem to be attracted to me. Which is why I was surprised that you . . . well, you were here. In my room. But I was wrong about your intentions for being here, and for that, I apologize."

"You get points for being adorably endearing and frank, but they will not be applied to your total until morning," she told him, and returned to her original position. "Good night, Alden. Would you turn off the light? It's too bright to sleep."

"Erm . . ."

"Again with the 'erm.' What is it this time? You want me to do it because I'm closer to the light?" She snuggled into the bed, pulling the duvet up to her nose. "I'm traumatized by the monstrous behemoth charging around my room. Besides, I'm still a bit hurt. You get to turn off the light."

"I'd really rather not," Alden said, well aware that just the thought of Mercy in his bed had returned his penis to what he thought of as a raging state.

"Don't be so lazy." She snuggled deeper. "Not to mention ungentlemanly."

"Fine, but don't say I didn't warn you." He got out of the bed and padded barefoot to the door.

"Why would I—oh. You sleep in the altogether."

He stopped at the light and turned to face her.

Her eyes widened. "And you're . . . hoo! Sorry. I didn't realize you were fully . . . uh . . . engorged."

"Aroused is, I believe, the preferred term." The way she looked at him made him harder than ever. He reached for the light switch.

"I don't know," she said, her gaze firmly affixed to his privates. "That looks pretty gorged to me. I never understood how men could walk like that. It looks . . . painful."

"It can be. It is." He clicked off the light and, holding out his hands so as not to stumble into the chair, made his way back to the bed. "And to answer your earlier accusations, I fully realize that there are words for men who jump into bed with women they just met, but I like to think of it as a meeting of two like-minded adults who wish to explore their sexuality with each other rather than something disreputable and unsavory. Not that we are going to do that, but I do feel obligated to mention that."

"Now, you see, I like that description. And if I knew you better, and you were still inclined that way, I might have been tempted to indulge in that meeting of minds, so to speak. Only with bodies. Oh well. It is what it is."

He climbed under the duvet, still warm from his body. "I don't suppose you'd like—"

"No. I mean, it's not that I'm against it, per se, but even if I was willing to throw caution to the wind, there's nothing like almost being called a ho to deflate a girl's lust."

"I didn't! I wouldn't call you a ho—"

"OK, OK. No need to get riled. I said I'd forgive and forget in the morning."

She wiggled down into the bed. He lay on his back, looking over at her dark shape, so tantalizingly close, and yet just beyond his (figurative) reach, and wondered if she was really here because of the note he'd slid under her door. "Will that happen before or after you accidentally roll onto me while we're both asleep?"

She giggled. "Let's hope it's before. Good night, Alden."

"Good night, Mercy."

The scent of her, warm and soft and so near, seemed to cause little silken cords of desire and need to wrap tight around him. His penis grew even harder, something he thought would have been impossible. A joke about using it in lieu of a sledgehammer occurred to him, and he was on the verge of sharing it with her, but didn't when he wasn't sure how she'd take it.

Mercy shifted slightly, her foot brushing his leg. The contact sent fire skimming through his veins.

He sighed. It was going to be a very long night.

SEVEN

I wasn't sure if I was happy or sad that I woke up to find myself on the mattress, and not lying on Alden as I had joked. I looked over at where he lay sprawled on his belly next to me, with one arm under his pillow, and the other on my stomach. Likewise, one of his legs rested on mine, causing little pins and needles in my foot.

I gently slid my foot out from under his, wiggling my toes and wincing at the sharp sensation as feeling came back to it.

Alden's eyelashes lay thick and dark on his cheeks, his two eyebrows arched in a manner that made my straight brows green with envy. He had a faint russet brown stubble on his lower cheeks and chin, and lips that were neither thin nor plump, but pleasingly in between. And oh, how soft they were . . . and what fires they could stir.

His shoulders were definitely on the broad side, with nicely defined muscles that avoided being bodybuilder extreme, while still making my fingers want to stroke down his shoulders and biceps. He had a little scar on the back of one shoulder blade.

What was it about him that interested me so much? Was it just my need to help someone who was hurting? I shook my head even as that thought occurred. There was more to my interest in Alden than just that—I didn't want to admit that I was physically attracted to a man I had just met, but the sad truth was that he really did turn my crank. And if that made me the sort of woman who jumps into bed at the drop of a hat, then so be it.

I couldn't help but smile. I was, after all, in bed with him. And what was wrong with the idea of allowing myself to act on my desires? Oh, sure, the right thing, the reasonable thing, would be to give Alden the space he needed to see if he would hit it off with this blind date who was on her way.

But she wasn't here, and I was. And more important, Alden was a big boy. He could turn down any offer I made. Surely I owed it to him to allow him to make his own decisions?

My gaze strayed to the lovely curves of his shoulders and back. It might be wrong, but I really did want to touch him. And kiss him. And lick him . . .

I wondered if his behind was really as nice as I remembered it from the night before. With a quick glance at his face (his eyes remained closed), and a moment to monitor his breathing (still steady and slow), I casually stretched and shifted my leg in a way that would cause the duvet to slide down.

Yes, it was just as nice as I remembered. Very nice. Worthy of admiration, even. Except . . . I moved a little to better see the far side of his butt, where a dark mark caught my attention. He had a tattoo! An ass tattoo. I couldn't quite make it out, though. And suddenly, I really wished to know what it was.

With another careful glance at his face, I sat up and leaned over his butt, careful not to touch it. The light in the room was too dim to see clearly. Carefully, I got onto my knees, and braced a hand to support myself, while holding my hair and nightgown back so they wouldn't brush against him when I leaned down to examine the tattoo.

"It's a hedgehog."

"Eep!" I said, jumping a little, which, given my off-balance and awkward position, meant I tumbled down on top of him. "Gloriosky, Alden! You could have given me a heart attack."

One eye opened to consider me. "I didn't think my ass was that bad."

"No, it has nothing to do with . . ." I pushed myself up, and only just kept myself from patting the body part in question. "It has nothing to do with your butt. You scared me. You could have warned me you were awake."

"Why? You seemed to be enjoying staring at my ass."

I sat back down, and pinched his arm. "I wasn't staring at your ass. Not specifically. I was trying to figure out what the tat was. Why, if you don't mind my asking, do you have a tattoo of a hedgehog on its back legs on your behind?"

"It's a hedgehog rampant, actually. It's part of my personal coat of arms that my brothers had created for my twenty-first birthday, the same birthday where they took me out and got me so drunk that I agreed to honor the hedgehog in the only way I could: with a tattoo on my ass."

"I think it's cute."

"Thank you." He flexed his butt cheeks. "I have no complaints."

"Silly. I meant your tat, not your butt. Although . . ." I cleared my throat. His eyes were closed again, which made it a bit easier to ask what I wanted to ask. "Would you mind . . . I know this is seriously inappropriate, but since we are here in bed together, and you're naked, and I'm in my good nightie, would you mind if I touched it?"

"My tattoo?"

"Yes. Well, that and your butt."

His eyes opened at that. "You want to touch my ass? Why?"

I cleared my throat again, and tried not to wiggle my fingers in a blatant show of grabby-ass. "It's . . . nice. And I would very much like to touch that swoopy part on the sides where it indents."

He glanced over his shoulder at his butt, and gave another flex before turning his attention to me. "Do I get to touch yours?"

"I'm not lying here naked and exposed."

"You exposed me."

Dammit, he had a point.

"True, but I am wearing appropriate sleeping apparel."

"Sweetheart," he said with a twitch of his lips that made me feel a good ten degrees warmer, "that bit of nothing you have on is anything but appropriate."

"I notice that you're not having any problem talking to me now," I said in a blatant change of subject, then decided that wasn't fair. I couldn't play coy with him, not when the reality was that I wouldn't mind in the least if he touched my butt. And legs. And breasts, and pretty much all of me. "I'm sorry, that was wrong of me."

"Why?" he asked, frowning. "I am talking to you, but it's due to the fact that I'm feeling quite a few emotions that are blocking out my social anxieties. I believe I explained that phenomenon to you."

"You did, but my apology was about me pretending I wouldn't like for you to touch me, when the reality is that I would."

"Mercy," he said, giving his butt another flex.

Twenty degrees. Maybe I felt twenty degrees hotter. "Hmm?"

"Is there a reason you're talking and not touching?"

"You didn't say I could. I wouldn't wish to presume, especially after I made such a big deal last night about telling you I didn't do the very thing that I want to do now."

"I can say with all honesty that at this moment, you may consider my ass your own to do with as you like. So long as you offer me the same consideration."

"Deal," I said, and got onto my knees to commence fondling. "I don't know what it is about men's butts when they have this swoopy part, but hoo mama, do I like it."

"And I like you liking it." He groaned into the pillow when I put both hands on his cheeks, and gave a little squeeze.

I had the worst urge to bite him, but decided to keep that rather shocking reaction to myself. "Would you mind if

I . . . er . . . expanded the territory?"

"That depends. Where do you intend to go? Up or down?"

I gazed upon the wonderful smorgasbord of Alden that lay before me. I just wanted to touch and taste all of him, but again, I didn't want to admit that. At least, not just yet. "Can I do both?"

"Yes, but I warn you, when it's my turn, you're going to have to face the consequences of all this exploration."

"I hope you don't mean that literally," I said, sliding my hands up his warm, satiny flesh to his lower back. He was hot, but with every touch, I was growing even hotter. "No one likes a face full of unexpected penis."

"Unexpected Penis is my grunge band name," he said when I scooted over slightly, and spread my hands along his rib cage.

I paused and looked down at him.

He opened an eye and rolled it back to look at me. "Didn't you ever play the fake band name game?"

"Oh, that, yes. Grunge band. Heh. Would you mind rolling over?"

"Much as I'm enjoying this unanticipated massage—you may have that for your grunge band name—I hesitate to point out that if you continue, I will feel obligated to do everything I can to seduce you."

The secret, hidden parts of me gave a thumbs-up to that idea. Just the thought of that magnificent body lying next to me doing all the things that I'd been thinking of the night before had me restless with need. "The way I see it is that we're both consenting adults, and although we've only just met, we have had a lot of conversation, and beyond that, we have a spark going on between us—we do have a spark, don't we?"

"I believe so, yes."

"We have a spark, so that means it's perfectly OK if we want to build that spark into a fire. Or in your case"—I stroked his behind again—"an inferno."

"You've forgiven me for my verbal faux pas last night?"

"Forgiven and forgotten." I wanted to urge him over onto his back so I could frolic on all the good parts of his front side, but didn't want to shock him with my wanton ways.

Then again, I'd just announced that I wanted to have sex with him after knowing him for a day, less than eight hours after stating the opposite. So much for high morals.

"Excellent," he said, and before I could so much as tickle his hedgehog, he flipped over onto his back, and had whisked my nightie off over my head, pulling me over his body as he did so.

"Oooh," I said, giggling a little as his very aroused penis poked me in the hip. "You weren't lying about your unexpected penis. Are you sure 'engorged'—"

"Quite sure. 'Engorged,' 'swollen,' and 'throbbing' are three adjectives that I'd prefer not be used when referencing my penis. You have lovely breasts. I take it you don't mind if I reciprocate all the tormenting you've been doing to my poor body?"

"Reciprocate away." I spread my hands across his chest at the same time his hands slid down my back and squeezed my butt. "I love how you talk, Alden. And before your anxiety tells you that was my subtle way of saying you're talking too much, I didn't mean that at all. The opposite, as a matter of fact, especially since I'm the same way. My last boyfriend says I wasn't so much a moaner as I was a talker when it came to sex."

"I will admit," he said, tipping his head so as to be able to reach my right breast, "that a woman I was with once told me that the fact that I talked during intimate times caused her to strike me off her list of partners."

"Silly woman," I said on a gasp when his mouth closed around one of my nipples. I arched back, rubbing my thumbs across his nipples, giving them gentle little tweaks that I was pleased to see made his eyes cross. Small rivulets of fire seemed to trace along my veins at the touch of his mouth to my flesh, sending my libido into overdrive. Rather than the pleasurable tingle of anticipation I'd felt at the thought of lovemaking with him, I was suddenly cast into a raging blaze of pure, unadulterated desire. It left me breathless and speechless and writhing with mingled passion and need.

"Hmm?" he said when I made an inarticulate sound in my throat.

I twisted so that my other breast could receive its due attention, shivering with the heat that his mouth seemed to generate inside me. I clutched his shoulders, my breasts heavy and sensitive, and just when I was thinking seriously about spontaneously combusting, his fingers stroked their way up my thigh, and hit ground zero.

"Hrn," I said, my body tightening around his fingers in a way that warned me an orgasm was imminent.

"Pardon?" His fingers stopped moving in me.

I opened my eyes, and glared down at him.

"What did you say?" he asked, a tiny frown pulling his brows together.

I searched my mind. Had I spoken? Despite my declaration to the contrary, at that moment I didn't think I could form actual words. At least not ones that made any sense. "Hrn?" I asked, and wiggled my hips on his now stilled fingers.

A slow smile turned up the corners of his lips. "You like that, do you?"

"Hrn!" I said, my toes curling when his fingers moved again.

"Then you're going to love this, my talkative little minx." He rolled me onto my back, kissing his way down my chest to my belly, and then lower, moving until he was between my knees. "I can't tell you how nice it is to have someone who enjoys talking during lovemaking. There's so many things to say. And ask. Oral sex, for instance. I assume by the way you are trying to pull me down to your . . . erm . . . lady parts . . . that you are happy to participate. Now, let me tell you what I plan to do, and if there's something in particular you'd like, I'd be happy to oblige."

"Alden," I snarled, glaring at him down the length of my needy, desperate, deprived body. "Too. Much. Talking!"

He laughed, and gently nipped my hip. "All right, my demanding one, I shall stop talking, and give you the pleasure you so obviously want."

I collapsed back onto the bed, my body buzzing with anticipation as his warm breath approached the parts that were so desperately awaiting him. Just as I was grabbing the sheets to brace myself for what was sure to be a hell of a sexual experience, there was a creak outside Alden's door, a brief tap, and the door opened.

I had just enough time to grab the duvet and fling it over us, leaving my shoulders and head exposed.

"Alden? Just wanted to let you know—" Vandal stopped at the sight of me, frowning as he looked around the room. "This is Alden's room, isn't it? Where is he?"

Alden, who had stiffened at the noise, jerked upright. Vandal's eyebrows rose when the bottom half of the duvet moved apparently of its own accord.

"Ah. Just so. Well, when he's done, would you tell him the kitchen is on fire? Fenice has it confined to the pantry area, but she thought he'd like to know." Vandal closed the door before I could do more than clutch the duvet to my chest.

"It's on fire?" Alden emerged from beneath the duvet, his hair ruffled, his face furious. "Bloody house! It's gone too far this time!"

"What?" I asked stupidly, trying to understand what was happening other than Alden had been interrupted during a moment I would have preferred to have been allowed to continue. "What is going too far? Should I call the fire department? Alden! You can't go out like that!"

He paused at the door, glanced down at himself (still aroused, I was pleased to note, although why, I didn't know— it wasn't likely I was going to see any action now), and with a tsk of annoyance grabbed his jeans, and pulled them on while hopping his way to the door.

I sighed, looked up at the ceiling for a few seconds, and

mentally apologized to all my girly bits for getting them worked up over nothing. "Next time I won't let there be any interruptions," I promised them, and with a muttered oath grabbed my nightgown, Alden's shirt, and my slippers, and donned them all while making my way downstairs to the kitchen.

"Ah. There you are. I was looking for you." Lady Sybilla emerged from a door once I'd made it downstairs, causing me to jump and clutch Alden's shirt, which I'd put on over my nightie. She eyed me with a critical look. "That garment is inappropriate."

"Yes, I know it is, I'm sorry, but—"

"You will get chilblains in the library dressed like that," she continued, just as if I hadn't spoken. Waving an imperious hand, she added, "Adams! Bring me the coat Sir James bought in Saint Petersburg."

The equally ancient old woman who I suspected was more of a friend than an actual servant to Lady Sybilla sucked her teeth at me, then disappeared into the gloom of their shared sitting room.

"That's really sweet of you, but it's not necessary," I explained, trying to do up the buttons on Alden's shirt. "I just threw this on when Vandal said the kitchen was on fire. If you don't mind—"

"Here it is, your ladyship." Adams's voice came from beneath a mountain of fur the size and approximate texture of an Irish wolfhound. The fur was projected toward me, and with Lady Sybilla watching me, disapproval dripping off every wrinkle, I took the horrible coat.

"You would be unable to do your work if you were to take ill. Put it on, gel."

I sighed to myself and, with a disgusted wrinkle of my nose, slid into the beastly thing. It smelled of long-dead animal (what was it? badger? plagued wolf? yeti?), mothballs, and something vaguely skunky, and I swore to myself as I tottered under the weight of it that I was going to ditch it as soon as I was out of sight.

Unfortunately, that wasn't until I reached the kitchen door. With a little wave down the long hall to Lady Sybilla and Adams, silently watching me, I pushed open the kitchen door and entered what I figured would be a room full of smoke.

It wasn't. But that was only because the pantry door had been closed, so only a bit of smoke had leaked out.

"Is the fire . . . ack." I stopped to hack and wheeze. Although the small window a good six feet up the wall had been opened, the room was still hazy with smoke. I coughed a couple of times, and asked hoarsely, "Is the fire out?"

"Yes. We're just checking the wall to see if the fire reached it." A shirtless Alden, his chest glistening with sweat, and black with soot, pulled out a bin of what looked like potatoes, and stacked it with a collection of assorted kitchen paraphernalia. He knelt and felt the wall. On the other side of the pantry, Fenice, clad in what I thought of as Renaissance Faire wear of black leggings, ankle boots, and some sort of leather jerkin, was one-handedly trying to toss foam-laden items into a large black trash bin.

"Here, let me do that," I said, hurrying forward. "Your shoulder must be hurting like hell if you were trying to put out the fire on your own."

"It wasn't that bad, and I had an extinguisher," she said, nodding to where a home fire extinguisher sat in a stack of blackened cardboard and charred wood. "It was just the flour bin, although how that caught on fire is beyond my understanding."

"It's the house," Alden said, sliding his hands along the wall. "It hates me, and would rather self-destruct than have me repair it."

"Heh." Fenice shoved a soot-stained wad of wet paper towels into the trash can. "Still, I wouldn't mind if you— goddess above and below! What are you wearing?"

"I think it's part of a Russian wolf," I said, struggling out of the monstrous coat.

Alden glanced over to me, his expression turning to one of horror. "That looks like a dead musk ox. Where did you get it?"

"It's not mine, if that's what's worrying you. I don't do fur. Lady Sybilla forced it upon me because she was under the impression I was dashing off to work in the library clad in nothing but my nightgown and your shirt." I dragged the coat over to the wall where pegs held various gray and faded aprons, and hung it on one of them. The peg promptly fell off the wall, taking the coat with it. I pretended I didn't notice. "What can I do to help?"

An hour later Alden and I dragged ourselves up the stairs to our rooms. I paused at the door of mine. "I think I'll take a shower, since I'm supposed to start work soon. I'd ask you if you want to join me, but the shower is small, my skin itches like crazy because I think that musk ox had mange, and I never really did get into the idea of sex in a shower. I mean, it's slippery in there. Someone could fall."

Alden gave a short bark of laughter, but didn't meet my gaze, a sure sign he was feeling awkward again. I thought about just letting him cope with that—after all, it really was not my problem to constantly be fixing. But then the memory of what a nice time we'd had before the flour bin caught on fire returned, and I strode over to him, grabbed his head with both hands, and kissed the living daylights out of him.

His mouth was as hot as I remembered, and spicy, due to the package of cinnamon candies that Fenice had offered us (evidently she was addicted to them) while we were cleaning.

"You taste like gingerbread," I said into his mouth, growling a little when he dug his fingers into my hips and pulled me up tight against his groin.

"Are you sure you don't want to shower together?" he asked, his eyes changing from shy to passion-filled in an instant. It made me warm just seeing how much he wanted to continue our previous activities. "We could pick up where we left off."

"Tempting, very tempting, but it is my first day on the job, and I hate to be late because I was having mind-blowing sex. I mean, that's a pretty good excuse for being late for most things, but Fenice and Vandal already think we're a couple, and I don't think we need to reinforce that. Because this is just . . ." I made a vague gesture.

"Consenting adults indulging themselves?" he said, releasing my hips.

I bit the end of his nose. "Exactly. We're just scratching a mutual itch. Right?"

"Right," he said, nodding.

"Tonight, however, is another matter." I waggled my eyebrows at him. "Assuming you're up to it."

"I suspect I'll be aroused to the point of engorgement," he answered. "Assuming the house doesn't self-destruct around my ears while I'm trying to renovate it."

"You could always come out to the garden and play medieval knight," I told him, forcing myself away from his tempting self. "I'd be happy to teach you archery."

"Another time, perhaps," he said, squaring his sooty shoulders. "I'm not going to let the house beat me. I'm going to renovate it if it kills me!"

"So dashing!" I said, giving him one last little nose nibble. "I'll see you later, then. Happy painting and building and whatever-else-ing you are doing."

A half hour later I was present at the garden when the clock struck nine. I met Alec, the man who handled the armor and took care of the weapons, and was briefed on the day's schedule.

"The combat classes will be ongoing throughout the day," Vandal told me as he handed me a sheet of paper showing the day's schedule. "Your classes will be held five times a day for an hour each session."

"Gotcha," I said, tucking away the paper in the pocket of my jeans.

He frowned at the gesture. "You'll be expected to help out Fenice with the clothing booth when you are not giving classes. There may be some drop-ins, but we are limiting those to the times between the first and second scheduled classes. Is that what you plan on wearing?"

I glanced down. My T-shirt was a size too large, which I preferred since it gave my arms unobstructed movement. "Yes. I'm not very medieval, but it's comfy."

Vandal's outfit was about as authentic as you could make it—leggings complete with cross-garters going up his calves, a long tunic, and a flat-topped wide-brimmed hat that curled upward at the ends. A little smile played along his lips as he leaned close to say, "It may be comfortable, but it also offers anyone who cares to look a view of your lovely breasts."

I glanced down and realized he was right—the shirt was baggy enough that when I moved, it was fairly easy to see down it. "Oh, crap."

"Nothing of the sort. I quite enjoy the view." He leaned in a little closer, and I was reminded of Fenice's warning about the flirty nature of her brother. "If I told you that you had lovely eyes, would you consider that inappropriate?"

I looked at him, puzzled. "You like my eyes?"

"I do." His smile grew. "I find them irresistible."

"Oh, so it was you who wrote that note?" I felt oddly deflated. I'd assumed that it was Alden who had slipped the sweet note under my door, but now . . . I rubbed my arms. The note didn't seem nearly so nice now.

"Note?" He frowned, then suddenly his expression cleared. "Ah, the note. You enjoyed it?"

"Well, of course I did," I said lightly. "It was very flattering, but really, Vandal, I have to say—"

"Good, good." He bustled past me when Fenice appeared and beckoned him. "We can talk more later about how it made you feel, and what you'd like to do about it, but right now, I must go heed my sister's call. She looks frazzled."

I stood for a few minutes, bothered by the idea of Vandal sending me little notes of admiration. It seemed all right with Alden, since he wasn't a flirty soul, but Vandal . . . I shook my head. He was handsome and all, but I wasn't particularly interested in him.

"Patrick, two cars just pulled up, full of what looks like a rugby team."

"That would be the morning session," he said, and hurried off to greet them.

Fenice fussed with the registration papers at the small desk that served as our administrative center, before eyeing me. "You should get dressed."

"Well, I thought I'd wear this—"

"That's not the Hard Day's Knights way. People expect us to be in some sort of costume, or else they feel cheated. Go pick out something from the wardrobe bins to serve as your official on-duty ensemble. Oh, and I'd advise you to make it something practical," Fenice warned as the first of the attendees strolled around the side of the house from the designated parking area. "Not only are you going to be in it all day, but you have to be able to shoot in it. So don't go for anything tight or too revealing."

"Gotcha." I dashed to the section of a small storage building where Fenice had hung a long metal rod, from which a variety of Faire clothing hung in a number of sizes and colors. Most of it was laceable, which she had told me allowed them to cover a wide range of sizes by cinching it down to whatever circumference was needed.

"Let's see . . . full-on lady of the manor?" I shook my head at a lovely rose velvet kirtle. "Nope, not at all what an archer would wear. How about standard Robin Hood?" I held out a forest green leather jerkin that was likely the twin of Fenice's. "Naw, not me. Oooh, pretty blue . . . oh. It's torn."

A lovely summer-sky blue gauze chemise peeked out of a rattan basket that I vaguely remember Fenice telling me was for items that needed repairing. I held the chemise up, admiring the simple sleeveless scoop-neck design, but knowing there was no way I could wear it with half the skirt torn off and muddied. It looked like it had been chewed up by a lawn mower. I set it down again, unhappy that I would have to wear something that didn't appeal to me as much, but after browsing through the remainder of the items, I returned to the chemise.

Two minutes later, I emerged into the sunshine of a lovely late summer morning, pleased with the resulting outfit of chemise topped with a black under-bust corset. I'd cut off the mangled part of the chemise, leaving it at a very nontraditional above-the-knee length, which didn't scream Medieval Faire wear, but neither was it a T-shirt and jeans. "Plus, I like the blue," I said aloud to myself as I hurried over to where three people were waiting at the archery butts. "It's my lucky color, and if there's any day I need luck on my side, it's today. . . . Hello! I'm Mercy, your instructor for the day. Are you all ready to rumble?"

Three pairs of startled eyes turned to me. I gave them a bright smile. Maybe this wasn't going to be as easy as I'd first thought. "In an archery sense, that is. You know, nailing the bull right in his eye."

The three people—two women and a man—just stared at me.

I made a little jabbing motion toward the archery butts. "Bull's-eye? Anyone?" I gave a mental sigh, and upped the wattage in my smile. "Right, enough levity. Shall we get started?"

The morning flew by faster than I had thought it would. The year I'd spent instructing high school students was enough to get me over the hump of how to explain the art of the bow and arrow to newcomers. The first three sessions whipped past, after which I trotted to the shed to relieve Fenice from her dress-up duties.

There I found a gaggle of older ladies, a handful of teenage girls, and a couple of kids who were pulling everything out of tubs that Fenice had set aside for when other items had become worn or damaged. I directed the ladies to the section of lockers that Vandal had bought from some salvage yard, got the older women into full-length dresses, the teens into skirts and peasant tops, and the kids into tunics and hats, along with their plastic replica weapon of choice.

"Is there jousting?" the mom of one of the more obnoxious boys asked. The kid whacked me on the shin with his plastic sword, and ran screaming bloody murder out of the shed. "Tibby does love jousting. We saw it last year, and he was just crazy for us to get him a horse."

"Samantha wants to shoot a bow and arrow. Do you teach that?" the second mom asked, nodding toward her daughter, who was wearing a tiara and a gauzy, Princess Elsa from Frozen rip-off dress while galloping after her sword-wielding buddy.

"I am the archery instructor, yes, but we do not allow children to participate for insurance reasons," I said, sending thanks to Fenice that she had nixed Vandal's idea to include kids in the lessons. "Adults only, I'm afraid."

"What a shame," the woman said, and hurried off to collect her child when she got in an argument about an antler battle horn that was meant to be an accessory for another outfit.

Fenice returned not long after that. "The caterer is here. It's your choice of egg and tomato sandwich, or salmon paste sandwich."

"Ah. Both sound delightful," I lied, "but you know, I think I'll just trot up to the house and grab a quick something if you don't mind."

She shrugged. "It makes no difference to me. Just be back in half an hour. You have another class at two, and then if you could help Patrick with the arming, that would be lovely."

"Arming?" I asked, handing over the cashbox used to store the rental fees.

"Helping pull off the armor that's been damaged, and replace it with fresh stuff. Alec is already busy repairing the damaged plate, and Patrick said he could use a hand since today's melee group are a bit mace-happy."

"Not a problem," I said, and trotted off to the house, my mind divided between wondering what Alden was up to and what I could scrounge up for lunch in my allotted time.

"Lunch first, then Alden . . . Oh, hello." I stopped at the entrance of the kitchen, pleased to see Alden standing on a chair, a screwdriver in one hand, and a light fixture in another. He was clad in a black T-shirt and a knee-length pair of walking shorts. I admired his calves (slightly hairy with nice bulgy muscles) before asking, "Decided to start here, did you?"

"No."

I watched him a moment. He kept shooting me little glances that made me think he was feeling shy again.

"What are you doing?" I asked, giving him a supportive smile.

"The light . . . it stopped working. It . . ." He shrugged.

I wondered if I'd get tired of helping him overcome his shyness. I decided, as I reached out and stroked the bare part of his leg, that I wouldn't.

He almost jumped off the chair. "What are you doing?"

"Getting you annoyed or aroused enough so that you'll talk to me without feeling weird. The choice of which emotion to go with is yours."

He made a face. "I'm not a child who needs soothing, Mercy."

"Of course you aren't. But you have to admit, you get downright chatty when I touch you."

"That's because I like you touching me."

"Good." I gave his calf another stroke, then leaned against the counter to watch him.

Silence filled the kitchen for about three minutes.

"It doesn't like me."

"The light?" I asked, my smutty thoughts about what I'd like to do with Alden evaporating.

"No, the house. I think it's depressed."

"Huh?" I hoisted myself onto the counter, and watched him work while he screwed in the fixture. I liked the way his shirt moved over his back and arms.

He slid me a sidelong look. "You think I'm exaggerating, don't you?"

"Not necessarily." I fiddled with a box of lightbulbs. "What I think that you might have is a bias influencing your perception of what's happening in an old house that is likely to have decrepit fixtures, and interpreting that as being a personal vendetta against you, due to the fact that you are stressed over the amount of work to be done, and thus are looking for outside forces to blame for any potential failure."

"You really took away a lot from those psychology classes, didn't you?" he said, climbing down from the chair and going over to where an electrical panel darkened the wall between the kitchen and the pantry. He flipped a switch. The light fixture made a humming noise, then popped, and the light went out.

Alden sighed.

"Sorry," I said, holding out the box of lights. "Try again?"

He shook his head. "It won't do any good. The house doesn't want to be fixed. What are you doing here?"

"I assume you mean here in the kitchen when I should be out working?"

"Yes."

"I'm on my lunch break."

He set down his tools and stretched, wiggling his shoulders around in a manner that warned they were feeling tight and uncomfortable. "I could use a break, too."

"Good. We can have lunch together, although all I was going to make was a grilled cheese sandwich."

"That sounds fine to me."

I got off the counter and went into the still faintly smoky-smelling pantry to get the necessary ingredients. While I assembled the sandwiches and got them onto a small skillet to cook, Alden put away his tools, and tidied up the bits of broken glass that came from a bulb he said had been stuck in the fixture.

"What are you going to do next?" I asked when we sat down to our sandwiches, a bowl of grapes, and corn chips. "More fixing things, or renovation work?"

"I can't renovate anything until I get some supplies," he answered around a mouthful of sandwich. "I may try to do that later today."

"I have an idea," I said, popping a grape into my mouth.

"Oh?" He shot me a look that was partly wary, and partly steamy. "Does it involve touching my leg again? Or any other part of me?"

"Actually, it does." I wiped my fingers, and smiled at him. "I thought you might like to try the melee shindig this afternoon. Vandal is taking walk-ins for the afternoon class, and I figured it would be a good way for you to work off some stress."

"Pretending to be a medieval knight?" Alden said, and shook his head. "I'm not one for playacting."

"I meant the combat part of it. I watched a bit of it earlier—guys put on all sorts of armor, and learn how to beat the tar out of each other without actually killing the other man. Or hurting him seriously. It's pretty awesome-looking."

Alden pulled a face. "That's not my idea of the best way to spend an afternoon."

"OK. It was just a suggestion." I finished my lunch, gathered up my plate, and gave it a quick wash. "Have fun fixing up stuff."

"Thank you. I suspect it will be a nonstop laugh-fest."

I paused as I was leaving the kitchen, glancing back to where Alden sat alone at the table. He looked a little forlorn, sitting in the big empty kitchen all by his lonesome, tempting me into offering to teach him archery, but I reminded myself that although I was trying to show him he didn't have to be awkward around me, that didn't mean I could pressure him into doing things that I thought he'd enjoy.

"Which is just a shame," I said aloud, then glanced at my watch before trotting down the hall toward the back of the house. "Because I bet he'd be sexy as hell as a knight."

EIGHT

Dear Mercy.

Alden consulted the slim volume of obscure Edwardian poetry he found propping up a coal scuttle in what used to be a maid's room on the uppermost floor of the house. *I saw this, and thought of you.*

I sit and watch the shadows pass,
Grey shadows on a grey water.
None comes ever to my door,
Or stirs the rushes on my floor.
Only memory with me stays.

Alden eyed the words, frowning.

He decided that he was too ambiguous, and added, *When I say "thought of you," I meant that the words applied to me, and how I feel around you. Not that they applied to you.*

Was that making it less clear? He was unsure, but decided to slide the note under her bedroom door and hope that she understood what it was he was trying to say. After all, she'd had a pretty good sense about his thoughts thus far; no doubt she'd get the reference.

He was halfway down the hall when he turned around, went back to his room, and on a piece of scratch paper, wrote, *The poem is by Ethel Clifford, by the way. Just in case you thought I'd written it.*

An hour later, his knuckles were scraped raw from stripping the stained and mildewed wallpaper from the old music room. Twice he slipped with the putty knife he was using to peel off the wallpaper, leaving him with a couple of bloody gouges on his left hand.

"Son of a—"

"None of that, now, there are ladies present!"

Alden jumped at the loud voice, spinning around to see Barry Butcher's eyebrows at the door, with Barry not far behind. He had a big smile on his red face, and clutched in one hand the size of a respectable ham was the arm of a slight woman with short red hair, a pair of expensive sunglasses, and lips the color of lacquered cherries. "Oh . . . I . . . erm . . ."

"Knew you wouldn't mind if I dropped by to give you the latest report by the HTC, and found this young lady wandering around looking for you." Barry released the woman's arm, glancing around curiously. "Stripping the walls, eh? Needs it."

"Yes to both. Er . . . are you here for the medieval classes?" Alden asked the woman. Everything about the woman reeked money, from her stylish wedge sandals to the chiffon summer dress and a handbag with a well-known name.

"Heavens, no." She pulled the sunglasses down, her bright red lips parting to reveal very white teeth. Her eyes, a rather unremarkable shade of brown, twinkled at him. "I'm Lisa Hauf, and I'm here to help out."

"Me?" Alden stared at her for a few seconds, trying to work out who she was, and what she wanted. Just as he was about to ask those questions, it struck him—this was Alice's friend. This was the woman she had chosen specially for him. He fought back the urge to make some excuse and run from the room, taking a couple of deep breaths while remembering what Mercy had said about her experience at college. If she could stand an embarrassing scene, then he could deal with this situation. "Ah. You're from . . . yes."

"Wish I could get this kind of help around my house," Barry said with a loud bark of laughter. "Lucky sod. Well, now. Here's the report I promised you yesterday. I think you'll find our research on the nesting grounds of the Hairy Tit is above and beyond what you'd expect to see. We really pulled out all the stops on it, and I just know you'll read it and see the reason behind our offer. Which still stands, by the way. I had a little chat with the board last night, and they all feel it's vital to the well-being of the tit to spend the money on the land."

"Tit?" Lisa slid a questioning look toward Barry. "Did I hear that correctly?"

"It's a wee bird about so big," Barry said, indicating three inches. "Very rare, and makes their home here at Bestwood in the north pasture. It's all in the report—a qualitative analysis of the likelihood of survival if the Bestwood nesting area is disturbed, and a point-by-point examination of the offer to purchase the land for preservation."

"How very interesting." Lisa turned to Alden, her eyes doing a smiling thing at him that instantly tied his tongue up tight. "Dumplin', my feet are killing me. Is there somewhere I can get into something a little more suited to work?" She had a Southern U.S. accent, one Alden thought of as being stereotypical Deep South, but with an odd habit of stressing certain words.

With a start, Alden remembered his manners, and murmured a welcome, and that he'd be happy to show her to a room.

"I can see I'm de trop," Barry said with an obvious wink at Alden. "So I'll take myself off. Give me a call if you have any questions. I'll be back tomorrow to discuss with you some recent geographical survey results that we have showing just how fragile the ecosystem is for the poor little tits."

"That's really not necessary," Alden started to object, but Barry cut him off.

"No trouble at all. It's worth taking the time to ensure you're fully cognizant of what our plan is, and why it's so important that we save the tits for future generations."

Lisa snickered. Alden was too distressed by the arrival of Alice's protégée to appreciate the assumedly unwitting pun. "This way," he said miserably, and accompanied Lisa to the habitable wing, showing her an available room.

"Oh, it's charming, just charming," she said, glancing around the powder blue room containing only a dark Victorian bedstead and mattress, a massive wardrobe that was no doubt too large to get through the doors, and a broken ladder-back chair with only three legs. "A little sparse on the furnishings, but I could just eat it up with a spoon—it's so cute."

Alden murmured something about finding her blankets and bed linens.

"That would be much appreciated," Lisa said, strolling around the room, her fingers trailing along the blue and white patterned wallpaper. "I do hope you'll show me around the rest of the house this afternoon. I'd love to see the rest of it. That nice Mr. Butcher, bless his heart, says you are renovating? I do love the thought of a historical home being brought back to life for all to enjoy."

Panic swamped him, leaving him a bit startled by the strength of the emotion. He might not be comfortable around women, but he seldom felt quite so uncomfortable. He took firm control of his emotions, and said, "I'm afraid I can't do that."

"No? But I will be so very sad if you can't find a few minutes to spend showing me around your wonderful house. And speaking of wonderful, this room has lovely dimensions. I can just picture it done over in shades of rose and a pale gold. Perhaps with a touch of cream? Ah, I see I have a view of the garden. Or is it the garden? Some sort of event seems to be taking place out there. Is it a fete?"

"No, that's—" Alden paused, a thought occurring to him. "That's a medieval combat fair. That's why I can't show you around the house. I will be down with the medieval combat class. In fact . . ." He made a show of looking at his watch. "In fact, I should be down there now. You're more than welcome to poke around the house as you like. The kitchen is on the ground floor, on the south side. Please help yourself to anything there. Tea is in the cupboard above the electric kettle. If you wish to know more about the house, you can visit Lady Sybilla. She's also on the ground floor, in the west wing."

While speaking, he had been sidling toward the door, a sense of relief swamping him when he reached it.

"Well, yes, of course I'll visit Lady Sybilla. You see—"

Lisa turned a surprised face to him when he bolted out of the door, saying over his shoulder, "Excellent. I'm sure I'll see you later."

"But, sugar, you didn't let me finish—"

He ran down the hallway at a full gallop, making a mental promise that he'd devote himself to Lisa later to make up for his atrocious manners. His footsteps reverberated loudly in the empty great hall, echoes bouncing from crackled marble floor to dark wooden panels, and back, in a growing crescendo. Just as he headed to the rear of the house, a door opened, and Lady Sybilla's grim-faced maid looked out. She frowned at him, and turned to say into the room, "—think you'll be very pleased with her, my lady. Oh. It's not her. It's just the new master running pell-mell like a madman."

"Good afternoon," he called politely, not pausing to converse with the elderly ladies. He dashed through the library, stumbled over a parquet floor tile that had chosen that moment to disengage its hold on the subflooring, and continued on through the doors to blessed freedom.

The warmth of the afternoon sun caught him full-on when he arrived at the garden, the mingled scents of hay, flowers, and grass having a soothing effect on his jangled nerves. The scene before him was oddly anachronistic. Ladies in long, flowing dresses with laced-on sleeves strolled around; children in a bewildering array of costumes varying from what he thought of as Robin Hood–esque to outright fantastical leaped and yelled and ran around with plastic swords, shields, and, in one case, a light saber. To his left, the archery butts had been set up, but were currently empty of all but a couple of children chasing a large Saint Bernard dog.

On the right, a grassy expanse had been turned into some sort of a battleground, with bales of hay serving as a barrier to the rest of the garden. Standing in the middle of the battle area, Vandal, clad in full plate-metal armor—all but a helm—stood waving his sword and shouting at a pair of men.

Alden descended the three stone steps into the garden proper, heading for the men, when a voice called out over the general noise and confusion. "Hey, look who showed up after all."

Mercy emerged from one of the small sheds, on the heels of two tittering teenagers in what vaguely looked like harem-girl outfits.

"I decided that a little exercise would help counteract all the centuries of dust I've breathed in during the last few hours," he told her, nodding toward where Vandal still chastised two of his students. "What's going on there?"

"Evidently one of the guys decided to disregard the rule that says you can only bash other people with swords, and not do any sort of stabbing. Dude on the ground was knocked down by Vandal when he stabbed at the guy over there, seeing Alec." She nodded to their left, where Alden noticed a couple of women clustered around a man seated on a bale of hay, having his armor removed by a man who closely examined each piece. Fenice was one of the women, her good hand gesturing as she spoke to the injured man.

"Was he hurt seriously?" Alden asked, images of lawsuits floating through his head.

"Not hurt at all, just winded, or so his daughter told me. She's the one over there." Mercy nodded toward where a heavily pregnant woman in a medieval kirtle and a flowery wreath on her head strolled around with another woman. "I gather Fenice is trying to convince him to go see a doctor just in case, but his daughter says he just wants to get back at it."

"If there is any risk that he might be truly injured—" Alden started to say.

Mercy shook her head even as he spoke. "Evidently he's not. Fenice is just being overly cautious, which I gather she doesn't need to be, since the students here sign all sorts of waivers saying they are aware of the physical risks they're taking, and that they can't sue if they get hurt. Fenice made me sign one yesterday afternoon, not that I'm likely to shoot my own eye out. But I have a list of rules a mile long about where my students can stand while I'm teaching them, just to keep the Hard Day's Knights insurance company happy. Are you going to try fighting?"

Alden resisted the urge to glance over his shoulder at the house to see if Lisa was watching from her bedroom window. "I thought I might give it a few minutes."

"Excellent. I'm sure that Fenice and Vandal will be willing to let you have a go without charge, since you're not making a fuss about them being here, and staying in your house. Let's go see Alec and he can fit you with some armor."

An eye-opening twenty minutes followed, in which Alden learned the difference between a bazuband and a gauntlet and why the heavy cotton arming tunic and hose were necessary.

"OK, let me see if I get my spiel right." Mercy consulted a sheet of handwritten notes, and pulled out of a bin a weird-looking jacket that appeared to be made up of bits of sheet, cotton batting, and leather. "This is the arming doublet, or gambeson. Let's have you slip into it. No, over your T-shirt is fine."

Alden stuck his arms through the thick padded sleeves, and immediately started sweating. "Is it supposed to be this heavy? I thought the armor was supposed to protect me."

"It is, but this is to keep you from being hurt by the armor. And it has ventilation holes on it so you don't drown in sweat. OK, see these things?" Mercy pointed to little squares of leather with leather laces hanging from them. They were situated around his waist, on his shoulders, and at the collar.

"These are called arming points, and are what we use to attach the armor to you. And here are the pants, which Vandal insists I call hose."

"It is an arming hose," Alec told them, before dumping another bin of armor at their feet and hurrying off to answer a call by Vandal.

"We can tie them on over your jeans. They also have the little ties on them. Just buckle it at the waist . . . excellent. Aren't you pretty as a picture?"

Alden rolled his eyes while Mercy beamed at him. He felt hot and bulky, and slightly claustrophobic. "I'm sure I'm ready for the cover of GQ. What's next?"

"We start at the bottom and work up," Mercy said, having had a quick peek at her notes. She gestured to a bale of hay. "Take a seat, and I'll get your shin thingies on."

"Shin thingies?"

"Technical term," she said loftily, and strapped greaves to his lower legs. "Vandal says we don't do sabatons—the things that cover your feet—unless you are in competition. These go on your upper thighs, and strap into the arming points. OK, now stand up."

Alden got to his feet, shaking his legs. They felt like they each weighed ten stone.

"Here's the breastplate. No, don't try to hold it. I'll tie it onto your shoulder straps. See? The extra padding up there takes the weight so it doesn't hurt you."

"That's what you think," Alden said, shifting the armor a little so it didn't dig into his tendons.

"Now for the arms and hands, and then the helm, and you're ready to do battle!"

"Assuming I'd be able to move, yes, but with all this on, I doubt if I can even take a step, let alone raise my hand and strike a blow."

"I bet you will. Alec says your adrenaline kicks in as soon as the lesson starts. Why don't you practice walking around while Vandal finishes up with that class? The next one is due to start in ten minutes."

Alden spent the next ten minutes walking up and down along the line of hay bales, wondering if avoiding Lisa was worth the heatstroke he was sure to acquire by standing out in the sun in full plate metal.

"Going to join us today?" Vandal asked, clanking his way over to where Alden was sweating profusely under all his armor. Both men were helmless, since Vandal evidently didn't wear one, and Alden couldn't bear to be closed into it with the heat of the day.

"Mercy talked me into it. I trust I am an acceptable student? I don't have any experience at combat with swords."

"This is a beginners' class," Vandal answered, and gestured to three men who were sitting in various poses of exhaustion on the bales of hay, sipping from bottles of water. "You're a bit behind the others, but let's give you an introduction to the art of melee combat while they're taking a break. I believe there is one other newcomer—you, sir?"

"That's right," came a familiar booming voice from inside a conical helm. One metal-encased hand lifted up the visor to reveal Barry Butcher. "Heard about the fighting classes, and decided it was an opportunity I couldn't miss."

"You know each other?" Vandal asked with a raised eyebrow.

"Yes," Alden replied with a weak smile, then continued before Barry could go into detail. "I don't intend to do more than just have an introduction, if that's all right. I do have a house to renovate, after all."

Vandal made a gesture that Alden assumed was a shrug under what had to be at least a hundred pounds of armor. "Whatever you like. Now, I'll need you two to each pick a weapon. Beginners are limited to sword or mace. You'll find the practice weapons behind you."

"Ah, a mace. I like the looks of this," Barry said, hefting a long-handled mace in one hand. "This could take the legs out from under a man in one blow. Yes, this will do nicely."

Alden bared his teeth in another smile at the speculative look Barry cast his way, and took a sword. He felt that, somehow, a sword was a more gentlemanly weapon.

"Good. Now we'll go over some of the basic rules of melee combat. If you violate any of them, you are out of the class, understand?"

Both men nodded.

"First thing: no stabbing motions of any sort. Doesn't matter where or with what weapon you're using—no stabbing. Likewise, no horizontal blows to the back of the neck. In addition, for the purposes of this class, we are declaring the following areas off-limits to blows: groin, feet, and back of knees."

Mercy came forward with two shields, handing them to each man. She grinned at Alden, and gave him a thumbs-up.

"Shields up," Vandal said, and just as Alden raised his, trying to get used to the weight of it, Vandal lunged forward with a sword, and viciously attacked the shield a number of times. Alden staggered backward, not expecting the assault, and also not braced for the strength needed to keep the shield in position.

"What the hell?" he said when Vandal stopped. His hand felt numb for a few seconds.

"You need to get used to taking blows with your shield. Remember to use it as a barrier. The fewer blows that get through to you, the longer you'll last."

He repeated the process with Barry, who was ready for it, and didn't seem to suffer from any difficulty in fending off the blows.

"Right. Mercy, the helms."

Mercy returned with a box containing padded cotton helm linings, a couple of mail collars, and the two helms.

"Collars first, then arming caps, then helm," Vandal instructed.

Alden donned the mail collar, which was supposed to protect his neck, then the thick padded arming cap, which tied under the chin, and finally, the helm fit snugly over the cap.

"Ready?" Vandal asked, and closed the visor on Alden's helm.

Instantly, Alden was pulled to a different world. Sounds were muffled and distant, and his range of vision was extremely limited to just what was directly in front of him. He could see Barry's eyes glittering through the narrow slit of his helm, and felt a jolt of adrenaline.

"Go!" Vandal shouted.

Barry swung his mace before Alden could even raise his shield, taking a blow to the head that didn't hurt, but left him reeling a few steps nonetheless. He saw Barry raise his arm again, and this time got his shield up and, struggling under the heavy armor, managed once again to block the blow. His breath sounded harsh in his ears, drowning out all other sounds but that of the frantic beating of his heart. Barry swung again and Alden blocked, lifting his sword in the air in a menacing fashion.

He couldn't bring himself to swing it, though. It didn't seem right to be striking a man with a huge sword, even if they were wearing armor, and the weapons were blunted.

Then Barry swung the mace again, catching the edge of Alden's shield, and ripping it from his hand. Barry didn't wait for a reaction—he slammed a shield into Alden's chest, and a big metal-covered fist into the visor of his helm.

Fury rose in Alden, adrenaline spiking him hot and fast, causing him to whirl around and slice at Barry's rib cage with his sword, sending the older man stumbling to the side. He used that moment to reclaim his shield, then, when Barry lifted his mace, lunged forward, slamming both shield and sword against the man's head.

Barry almost fell backward, but retained his footing, and gave a little shake of his head. Mindful of the off-limit zones, Alden whacked Barry across the knees with the sword, while striking again with the shield, this time knocking Barry's shield away.

Alden took a blow to the shoulder, but it almost didn't register, so focused was he on defeating his opponent. He kicked out, his foot landing on the center of Barry's chest, causing him to stagger backward several steps before falling onto his back. Alden leaped forward—as much of a leap as he could accomplish clad in all that metal—and held his sword over Barry's head.

Vandal came into his field of view, waving his hands, which Alden took to be the cease-fire gesture.

"Nicely done," Vandal said a minute later, having pulled off the helm and arming cap. Alden was sweating profusely, his breath coming in fast, short gulps, but he felt absolutely wonderful, just as if he'd really fought off a vicious attacker.

That feeling lasted until Mercy helped him off with his armor, some forty minutes later. By then, the blows that he'd taken first from Barry, then from the other students as they'd plunged into a free-for-all melee, began to take their toll.

"Ow," he told her as she began to unbuckle all the bits of armor. Vandal and Alec were doing likewise for the other students. "That hurts."

"What does?" She paused in the act of removing his chest plate. "Your shoulder?"

"No. Breathing. Also, living. Living and breathing hurts."

"Uh-huh. Bet you're going to be a mass of bruises tomorrow," she answered without the slightest hint of sympathy. "You looked like you were having fun, though. Were you?"

He thought about that while she peeled off the rest of his armor. "I suppose so. It was difficult at first, but then some sort of primal fight-or-flight instinct seemed to kick in, and all I wanted to do was bash the others to bits. It's a bit unnerving just how much I wanted that."

"Supposedly, melee fighting like this relieves tensions and stored aggressions. Perhaps it was good for you to work all that out of your system."

"Perhaps." He was about to say more when a voice cut through his thoughts.

"Well, didn't you look the perfect knight in literal shining armor? I've never seen such a manly-man sort of activity before in all my born days. It just thrilled me to my very core, it did indeed! I declare I could just fall at your feet with admiration."

Lisa moved around to where he was sitting. Mercy shot her a curious glance, but continued to remove his greaves.

Alden's tongue immediately tied itself into a knot. He was very aware of Mercy silently working to free him from the grip of the armor and the thick cotton arming clothes, but she wouldn't meet his gaze.

"How long is this fair going on?" Lisa asked, glancing around. "I do hope you're going to fight again. I'll be sure to cheer you on if you do."

His shoulders slumped when Mercy slipped off the arming doublet.

Now what the hell was he going to do?

NINE

"Alden," I said softly.

He sat frozen on a bale of hay, his eyes wide and startled, his hands fisted on his knees.

"Hmm?" His gaze shifted to me.

I tapped his hand with my finger. "I can't get your gloves off if you don't relax."

He looked down. "Oh. Sorry."

"I just love all this, I truly do," the woman who had approached us said in a thick Georgian accent. "I did drama while I was in college, you know? And I loved dressing up and pretending I was, oh, just all sorts of people. It's just ever so much fun. Since you're done with the show, when your servant there gets done undoing all those bits and pieces, Alden, perhaps you can show me around?"

"I'm not a servant," I said politely, holding back a snippy answer. I had enough experience working in the service industry to know how poorly sarcasm goes over with the customer. "My name is Mercy, and I'm the archery instruct—"

It was my turn to freeze. The woman's sentence had finally filtered all the way through my brain. Alden? She knew Alden's name? I looked up from where I was kneeling at his feet. He was watching me, not the woman, but with an expression in his eyes that I couldn't read. Was it a plea for help? Sympathy? Anger, betrayal, disinterest? I simply couldn't tell, and didn't want to embarrass him in what was sure to be an awkward situation, so I kept quiet.

Alden must have realized the silence was stretching far too long, and finally, as I got the last bit of armor and arming gear off him, said, "Erm."

I got to my feet, stowing away everything but the arming items back into their appropriate tubs. The heavy cotton doublets and hose were laid out to be aired overnight, and laundered by an industrial laundry every week.

"I'm Lisa," the woman said, giving me a saccharine smile. "I'm here because—"

"She's here to help me with the renovations," Alden said quickly, at the exact same moment that Lisa finished her sentence with, "—Lady Sybilla needs some help."

An awkward silence fell. Alden cleared his throat, and said hurriedly, "Yes. Lady Sybilla does need help with . . . er . . ."

"She's writing her memoirs," Lisa said, showing a lot of her teeth in a smile. Far too many teeth, I thought. "And of course, I'll be happy to help you in whatever way you'd like, Alden."

Alden cleared his throat a second time, and made an abrupt gesture. "Shall we . . . urm . . . shall we go to the house? Er . . . Lisa?"

I alternated between empathy and irritation at his attempt to hide the truth from me. This was clearly the woman he'd been waiting for, the one he wasn't sure he wanted a relationship with, but if the way she clung to his arm as she all but dragged him off to the castle was anything to go by, she certainly wanted him.

"Well, that was interesting," a voice said behind me.

"Wasn't it, though?" My teeth ground slightly. I made an effort to stop, and cast a glance at Fenice, who moved up to stand next to me, watching as the two figures drifted into the house. "I wonder if that accent is as phony as her hair color."

Fenice laughed. "Oooh, jealous? I thought you said that you and Alden weren't a couple?"

"We're not. We just . . . we have mutual . . . uh . . ."

"Interests?"

"Yeah, that." I lifted my chin and tried to look like I hadn't just been daydreaming about stripping Alden and having my way with him. "What he does with redheaded hussies is no business of mine."

"A hussy, is she?" Fenice laughed again, and then punched me in the arm with her good hand. "I like you, Mercy. So I'm going to give you a piece of advice that I learned from a friend of mine named Pepper. She told me once that a life filled with regret for all the desires left unexplored was a form of early death, and the only way to truly live was to take the opportunities presented."

"A suitably vague statement that could apply to just about any situation, but which I gather is intended to encourage me to go after Alden?"

"Only if you really want him." She gave a little one-shoulder half shrug. "I can only offer Pepper's advice, since I've seen it in action, and I know it has some merit. Ugh. What is that brother of mine doing now? Patrick! You can't start another class now—people need to eat sometime, you know, and it's after five!"

"Do you still need me to help disarm?" I called after her.

"No, Patrick can do it," she answered, storming off to free the students Vandal had herded back into the center of the fighting area.

"Okeydoke." I started to leave when the man whom Alden had been fighting limped over to me. He was quite tall and very wide, and had a red face that clashed horribly with his ginger hair.

"Do you work here?" he asked, wiping his sweaty face with a towel. "I'm looking for someone who can take a message to Alden Ainslie, the owner."

"I work for Vandal and Fenice, but I'm staying at the house, so I can take a message if you like."

"Staying at the house, eh?" He gave me a piercing look. "How'd that happen?"

"It's something that Vandal and Fenice arranged."

"Ah." He glanced around. "They're just here for the month, yes?"

"Three weeks." I was starting to get a bit irritated by this man. Although his manner was pleasant enough, I felt that in some way he was giving me the third degree. I slapped a smile on my face to cover up any hostility that might have shown, and asked, "What message is it you wanted to give Alden? A note, or a verbal message?"

"Verbal will do. Remind him that Barry Butcher—that's me—will be by tomorrow to talk about the terms of selling the tit reserve."

I gawked at him for a moment, then realized he must be talking about birds. "I didn't realize Alden was selling land off."

"It would be best if he'd sell us the whole package of house and land," Barry said, tossing the towel in a garbage bucket set up for that purpose. "We had a study made, and it was decided the house would make an excellent administrative center for the Hairy Tit Conservancy, as well as house a first-rate interpretive center that would explain to tourists the importance of local birds in the ecosystem."

"That sounds awesome," I said, wondering if Alden was considering Barry's offer. It was a shame if he was—I'd much prefer to see the house restored to its former glory than be converted into offices and a tourist facility.

He shot me another keen-eyed look. "Glad to see a woman with a good head on her shoulders. You be sure to tell Alden I'll be back tomorrow."

"Will do," I told him, watching for a few moments after he took himself off.

Something about the way he grilled me still rankled, but a review of the conversation left me shaking my head at my paranoid thoughts.

Since I was officially done for the day, I went back to the clothing shed to make sure everything was tidied away there, chatted briefly with some of the family members waiting for their men to disarm, and double-checked that I had put all the archery equipment away.

"I don't give a damn what Alden does," I told myself as I marched to the house, intent on taking a shower, washing that man right out of my hair, and fixing food that I could eat somewhere private.

My inner self asked me why I would make such a patently untrue statement when it was clear I very much did care what he did. Was it because I had planned on hooking up with him, and thus felt that in some way he was "mine"? That made sense, more sense than the idea that I could have a deep connection with a man I'd met twenty-four hours ago.

There was no sign of Alden or the Southern belle, but I did meet Lady Sybilla's maid, Adams, while she was carrying a large vase of flowers, walking slowly and carefully, the vase way too overloaded for someone with such gnarled hands.

"Here, let me help you," I said, hurrying up to her. "What pretty flowers. The roses are gorgeous, but, oh, the carnations smell heavenly."

Adams gracefully let me take the vase, inclining her head in a pretty good imitation of her mistress. "Her ladyship has always insisted on fresh flowers when they are in bloom."

"She's a wise woman to enjoy them. I never can seem to bring myself to buy them, since they last such a short time, but they are lovely to look at."

"Are you on your way to organize her ladyship's papers?" Adams asked as she paused next to the door leading to Lady Sybilla's suite of rooms.

"Not just yet. I hope to put some time in on them tonight."

She sniffed. "I will lock them away safely, then."

"I didn't think they were particularly valuable," I protested, feeling guilty nonetheless. "From what I saw, they were just a bunch of household accounts going back a few centuries, and some notes of tenants, and cattle, and horses."

"All of Lady Sybilla's possessions are valuable," she replied with a pinched expression. "Even if you do not value them. Thus I will lock them away until you can find the time to fulfill your promise to Lady Sybilla."

The accusation in her tone was all too clear.

"I have a paying job that I have to do during the day," I pointed out. "And I have every intention of doing what I said I'd do, which was sort through the papers and put them in some semblance of order, but it's not going to be an instant thing. Please tell Lady Sybilla that I'll do my best as quickly as I can."

"Hrmph," Adams sniffed again, her curled lip saying much about what she thought of people who did not put Lady Sybilla first in all things, and taking the vase without another word, she left me, closing the door firmly behind her.

"You're welcome," I told the door, and continued on to the back staircase that provided a shortcut to the wing with my bedroom. I banged loudly on the door a couple of times, then flung it open and stomped my feet until I felt like a deranged flamenco dancer.

"All right, all you mice. Just get the hell out of here long enough for me to grab some clothes and take a shower."

I listened intently, but didn't hear (or see) anything moving, so entered the room. There was another note that had obviously been slipped under the door. I wondered what I had to do to get the message across to Vandal that I wasn't particularly interested in him.

Dear Mercy,

I'm sorry.

I stared at the bizarre note, and wondered what the hell Vandal was apologizing about. A thought occurred to me that so startled me, it had me rooted in the center of the room while my brain turned it over and over. What if it wasn't Vandal sending me the notes? That meant it had to be Alden. But why would he send me notes?

"For that reason," I said aloud, still mulling over the idea, "why would Vandal? No, I think it must be Alden. Which is oddly sweet of him. I think I'll reply."

I stomped my way over to my luggage, which I'd left closely zipped shut against mousey intruders, and dug through my duffel until I pulled out a small journal and a nibbed pen that I used whenever I felt overly introspective. I also gathered up clean clothes and my bath things, and entered the bathroom I shared with Fenice.

A mouse sat up in the bathtub, and gave me a startled look.

I screamed, slammed the door shut, and, grabbing my duffel bag, raced out of the room, the hairs on my arms standing on end in horror. I ran to Alden's room and, without even knocking, flung open the door and ran inside.

Alden stood next to the bed, stark naked and wet, a towel in his hands as he dried off his chest, the surprised look on his face quickly fading away to something unreadable (damn him—I liked it much better when I could read his expressions).

"Sorry," I said, panting a little despite the short distance between our rooms. "There was a mouse in the bathtub, Alden. A mouse. In the bathtub. It mocked me—it sneered and mocked and waved its mousey claws at me as if it was inviting me in so it could ravage me. You must have just had a shower. You look good naked."

I slapped a hand over my mouth at the last sentence, not having intended on saying it out loud.

"I have had a shower, yes, and I'm sorry you were nearly ravaged by a wild mouse," he said, much to my sorrow wrapping the towel around his waist. "I called an exterminator earlier today, but he won't be out until tomorrow."

"Well, I hope you don't mind if I stay here until he demouses my room," I said, setting my bag down on the hard wooden chair. "Or rather, I hope your girlfriend doesn't mind."

"My . . ." He stopped, a little frown pulling down his eyebrows. "I gather you are referring to Lisa. If so, I assure you that she is just an acquaintance. She was sent to . . . well . . ."

"I heard her cover story," I said, holding up a hand to stop him. "It's none of my business what you do even if we were about to hook up before your kitchen caught on fire."

"Why don't we agree to forget Lisa? She is my guest here, but nothing more than that," he said, moving over to where I stood. A shiver ran down my back at both the heat in his eyes and the way he brushed a strand of hair off my cheek. "I'd much rather talk about you staying with me in this room, and how you suggest we set up the sleeping arrangements."

I reached up and pulled his head down to mine, laying my lips on his in a way that let him know I reciprocated that shimmer of passion in his eyes. His mouth was as wonderful as I remembered, but this time, rather than this just being a kiss, Alden's body got into the act. His hands were on my behind, pulling me tight against him, his legs as hard as steel where they pressed into mine. I melted against him, feeling all my soft, squishy bits making the differences between us obvious.

His lips parted from mine for a few seconds. "You taste spicy."

"Cinnamon mints," I murmured, nibbling on his lower lip. My body felt like it was filled with fire, making me restless and wanting, and missing something that I badly needed.

"I like it." He hoisted me upward a little, angling his head to better kiss me. I slid my hands up his bare back, careful not to dig my fingers into him as I wanted, since I knew he must be feeling the effects of his fighting earlier. "Would it be inappropriate if I suggested we conduct those activities that were interrupted this morning?"

"Not inappropriate at all, although you have to let me take a shower first. It was hot standing out in the sun all day."

"If you insist, although I don't find you in the least bit objectionable." He released me, giving my butt a friendly squeeze as he did so.

"Trust me, when you got to the part where the toddler with sticky grape lips decided to slobber on my knee, you'd object. Be back in a couple of minutes." I was in the act of peeling off my pretty blue gauze dress before I even closed the door behind me, and took what had to be close to the world's fastest shower.

When I stepped out of the shower to dry myself, I spotted a folded piece of paper on the floor.

You are beautiful.

I felt warm down to my toes, and not just because of the warm shower.

With nothing on but a towel, I opened the door to Alden's bedroom, and struck a pose, the letter in my hand. "Thank you."

He was lying on the bed, hands behind his head as he glared at the wall next to his bed. He shifted his gaze to me, the glare melting into a look that turned quickly to one of approval. "For what?"

I lifted the note. "I like your messages."

His gaze shifted, and I couldn't help but notice that his feet moved restlessly, a sure sign he was feeling embarrassed. "Ah. That. Yes. I thought . . . it seemed like a way to . . ."

"I know. And it's cute. And fun. Do you mind if I do some, too?"

"No, but you don't . . ." He waved a hand in the air. "You don't have problems talking."

"It's still fun, though. So. Here we are. Both of us wearing towels, and alone. Together. In a room with a big bed." I strolled forward, trying to appear worldly, as if it were nothing to be on the verge of having sex with a man I'd met the day before. "How do you want to do this?"

An indescribable look crossed his face. "I thought the traditional method would be appropriate."

"Traditional?" I shook my head, puzzled about what he meant. "You have a tradition for this?"

"Well . . . yes." Now he looked confused, too. "I don't know what sorts of things you like, but I'm fairly orthodox. Why, are you looking for something a bit more flashy?"

"Right," I said, sitting down on the foot of his bed. "I

think we're talking at cross-purposes. I asked how you want to do this because I'm feeling pretty uncomfortable since we just met, and although we have that spark, and I like how you kiss, and I want to do many things to your delicious body, it's a little uncouth to run at the bed, and leap on you the way I'd like to."

"Oh, that," he said with a little laugh. "I thought you were inquiring how I wanted to have sex. I was a bit worried you were going to want something kinky."

"Define kinky," I said, looking up the length of his body. "Do you have any playtime handcuffs? Or scarves? Scarves would work, too."

His eyes widened. "Are you talking bondage?"

"Mmm." I got to my knees and crawled up his legs until I could sit on my heels next to his hip. "Don't knock it until you've tried it. And I'd very much like to try it."

"Bondage?" he said, his voice rising on the word. "You wish to be my mistress?"

"Lover, I think, is the preferred term." I spread my fingers across his stomach, sliding them upward toward his chest.

"Mercy." His hand clamped down on my hand, stopping it from exploring all the territory it wanted to touch. I looked up to his face. There was an odd regretful glint to his eyes. "I'm not ... that is, I don't like ... I'm not into ... I don't get into erotica."

"Huh?" I asked, then made the obvious connection between his clear discomfort and his mention of the word "bondage." "Oh, you don't think I'm one of those women who read bondage books and wants to do that, do you? Because I'm not like that at all. OK, I will admit that the idea of tying your hands to the headboard—it looks very substantial, by the way; is it?—so I can molest you with abandon doesn't mean I want to do more of that sort of thing. I think it's a bit funny, to be honest. The bondage, that is, not tying you down so I can frolic upon your manly flesh."

"Good. I don't mind taking the dominant role, but I never found it enticing or even moderately titillating to control a woman. I prefer you to enjoy your experiences as you like, without reference to me."

I laughed. He looked appalled for a few seconds until I clarified, "I can have fun on my own, but I'm sure to enjoy it more with reference to you than without."

"Ah." A little smile curled his lips. "I agree, together is definitely more enjoyable."

"So you wouldn't even let me use some scarves on your hands to tie you down?"

He looked at his hands, then peered upward at the headboard. "I hadn't ever considered that. Perhaps another time?"

"Deal," I said, leaning down to nip at his hip. "It's actually kind of fun. I'll let you tie me down, too, you know. And I'm totally with you on the dominating thing. I mean, I want to know what you like, and don't like, and all that, but I don't get off on people telling me when and where and how I can enjoy myself. We're talking a lot, aren't we?"

"We could be doing so much more," he agreed.

"You make excellent points, sir," I said, pulling the end of his towel where it was tucked inside. "So much so that I believe you should be rewarded with some oral sex."

"That would be lovely," he said, his eyes filled with hope as I pulled the towel from underneath him. "Although I never got to finish what we started this morning."

"Don't worry, you'll get your turn later. Or rather, I will." I contemplated his nether bits. "Be sure to tell me if I do something that you really like."

"This!" he said, gasping when I grasped his testicles with one hand, while licking the full length of the underside of his penis. "I like this."

He liked it even more when I got both hands into the action, and by the time I was experimenting with technique and patterns, he was babbling nonstop, his fingers clenching and releasing the sheet beneath him.

"Stop," he said, panting, his hands on my shoulders. "You have to stop now, or it will be too late."

"For? Oh. Gotcha." I crawled up his body, kissing my

way along his stomach, enjoying the taste and feel of him beneath me. There was something about him that made me feel like I was charged with static energy, almost as if we were two atomic particles electrically attracted to each other.

His belly was very sensitive, causing him to contract it when I worked my way over to his hip, giving him a tiny bite there. I wanted to keep touching him, tasting him, learning all the sensitive spots on his body as well as finding out what it was that drove him to the breaking point, but there was no sense in ending our fun prematurely.

"Is it my turn?" he asked, his hands going for my breasts.

"Not yet. I think we'll save that for another time, because tormenting you ... er ... pleasuring you really got my motor running."

"Tormenting is the correct term," he said with a groan as I spread my hands across his chest, leaning down to lick a pert nipple where it sat surrounded by a light amount of chest hair.

"It's really amazing how bodies can be so different," I said, swirling my tongue around his other nipple. "You're so hard. And no, not just your bald-headed giggle stick."

His eyes popped open. "My what?"

"You know." I gently bit his nipple. "Your baloney pony."

He stared at me.

"Cucumber of love?" I asked, a little giggle slipping out as I said it.

"Do you feel better now?" he asked, one eyebrow rising. "Are there any more you feel you can't hold back?"

I thought for a moment. "Fun gun, kosher pickle, and Darth Vader. OK, now I'm done."

"Darth Vader?"

I laughed outright at the expression on his face, comforted by the fact that his lips were twitching despite his attempt to keep a straight face. He sighed a faux martyred sigh, and pulled me upright to kiss me the way I'd been wanting him to kiss me ever since I came out of the shower. "You really are the most unique woman I've ever met."

"I hope that's good," I said, squirming a little when his fingers went wandering up my thighs.

"Very much so," he mumbled, his mouth hot on my neck as he started nibbling there, making shivers go up my back.

"Do you happen to have any condoms?" I asked, arching my back when his hands slid up to my breasts, his fingers teasing them until they were two demanding little hussies who wanted his mouth that instant. "I have some, but they're somewhere in my bag."

"Nightstand," he said, the word muffled since he was now kissing the valley between my hussies, his thumbs and tongue torturing me with exquisite pleasure. I squirmed around on him, wanting him to touch all of me, but at the same time knowing I wasn't going to last a whole lot longer. I needed him suited up and ready to go, so I rolled off him, my breasts instantly singing a dirge of loss and abandonment, and dug around in his nightstand drawer until I found a package.

He was about to follow me, but I pushed him back, opening the package with a knowing waggle of my eyebrows. "Do you mind if I do this? I'm not very good at it, and I feel that I need practice."

"Be my guest," he said, waving a gracious hand at his crotch. "But be warned if you intend on trying anything fancy, like putting it on with your mouth or, god forbid, your breasts, I won't last past a few seconds."

"Duly noted . . . wait, my breasts? How do you put a condom on with your breasts?"

He just stared hopefully at me as I sat with my hand poised over his penis.

"I'll Google it later," I told him, taking pity on his now very aroused penis. I unrolled the condom onto him, making sure to touch him as much as possible in the process, and asking, "Was that enjoyable for you?"

"Very, but that's because you cheated and did extra tormenting things with your fingers. Can I return to your breasts?"

I lay down and held my arms up. He was there instantly, his cheeks, ever so slightly stubbly, rubbing on my still-sensitized breasts. "You are so smooth," he said, nuzzling the underside. "Like satin."

"It's what I was saying earlier about you being hard. You're like steel with a very soft covering, whereas I'm soft and smooshy."

"I like soft and smooshy. I like everything about you, especially your little belly," he said, nibbling a serpentine path down to that spot. "But I especially like your legs. You have lovely legs. I wish to kiss them all over, but I'm afraid that is going to have to wait for another time, because your breasts have pushed me perilously close to my breaking point."

I kissed his mouth as soon as it was in range, my legs moving along his when he settled himself for action, catching his moan of pleasure in my mouth when he slid into me. All my words left me then, leaving behind a body that was nothing but endless waves of ecstasy that started deep in my center, spreading out with every flex of his hips. I moved along with him, my body welcoming him with a thousand minuscule muscles, and just when his mouth moved to my earlobe, his breath as ragged and rough as mine, I let go of my control, and bit his shoulder, crying wordlessly when he thrust harder and faster until I went spiraling off into an orgasm that tightened all my muscles around him.

He didn't last long after that, giving his own hoarse cry, his hips giving a couple more thrusts before he collapsed down on me, his body heavy and damp with perspiration.

I relished every bit of him as I let my hands stroke down his sides and back.

"I'm sorry," he murmured into my shoulder.

"For what? The orgasm of my lifetime?"

"I'm heavy. I should move. I think my muscles are gone, however, because I don't feel like I can."

"You're fine," I said, giving his shoulder a little nibble. I was vaguely surprised to see that my love bite earlier had left a mark, and reminded myself to be less aggressive in the future. "Alden, I'm sorry. I bit you too hard. You've got a hell of a hickey."

With a groan, he rolled off me, and onto his back, where he lay splayed out like a man well loved. "I don't particularly care what marks you left on me."

"You might if Fenice or Vandal sees it. They might think we have something going on other than just this."

"Do you care what they think?"

"No, not really. I mean, it's not going to affect my job, so the itches we scratch in private aren't any of their business."

"Exactly."

I bit my lip, the pleasant buzz of orgasmic afterglow fading, leaving me feeling . . . I wasn't sure what I was feeling, exactly. Kind of let down. "Then there's Lisa. She'll know what we're up to as soon as she sees that hickey."

He opened one eye and turned his head toward me so he could pin me back. "You're not really jealous, are you?"

"No. But I don't want to come between you and a potential girlfriend just because we started something before she got here."

"You're not doing anything of the sort," he said, closing his eye again. "And I don't give a damn what anyone else thinks."

"Good. Then we're in agreement." But even as I spoke the words, I wondered if that was true.

Don't be ridiculous, I told my inner doubt. You knew going into this that it was just a little fling. You need to find a more permanent job, and he clearly needs someone who can spend her life with him. You can't have it both ways. Either you accept the relationship for what it is—a pleasant diversion that may have the side effect of giving Alden a bit more confidence with women—or you stop it now. What's it going to be?

I got up and went into the bathroom to tidy up, not liking the path my thoughts were taking.

TEN

Our pleasant interlude seemed like it lasted days, but at long last we realized that it was still early evening, and we were hungry.

"We could go out for dinner," I told Alden after we got dressed again. "Go to that pub you mentioned yesterday."

"We could, but I'd feel bad about leaving Lisa at the mercy of Vandal."

"Oh, I meant that we'd take her, too," I lied, feeling immediately guilty that I hadn't even thought about what Lisa was going to do for dinner. Here I'd been selfishly thinking of having Alden to myself, and he was being a considerate and thoughtful host.

He rubbed his face, his whiskers rasping in a way that sent a shiver down my arms. "We could do that if you like."

"Sure." I slapped a cheerful smile on my face. "Do you think we should invite Fenice and Vandal, too?"

"Why?" he asked, narrowing his eyes on me. "You don't . . . er . . . you're not . . ." He made an oddly abrupt gesture.

"You pick the weirdest times to get tongue-tied," I told him, leaning in to kiss him. "Here you've been chatting away without so much as a twinge, even while doing the most intimate things two people do, and whammo! One mention of Vandal and you're Mr. Hesitant. Do I need to ask you if you're jealous?"

"No," he said quickly, straightening his shoulders. "Of course not."

"OK, then," I said, and opened the door of his bedroom. "We'll ask Fenice and Vandal to come with us."

"Fine," he said, following me as I headed downstairs. Silence accompanied us until we were just outside the kitchen, from which voices could be heard. I put my hand on Alden's arm and stopped him. "Alden, I feel kind of odd."

"Odd how?" His brow wrinkled. "Sick? Or sore from . . ." He waggled his eyebrows, but stopped when a thought obviously struck him. "I wasn't too rough on you, was I? I know I got a bit carried away at the end, but I assumed you'd tell me if I did something you didn't like, or that hurt you—"

"No, nothing like that," I said with a reassuring smile, and a little bite on his chin. "That was fabulous. Especially you being enthusiastic. I meant that I feel like I'm using you, somehow. It's like you have this magic button, and I press it, and hey nonny-nonny, you can talk. Do you . . . does it irritate you when I do that?"

"Press my magic button?" His lips twitched. "Far from it."

I smacked his arm. "You know what I mean. When I kiss you to distract you from feeling weird. Is that abusing you? Should I stop? It's almost like I'm taking the choice away from you, and I don't want you thinking that's what I'm doing."

He looked thoughtful for a few minutes. "I don't feel used. And I don't think you're taking my choice from me—if I didn't want to talk to you, I wouldn't, no matter what you did."

"Does it help you when I refocus your anxiety away from the situation?" I asked, still worried that I wasn't doing him any good by bypassing his social awkwardness.

"I think it does," he said, still thoughtful. "It's not so much that you're refocusing, but reminding me that I'm getting caught up in frustration when I don't need to be."

"Oh, good," I said, relaxing. "I really do want to help you, you know."

"I know," he said, and gave my butt a little squeeze. "And I appreciate it. You're the only woman other than my mother with whom I've felt this comfortable."

"That's slightly creepy considering what we were just doing upstairs, but I'm going to ignore that, and take it for the compliment I'm sure you meant it to be."

"Good," he said, and opened the door for me. "Because that's how I meant it."

"That's how you meant what, darling?" drawled Lisa, now perched on one of the kitchen stools while she picked at a clump of grapes.

Alden stopped, and looked mildly appalled.

I smiled, and went over to the counter next to which Lisa sat. "Alden was just talking about his mom. Fenice, we were thinking about going to the pub for dinner. Would you and Vandal like to join us? And you, too, of course, Lisa."

"Pub?" Fenice, who was flipping through a well-worn vegetarian cookbook, looked up eagerly. "Sure, so long as they have something I can eat. And Patrick is probably already there. He said something about needing a pint after the classes today."

"Thank you for such a thoughtful invitation," Lisa drawled, her words as pointed as she could make them. "But I'm having supper with Lady Sybilla."

"Really?" I cast a quick glance at Alden. I had assumed her cover story was just that: a story. "You know her?"

"Actually, we just met." Lisa stood and stretched, making sure to aim her boobs at Alden as she did so. "Adams, her companion, suggested I help Lady Sybilla. And as I'm working for her, I thought it would be best to accept her dinner invitation. I'm sure we'll also talk about her memoirs."

"That memoir sounds like an excellent idea," Alden said, wholly to my surprise. "I'm sure Lady Sybilla will benefit from having a project with which to focus rather than what

I'm doing to the house. If you could convince her to move out to the gatekeeper's lodge, I'd be grateful."

"Really?" Lisa drawled. "And how do you plan on thanking me if I do get her moved?"

Alden looked like a deer caught in headlights.

"I'll pop upstairs and change my clothes if we're going to the pub," Fenice said, casting me a significant glance as she scooted past me. "Be down in a couple of minutes."

Lisa watched her leave with an amused smile, turning back to us to say to Alden, "Alone at last."

"Seriously?" I asked, shaking my head at her blatant flirting. I wanted to tell her to back the hell off, but decided that I wasn't going to play the jealous other woman. If Alden wanted her, then he could have her . . . but he couldn't have me at the same time. "OK, you know what? Clearly you want to be alone with Alden to flirt with him, so I'll just go wait out back by the car for when you two are done and ready to go to the pub."

"I'll come with you," Alden said quickly, halting me at the door to say to Lisa, "I know you came here to . . . you came because . . . but that's not needed. Mercy is here, you see." He waved a hand at me. "I'm sorry you traveled all the way to Cornwall, but you see how it is."

"No," Lisa said, oiling her way over to us. "How is it, Alden?"

He stiffened, and gestured toward me again. "Mercy is here now."

"I'm sorry, darlin', you're not making much sense. I see that sweet Mercy is here, bless her heart, but what is that to do with us?" She smiled a long, slow smile.

I said nothing. Alden was clearly in a panic, but I felt it was important that he make a decision without me pressuring him either way. "I'm happy to have you at Bestwood," he finally said, his voice very stilted. "Especially since you are helping Lady Sybilla. But that is as far as it goes."

His fingers tightened around my arm, not painfully so, but enough to have me flexing my arm. Instantly, his grip loosened.

"I see." Lisa's smile faded, and an odd calculating expression took over. "Well, that's put me in my place, hasn't it? I wish I'd known about this before I came out to Cornwall. Naturally, I won't stay where I'm not welcome."

Alden looked at a loss as to how to deal with that sort of emotional blackmail. I took pity on him, since he'd made it clear to Lisa where his preference lay.

"Oh, for god's sake," I said, taking Alden by the hand, and opening the door. "He said he was happy for you to be here and help Lady Sybilla. So stop making a play for him, and go be a secretary. Come on, Alden. I'm starving after a day of teaching people."

"Thank you," Alden said a couple of minutes later when we were crunching our way across the gravel drive to where he kept his car. "I couldn't get the words out to tell her that I wasn't interested in her in a sexual way. It's hard enough to talk to women, but to tell them that . . ." He gave a little shiver. "It's beyond me."

"I'd say we are going to have to work on your ability to reject women, but I don't think that's in my best interest," I said with a tight smile.

He shot me a look. "You don't need to worry about that."

"Aw. Thank you." I let my smile get warmer.

"After all, I can talk to you. If I wanted to dump you, I'd be able to tell you that."

"Hey!" I whapped him on the arm, but luckily for him, Fenice trotted up to us at that moment, so I couldn't chastise him any further.

Three hours later we were back in his bedroom, with me on the bed sorting through a collection of Lady Sybilla's papers that I'd snagged from the library before Adams had locked them up, and Alden at his small desk with a laptop, working on a spreadsheet that he told me was his renovation budget. I felt a pleasing sense of domesticity in our situation, and allowed myself to wonder for a few minutes what it would be like to have the relationship go on beyond the three weeks I'd be at Bestwood.

What would it be like to live with Alden permanently? To remain in England, at the side of a man who periodically got tongue-tied and frustrated with his inability to express his emotions? To spend my nights with him, snuggled up against him, feeling oddly safe and secure?

I sighed, and he looked up. "Problem?"

"Hmm?" I shuffled the papers, pulling out the small household journal that I'd been deciphering the night before. "No, just trying to read the spidery handwriting in this journal. I will say this for the Georgians—they had beautiful handwriting, but that doesn't mean it's easy to read. Especially as this journal appears to have been kept by not just the housekeeper and butler, but someone else who evidently wasn't quite as literate."

"Ah," he said, looking back at his computer and a stack of receipts. "Anything interesting about the history of the house in it?"

"So far, not a lot." I flipped through the journal. "Most of it is inventory of linens and candles and other household items—that's the part written by the housekeeper. Then there's a tally of wine and spirits, which I assume is the butler. It's the part in the third hand that appears to be the most interesting. This right here is an example." I tapped on a page, and to my pleasure, Alden got up and came over to sit next to me, his head angled close to mine to see the book.

"Good lord. How can you read that?" he asked, getting a glimpse of the handwriting.

"Two years of a history degree looking at primary sources," I told him.

The corners of his mouth crooked up. "You did that, too?"

"Too?" I felt my brows pull together in puzzlement. "You studied history as well?"

"European history. And English, and Latin. And I started law, but decided it wasn't for me."

I stared at him in wonder. "You're . . . you're a perpetual student like me?"

"If you mean do I have three degrees, and would be getting a fourth except my eldest brother cut my allowance so that I had to get work to support myself—not that I'm saying he was wrong, because he was paying for all of us, and I have a lot of brothers and sisters—if you mean that, then, yes, I'm a perpetual student like you."

"And they say opposites attract," I said, grinning at him. "I don't have any degrees, but I started on a whole lot of them. I usually get a year or two into it, and then decide it's not for me after all. And I was cut off, too! My dad told me that if I didn't have a degree by the time I was thirty, he was done paying my tuitions. And I didn't, so he stopped, and that's when I started taking jobs to pay my way. Which worked for a few years, but lately universities are telling me that I have to stick to one program and graduate, because I have over three hundred credits, and they're tired of me being a dilettante. Can you believe it? The last place actually used the word 'dilettante.'"

"That's unfair," Alden said, frowning. "You should be encouraged if you wish to educate yourself."

"Right? That's what I say. I mean, I get that they want people to graduate and all, but what's wrong with trying two or three or twelve programs before you settle on one?"

"Nothing whatsoever," he agreed. "If you were my daughter, I would continue to support you, no matter how old you were."

"If I was your daughter, we'd have a lot more to worry about than tuition," I said with a giggle.

"Point taken. What does this say? It looks like 'freeloader.'"

"'Free-trader,' I think." I squinted at the spot on the journal-cum-ledger where Alden was pointing. "I gather it means that whoever was the lord of the manor at the time was indulging in smuggled booze. Let's see. . . . I think it says, 'The Man o' War yesterday seized the free-trader Lopez and his vessel filled with wines by Accident and Folly of the people who in five row Boats were endeavoring to run ninety-one Casks of Wine. Will see to it that they will be set up a Trifle with far less than Duties so Lopez can make his voyage good.' Hmm. You know, that 'will see to it' bit makes it sound like the guy writing this was a local magistrate or something, which would mean he was the owner of Bestwood."

"Interesting. I knew there had been smugglers in the area, of course, but had no idea they operated here."

"Well, you do sit on a cliff looking over the water."

"True." He looked thoughtful, rubbing his forefinger over his chin in a way that completely distracted me. "I wonder if there are any of the old smuggling tunnels under the house. We'll have to ask Lady Sybilla what she knows about it."

"Definitely, although why would you care about tunnels?"

His eyebrows rose. "It adds value to the house if I can tell a potential buyer that there are historical tunnels underneath."

"Are you thinking of selling the hall once you have it fixed up?" I felt sad at the idea. I was starting to feel a certain kinship for the old place.

"That's the plan." He rubbed his chin a little more until I took the book away from him, causing him to look up in surprise.

I pushed him backward until he was lying on the bed with his feet on the floor, then straddled his lap, leaning forward to prop myself up on my elbows. My breasts were exactly at his mouth level. "A girl can only stand so much manly stubble flaunting. Kiss me."

He kissed the exposed part of my breasts. "I am happy to oblige, although I regret my stubble has taunted you to the point where you can't stand it any longer. What can I do to show the depths of my regret?"

"I think some intense, jungle-hot, slightly sweaty sex is in order."

"That sounds reasonable." He pulled my T-shirt up and off, cupping his hands over my bra-covered breasts. "But you have to let me indulge myself with you this time."

"The way I feel right now, I don't need any foreplay," I said, squirming around on his legs. I was speaking the absolute truth, too. The nearness of him, coupled with the way his finger had rubbed his sexy, sexy chin, had flipped my libido into high gear. "I really want to touch you, Alden. And taste you. And rub myself on you. And . . . oh, hell, let's just do it."

"I thought I was going to have the chance to drive you as insane as you drove me," he protested when I rose and unbuckled his pants.

"Next time, I promise. All of a sudden, you being right here next to me, smelling so good, and being warm and solid and raspy-faced, was just too much. I hope you are as ready as I am. . . . Oh, nice, you are."

I released him from the confines of his underwear and, doing a little dance on my knees, managed to rid myself of my underwear, praising myself for having the foresight to put on a skirt for the evening.

"I wasn't a minute ago, but then you started talking about your breasts, and thighs, and your legs wrapped around me with their strong, silken grip, and that was all it took."

I giggled as I positioned myself over him, leaning down to kiss him. "I didn't say any of those things, silly man."

"Ah. Then I must have imagined it. Here, let's get the rest of your clothing off."

"You still have yours on," I pointed out, but obliged him nonetheless, peeling off my bra, and pulling my skirt over my head.

"That's because you have me pinned to the bed, and besides, it's more important you are naked." His hands closed around my breasts, sending little shivers rippling down my back and arms.

I was in control until he took one nipple in his mouth at the same time his thumbs found very sensitive flesh.

"No!" I said, rising up on my knees, and reaching for his nightstand. I dug out a condom, ripped open the package, and slid it on him without mishap before positioning him exactly where I wanted him.

"No?" he asked, withdrawing his hands.

"No, not 'no, stop doing that.' No as in 'I am not going to be able to stand it if you continue, and I'd prefer to wait for you before jumping into the big O.'"

"I love your Americanisms," he said before swirling his tongue over my other nipple.

"I'm only half-American," I said, arching my back and rubbing the head of his penis against all those intimate parts of me that were clamoring for him. Wave after wave of tingles rippled out from my inner depths, my body already tight and on the verge of an orgasm. I wanted badly to kiss and touch and taste him, but even more than that, I wanted him deep inside of me.

I sank down onto him, my muscles rejoicing at the sensation, all my female parts clasping him with a fervent embrace, making it difficult to sink all the way down despite the fact that I was very anticipatory. Alden moaned with happiness, his fingers stroking my butt and legs as I moved on him.

I kept sinking. He kept moaning. I sank a little farther, expecting an end to him, but there still seemed to be more. I rose up and doubled over to look at him.

"What's wrong?" he asked, ceasing the moaning and stroking, a frown between his brows. "Why are you stopping? Why are you looking at my dick?"

"I could swear it's gotten bigger," I said, trying to do a visual measurement.

"Since when? This morning? I assure you that it is exactly the same as it was then."

"Hmm." I repositioned him, and slowly sank down, all my nerve endings roaring to life with his invasion. My back arched, my breath caught in my throat, and my breasts demanded the return of Alden's mouth. By the time I reached the end of Alden, I was squirming with ecstasy, needing to move, and at the same time wanting to stay exactly where I was. The urge to move won out.

"You're definitely bigger," I said, working out a lovely

rhythm. He groaned, his hands on my hips. I leaned down to nibble on his lips while one of his hands moved around to my front, sliding down my belly. "Sooo big. And hard. And oh dear heavens, did I mention big?"

Alden panted beneath me. "You did. Maybe it's because of this?" He held on to my thighs with both hands, and did an amazing, wonderful, astounding movement with his hips that had him pushing even deeper inside of me.

"Oh dear god, yes! Yes! Do that again!"

He did it again, and then twice more after that, which was all it took to push me over the edge. I didn't even have a chance to warn him that I was so close—my entire body suddenly slipped into a joyous explosion of orgasm. I was vaguely aware of his fast, short movements, but when I collapsed down onto his chest, it was the manic beating of his heart that filled my awareness.

Oddly, my own heart seemed to be beating at the same rate, not to mention the fact that our breathing was equally as rough and fast.

It's almost as if, my inner voice innocently pointed out, we were made for each other.

"You're going to kill me if you keep that up," I said between pants, biting the lobe of his left ear. "And don't tell me you didn't get bigger, because I know you did."

He started laughing, but because he was still trying to catch his breath, it turned into a case of violent hiccups. By the time I disengaged myself, got him a towel and a glass of water, and he managed to stifle the hiccups, my inner voice had stopped saying how perfectly suited he was to me, and I was able to crawl into bed and curl up with him in a fairly reasonable facsimile of calm acceptance of what we had together.

And how long do you think that will last? my inner self asked.

I ignored her. Sometimes, ignorance really is bliss.

ELEVEN

Two weeks passed during which Alden sweated in the house while tearing off old wallpaper in the library, the formal dining room, a small reception room in a gloomy corner of the first floor, and the kitchen. He sweated while he repaired holes in the walls, killed mold, cut out rot, rebuilt window seats, and repainted all four rooms. He sweated every afternoon for three hours while wearing full plate armor, learning how to fight with a sword and a shield, how to breathe in an enclosed helm, and, most important, how not to fall over in such a way as to leave himself vulnerable to attack.

And best of all, he sweated every night with Mercy either on top of him or under him, but always she was right there with him when the pleasure became too much for him, and he gave way to limb-shaking orgasms.

"Unfortunately," he told Mercy on the fourteenth night of such limb-shaking activities, "the house hasn't given up its attempt to do away with itself."

"I really think you need to stop viewing what must be perfectly normal experiences for a house this old as a form of personal rejection. The house doesn't hate you, Alden. If it had feelings, and I'm not saying it doesn't, but if it did, then it makes sense that it would like you, because you're working so hard to make it nice again."

"You and I know that, but it doesn't care." He looked up at the ceiling, upon which, four nights before, a long, jagged crack had appeared, moving from the far corner to the exact spot under which he lay. He thought of it as an accusing finger, marking him for the house's disapproval. "Just today a door in the attic tried to fling itself down the stairs."

Mercy, who he was pleased to note was lying bonelessly next to him, a sated, dreamy half smile on her face, roused herself enough to say, "That wasn't an attempt to get out of the attic. You said there was wood rot, and the weight of the door was finally too much for the damaged frame."

"Or it could have been trying to leave the house the only way it knew how."

Mercy gave a ladylike snort. "So you've had one little incident—"

"Two days ago, a branch came off the oak next to the third-floor bedroom on the north wing, and broke not just the window, but damaged the frame."

"OK, so you've had two little incidents—"

"And the day before that, there was the discovery that the water heater for Lady Sybilla's side of the house has been leaking for an undetermined length of time."

"Aha! That means it wasn't an act of self-harm," Mercy said, raising her hand.

He raised one eyebrow. "Although the leak is of long term, the fact that the water heater fell over onto its side and spewed a good six inches of water in one of the cellars before I could turn off the water makes it fit my parameters for suicide."

"Hrmph. A few events—"

"Don't forget about the hornet's nest I found burrowed into the wall in the old housekeeper's room. Or the mushrooms that were growing in the ground-floor guest loo. Or the family of bats residing in the north wing's attic, rendering that attic unusable, and most likely unable to renovate due to the amount of guano that has hardened on the floor."

"All right, I admit those are all bad things—"

"Not to mention the fact that every day, whenever I go outside, yet another piece of roof tile manages to slither its way off in what I can only describe as an attempt to brain me."

Mercy's hand fell back to the bed. "That has been kind of odd. I wouldn't have thought it could happen until I saw it for myself."

He turned off the bedside lamp that he had finally gotten working again and settled back on the pillows, waiting for Mercy to snuggle up against him. That she did so automatically filled him with a quiet sense of contentment. "I told you the house hated me."

"It's a mild animosity at best," she corrected, putting her hand on his chest, and tucking one of her legs between his. She kissed his ear, and settled against his side to sleep.

He said nothing, enjoying the drowsy pull of sleep, and her warm, comforting nearness, but before he could completely drift off, a dull thud penetrated his awareness.

He opened his eyes, frowning at the sight of the quarter moon just barely visible through the leaves of the tree outside his window. The moon hadn't been anywhere near to visible when they'd settled down for sleep. A glance at the clock showed almost two hours since he'd turned out the light.

Thud. Thunk. Kerwidget.

Alden sat up in bed, his frown increasing as he stared at the section of wall where the noise seemed to originate. As in the other bedrooms in this wing, the two windows in his room sat above a deep window seat, one with storage that he did not use, since he suspected that the mice that still occupied the walls despite the efforts of the exterminator might have access to it.

The kerwidget definitely came from the window seat.

He extricated himself from Mercy, gently easing himself out from under her arm and leg.

She murmured an inarticulate noise, and rolled over, wiggling her enticing ass at him until she evidently realized he wasn't there for her to back up into. She half sat up, saying, "Alden?"

"I'm here."

"What are you doing?" She shoved her hair back off her face. "Is anything wrong?"

"No. Close your eyes; I'm going to turn on the light." He clicked on the bedside lamp, squinting a little at the brightness that followed. It died away almost immediately with a gurgling fizzle of the lightbulb.

Alden sighed. "The house is just being mean now."

"Coincidence," Mercy said in the darkness.

Alden carefully made his way over to the wall, and clicked on the light switch there.

Mercy shielded her eyes from the overhead light, and asked, "Why are you up?"

"I heard a noise. I think it came from the window seat."

"What sort of a noise?" She yawned, suddenly snapping her teeth closed while yanking the duvet up to her chin. "You don't think it was . . . mice?"

He didn't answer, instead pulling off the cushions that sat on the window seat, and lifting up one of the two hinged seats.

There was nothing inside the storage area.

"Well?" Mercy asked, the duvet now up to her eyes as she sat huddled in bed, pressed against the headboard in a way that said she expected a great wave of mice to come streaming over the sides of the window seat. "How many are there?"

"None. That is, there are no mice in it. There's nothing in it. It's completely bare."

"Completely bare things don't make mysterious noises. What exactly did you hear?"

"Two thuds, one thunk, and a singularly alarming kerwidget."

She sat up straighter, lowering the duvet so that her mouth was free of it. "I can explain away the thuds and thunk, but I can see why the kerwidget is alarming. That's not a normal sound."

"No." He knelt next to the window seat, feeling more than a little silly when he ran his hands around the interior, pressing on the walls and floor of it to make sure there wasn't some sort of secret panel.

"What are you doing? I can't look because you're presenting a view of you that I'm not super crazy wild about, and that's saying a lot because I'm super crazy wild about all the other views of you."

Hastily, he straightened up from the bent position, and reached for the closest pair of pants, heat washing up his neck and cheeks. His voice came out stilted when he said, "My apologies."

She pulled the duvet down from where she'd been covering her eyes with it. "That's OK. And stop being embarrassed—I know you didn't mean to moon me. Besides, I like your butt. I just don't need to see . . . you know . . . all of it."

He grimaced, and was about to apologize again when she added, "What were you doing bent over like that, anyway?"

"Pressing on the walls of the window seat in case there was some sort of panel that slid back to reveal a secret hiding place."

"You mean like a secret passage?" she asked, her nose wrinkling in the most adorable way. He badly wanted to crawl back into bed and kiss her nose, wrinkles and all, but he knew that neither of them would sleep until they had a better idea of the origin of the noise.

"More like a hiding spot for a cache of untold wealth in the form of jewels, or even a small hoard of gold coins. Houses this age sometimes had little spots where the lord and master could tuck away bits of his wealth."

"Oh." She sounded disappointed, and slid forward, picking up from her bag the gossamer-thin garment she called her nightgown. "I think a secret passage is way cooler than just a hidey-hole."

"I suppose that would depend if something of value or interest is hidden in it." He tapped the walls of the storage area again, but they sounded perfectly normal, and not at all like the sort of structures given over to midnight kerwidgeting. "Perhaps I misheard—"

At that moment the overhead lights—both of them—gave whispered hiccups and went out, one after the other.

"You bastard house!" he shouted, raising his fist to the ceiling. "You're costing me a fortune in lightbulbs!"

"Come back to bed," Mercy said, and patted the duvet. "You must have been dreaming."

"Possibly, although I wasn't aware I was sleep—" He stopped in the midact of closing the seat lid.

"Hmm?"

"Mercy," he whispered.

"What?"

"Come see this."

The sound of a duvet slithering to the floor was followed by the soft padding of her feet, and suddenly, she was there, at his side, her warm, sleepy scent twining itself around him. "If you are planning on showing me a mouse—"

"Shh," he said softly, and pointed even though he doubted she could see the gesture in the dark.

"Why? What—oh!"

It hadn't been visible with the lights on in the room, but now that they were out, a soft golden glow definitely showed along the near bottom edge of the window seat.

"There's a light beneath it," Mercy whispered into his ear, distracting him for a few seconds with the warmth of her breath.

"There is. I suspect that I was overly hasty in ruling out a secret passage," he whispered back.

"Oooh!" She squeezed his arm excitedly, moving with him when he carefully edged his way over to the black shape of the desk, where his laptop sat.

On the seat of the chair was the tool belt he'd been wearing earlier in the day while trying to fix a leak in Fenice's bathroom. He extracted a screwdriver, and, as an afterthought, a hammer.

"What are you going to do? Pry it open?" Mercy asked softly.

"If I have to. I'd rather locate the mechanism that opens it, assuming there is one." He made his way back to the window seat, adding, "It might be that there's no opening, you know. The seams of the wood could have simply pulled away and are allowing some light to come up from below."

"Yes, but light from what? Lady Sybilla is over on the other side of the house."

"That is exactly what I intend to find out." Using the screwdriver, he gently felt along the front length of the window seat, but with no result. No panel opened, no secret switch was uncovered, and no hidden mechanism was triggered. It was simply an empty storage area with a glowing line of light along one edge.

"Well, that's just anticlimactic as hell," Mercy said in an annoyed whisper when he sat back on his heels.

"I'm not sure what else I can do," he said, staring into the dark void presented by the opened seat. "Short of bashing down the sides of it, that is."

"Don't do that."

"I don't intend to. I have enough fixing to do in this house without creating more work."

"Let me try. I was always good with those boxes that had secret drawers." Mercy took his screwdriver and proceeded to tap, prod, and attempt to pry up the entire front length of the seat before she, too, sat back in frustration.

"Maybe just a little bash at the side wall," she said, disgust filling her voice.

"No bashing walls. We'll leave this until morning, and take a look at it in the light of day." He put both hands on the edge of the seat in order to get to his feet, and was halfway up when from the depths of the seat came a clicking noise, followed by a groaning, low rumble.

The light burst upward into the darkness of the room, dazzling Alden for a moment.

"You did it!" Mercy said with a clap of her hands, then

immediately whispered an apology for speaking loudly, and added a more subdued, "Holy cow, it really is a secret passage. Look, stairs! In your window seat! Oh my god, this is just like something out of my childhood Nancy Drew books."

Alden knelt next to the window seat, one hand rubbing his chin as he tried to make sense of what he was seeing. It was indeed a staircase, a narrow spiraling wooden staircase that was illuminated from below by the golden light they'd seen in the seam of the window seat. The light didn't waver or flicker, leaving him to believe it was not a candle or a lamp. What was a staircase of all things doing leading up to his window seat? "Mercy, go over to the toolbox in the wardrobe. There's a torch in there."

"Torch? Oh, you mean flashlight." Mercy hurried over to the wardrobe, poking around in its depth until she came back with a flashlight, a small saw suitable for use on branches, and her dressing gown, the last of which she slipped on after handing him the flashlight. "I feel just like I'm Nancy Drew."

"Does that make me one of the Hardy Boys?" he asked, pulling on a T-shirt and his shoes before tucking the hammer into his back pocket.

"No, you're Ned Nickerson, Nancy's handsome but beefy boyfriend. Hang on, shoes are a good idea. Where are my sandals?"

Two minutes later, with a warning to Mercy not to descend until he told her it was safe to do so, Alden began his descent down the creaking, dusty wooden staircase. He had to duck to fit himself under the edge of the window seat, but since the spiral stairs had a steep descent, it didn't take but a few more seconds before he was able to straighten up. As he descended, he could see a light glowing along one wall, clearly hung there for a purpose. The stairs ended abruptly, the light disclosing a small alcove, with two narrow, dark passageways leading away into inky nothingness. He eyed the light closely, shining his torch on the wall to reveal black cables snaking off in either direction. "How very curious."

"Alden!" Mercy whispered loudly from above him. He looked up, and saw her pinched face peering down over the edge of the window seat. "What's going on?"

"I was just looking at the light. Someone has put in quite a bit of work to bring lighting to this secret passageway. Come down, but drag the duvet over to hang into the window seat before you do."

"Why?"

"It'll keep the floor from closing on us."

"Oh. Good thinking, Ned."

She disappeared, but was back in a few moments, her sandaled feet pattering down the narrow spiral stairs quickly, followed by a long, bulky shape of the duvet.

"Oooh," she said when she got down to his level. She rubbed her arms even though she was wearing her dressing gown over the nightie. "Secret passages! Do you think we're inside the walls of the house?"

"Possibly, although the windows would keep the passages from running the length. A bigger question is, who put in these lights, and why?"

Mercy examined the light on the wall. "Huh. Obviously, whoever did it meant to use the passage for something. Maybe wartime activities?"

Alden shook his head. "I can't imagine why. This house wasn't conscripted for use by the army. From what I remember of the records, it was simply shut up during that time."

"Huh." She touched the light. "Well, this is a modern bulb, so it had to have been someone in the recent past."

"True."

"What I don't get is who would do it. Not Lady Sybilla or Adams—I can't see either of them scampering around in the walls of Bestwood Hall."

He flipped off his torch. The lights were spaced along the wall in such a way as to light up the passageway quite well. "No, I don't think this is their doing . . . or at least, I don't think they placed the light here. I wouldn't put it past Lady Sybilla to have rented out secret passages, though. Let's go this way. I believe it should take us toward the great hall."

Mercy took hold of the back of his shirt, shuffling after him as he walked forward. Almost immediately, the passage took a sharp turn to the left, leading them away from the front of the house. Lights continued to glow at them approximately every twenty feet.

"You'll notice it's not super dusty in here," Mercy said softly behind him.

"I had noticed that." He kept to himself the fact that although the ground was littered with bits of debris—stones, small chunks of mortar and wood, and lots of rodent droppings—they had been pushed to the side, as if someone had cleared a path. The smell was close and dusty, which led him to believe although mice or rats had once been here, they hadn't been for some time.

"Ah. More stairs." He stopped at the top of another wooden staircase and looked down. Like the one leading up to his room, this one was lit from below. Beyond the top of the staircase was a blank wall and a small square alcove. He frowned, stepping forward to kneel and examine the wall and floor. On the latter, the dust lay heavy and thick, leaving the outline of several squares where something had obviously sat. Something large and bulky.

"What's that?" Mercy asked, peering over his shoulder. "Or rather, what was that, do you think?"

"I have no idea. Crates of some sort would be my guess, but what was in them I couldn't say."

"Hmm. Odd."

"Indeed it is." He gestured to the stairs. "I guess we go down. Are you all right with that, Nancy?"

"Right as rain, Ned. Lead on!"

He smiled over his shoulder at her, then carefully made his way down the stairs. This staircase seemed to be in worse shape than the other one, causing him to watch anxiously as Mercy descended, but other than creaking ominously and weaving a little, it held up under their weight.

"I feel like we should be leaving a bread-crumb trail,"

Mercy said when they set off down a slightly wider passage. This one dipped downward, and had a wetter odor to it, the smell of mold driving out the drier, dusty scents of the passage above.

"I wouldn't suggest that. It might attract mice," he said, and brushed against the wall. It was horribly moist, causing him to recoil in revulsion.

"What's wrong?" Mercy asked when he staggered backward a step. "Did you see a mouse?"

"No." He reached out and touched the wall with the tips of his fingers. "It's damp."

"The wall?" She mimicked his movement. "Huh. That's probably because we're near the ocean."

"We can't be near the ocean. That's a quarter mile from the house, and we've only gone half of that distance."

She peered over his shoulder. Just as with the original passage, this one was very well lit. "I wonder where this is going. To the old part of the house?"

"I have no idea. Shall we see?"

"Yes." She gave his back a little prod, and he continued forward down the passage, soon coming to another blank wall as the passage made a right-angle turn. This time, the floor was dust free in front of the wall, but there were a few torn scraps of paper, and a ghostly white object that lay forgotten in the corner.

"What on earth?" Mercy asked, picking up a milky white plastic bottle. "It's a wash bottle."

Alden gathered up the couple of bits of paper, frowning. "A what?"

"Didn't you ever do any chemistry classes?"

"No, the physical sciences are not my forte." He eyed the bottle she held. It had a red cap with a long tube bent at ninety degrees. "What does a wash bottle wash?"

"Anything you want." She turned it around in her hands, tipping it so as to catch the light. "In my chem classes, we used these for solvents. Which I bet is what this is—see here? Most of the lettering is rubbed off."

She held the bottle to him, pointing out where the letters CETONE were written in red.

"And what exactly would an acetone chemistry bottle and"—he glanced at the scraps of paper—"over-the-counter cold medication be doing in the walls of my house?"

"Maybe you have a mad scientist with sinusitis living in your walls?" she offered with a smile to let him know she was joking.

He snorted. "It would be more likely to be a homeless person conducting illicit drug activity than a mad scientist."

"True, but at least you know one thing: it's someone contemporary, not one of Sir James Baskerville's long-dead ancestors."

"I think I'd prefer the long-dead ancestors," he said, pocketing the scraps of cold medicine label. "They, at least, have a chance of hiding treasure. Shall we continue?"

"Onward, Ned!"

They continued down the passageway, the walls still damp and unpleasant. Before long, the change in air could be noticed.

"Salt water," he said, sniffing.

"Told you it was the ocean."

"Hmm." Another two minutes, and they reached an arched opening, through which they came into a cave. At their feet, an ebony rippling line of water lapped at what looked like a primitive pier. Here the lights hung drunkenly from a zigzagging copper pipe that had been bolted to the low ceiling of the cave, the lights moving gently with the breeze coming in from the entrance. "I'll be damned. Do you know what this is?"

"A cave? With water in it?"

"It's exactly that. And who would use a cave with water access in Cornwall?"

She sucked in her breath. "The free-traders! Holy moly, Alden, you have a smugglers' cave under your house! An actual, honest-to-god smugglers' cave! One with . . . electricity?"

"Exactly. Smugglers may be using the cave, but it's not free-traders. I'd be very interested to know who else is aware of the cave's existence . . . and why they're lighting up the insides of my house."

"Not to mention what they're doing in there. I mean, a homeless person wouldn't string lights all over."

"This is true." He took Mercy's hand, her fingers cold and stiff in his, but curling around his hand in a way that not only provided comfort but stirred his desire. "Shall we see if anyone is out at the cave entrance bringing in some contraband?"

She waved the heavy spanner she'd evidently taken from his tool chest. "You bet. I'm armed, so even if it's white slavers or ivory smugglers, we'll be safe."

"You have the oddest notions of the sorts of things people would want to smuggle in this day and age." With another quick glance around the area, he turned his back on the dead end to the left, and led Mercy along the stream, into the unknown.

TWELVE

"So you're saying you didn't find anything in the tunnel?" Fenice, who had listened to my tale of my nocturnal subterranean adventures with Alden, sat with her toast and tea getting cold, too riveted to consume the breakfast I'd interrupted. "Nothing? Not even so much as a clue as to what was going on? Or who put the lights there?"

"Nothing. The stream led out to an entrance in the cliffside, about eight feet above the beach. Alden said watermarks on the cave walls show that it used to be much more of a river than a stream, which would explain why the smugglers liked it. We couldn't see any signs of a person on the beach—no boat, no campfire, nothing—and likewise, when we backtracked our way to his bedroom, we didn't encounter anyone."

She blinked a couple of times before absently picking up her cup, and promptly setting it down again. "How utterly, utterly bizarre. And unsettling. It does sound like homeless people are using it."

"Possibly, although that doesn't explain the lights. There was a big switch where the cave meets the passageway to the house, and three others that we found at various points, but no clue as to who turned the lights on, let alone put them in. Alden thinks the lights have been there for several decades, though. They look kind of old."

"World War Two?" Fenice asked.

I shook my head. "We think earlier."

"Well, it's odd. And unsettling."

"I know, right? Just the idea that someone could be sneaking around in the walls of the house spying on us . . . it's creepy as hell."

"What's Alden going to do?"

I went over to the electric kettle to make myself a cup of spicy orange tea. "We talked about that for a while once we got back to his room. I thought he should nail everything shut that could be nailed shut—like the window seat—and block the entrance at the beach, but he figured that would let whoever was using the tunnel and secret passageways know that we were on to him. Or her. But probably a him, because honestly, can you imagine a woman sneaking around like that?"

"Yes," policewoman Fenice said, taking a bite of her toast.

For some reason, I thought of Lisa. I could picture her being up to something nefarious like poking around secret passages. I chastised myself for such ungenerous thoughts almost immediately, however, telling my inner bitchy self that just because I didn't like her, that didn't mean she would do something underhanded. "Anyway, in the end, Alden decided to put some stuff in the window seat—heavy books and some iron doorstops, et cetera, that he found in one of the attics—so that the lid wouldn't lift up when you pressed down on the latch. That should, at least, keep anyone from entering his room that way."

"What about the other rooms?" she asked, pushing away her half-eaten toast. "I have some pepper spray, but if I need a hand weapon—"

"Your room is safe," I said quickly. "We went all along the upper-floor passages to see where they went, and it just went to the lord of the manor's chamber—Alden's room—and to a staircase that led down to a small room that Alden thinks used to be the butler's pantry. He's going to map the passages over a layout of the house today, in order to figure out just where they are, so he can check those rooms for any secret entrances that we couldn't find."

"At least I won't have to move in with Patrick," she said. "But I'd still sleep better knowing there wasn't someone hiding in the walls."

"Well," I said, making a show of looking around before I leaned in and spoke quietly. "As a matter of fact, Alden and I came up with a plan last night. In one of the forensic detection classes I took, we did a project using this stain that fluoresces under black light. The police use it to find residual traces of human-based fluids, like blood and semen. Anyway, while I was taking a shower this morning, Alden got online and found a place in town that stocked the dye in powder form. He's off getting it now."

"What good is that going to do?"

"He's going to dust it on the light switches, so that whoever touches them will stain their hands. Only they won't know it because you can't see the dye unless you have one of those black light wand thingies, which Alden's also picking up."

"But how will you know whose hands to look at?" she asked, picking off a crust of her toast.

"We'll check everyone out. Naturally, you and Patrick don't have to worry, but to be fair to everyone, we'll just do a hand check every morning. I bet you that we'll get whoever is hanging out inside the walls in the next twenty-four hours."

"I wish I had your confidence," she said with a glance at the clock. "Lord, it can't be that late already. People will be here in ten minutes—we'd better make a move."

"I'll be there in a couple," I said, hastily stirring some lemon juice into my tea. "I have to have a cuppa or else I'm totally worthless."

"Right. Remember that today you've got that group from the Women's Institute to handle."

"Dress-up and archery, in that order," I repeated from our discussion the night before.

She grimaced and, grabbing her toast, headed for the door. She paused to say, "If I were Alden, I'd call the local police."

"We thought of that, too," I said, blowing on my tea and taking a tentative sip. "But as Alden pointed out, there's not a lot the cops could do unless we found someone in the passages or, at the very least, something that gave us an idea of who was doing it."

"I'd still let them know," she pronounced, and then hurried off to greet the people who were due to arrive that morning. I sipped my tea, and thought of checking on Alden, whom I'd left going through all the documents related to the purchase of the house in search of a floor plan, but the sight of a long van pulling up with a bunch of excited women had me bolting for the garden.

By the time my lunch break rolled around, I was hot and sweaty, and my ears rang from the constant chatter, laughter, and, at some points, song from the group of women from a nearby town. The ladies had brought liquid refreshments with them ("So we don't get heatstroke," one of them said, raising a not-so-frozen daiquiri at me), and were well on their way to feeling no pain by the time the catering lady arrived with the selection of sandwiches. The day's choices of beef tongue or cheese sandwich, even if I hadn't established a policy of eating lunch with Alden, would have driven me up to the house for food.

I found Alden in the library, which was bare of all except the table where I occasionally went through Lady Sybilla's old ledgers, journals, and file folders filled with everything from fifty-year-old society column newspaper clippings to receipts for hunting dogs, horses, and even a sloop named the Lady S.

Next to him, in the chair, sat Lady Sybilla herself, both of them bent over a large sheet of paper.

"—thought that it must be the space between the great hall and those three rooms along the south side, but that doesn't work out. I measured the width of the rooms, compared it to the width of the house from the door to the hall to the outer edge of the wall, and there's no lost space."

"I told you that there would be little call for your passageway to run along the ground floor," Lady Sybilla said with slow, perfectly enunciated measure. "If it runs to the smugglers' lair, as you assure me it does, then it must be the passage that my late husband mentioned his father using to store valuables during the Great War. James mentioned once that his father had access to a hidden location accessible only to him, where he placed all the family portraits because he was certain that the kaiser would be landing on our shores."

"I don't understand how that translates to the passage not having any branches on the ground floor," Alden said, nodding to me when I stopped next to him. "It seems a folly not to have done so."

"Ah, but you are not thinking like a baronet who enjoys his French wine despite the war."

"Which war?" I asked, confused. "World War One, or the Napoleonic Wars?"

"The latter, naturally," Lady Sybilla said with an arched eyebrow at me. "I thought you were going to put my papers in order?"

"I am, I am, but I do have a job to do, too."

"I shall have my secretary attend to it if you are unable to handle the task as you indicated you would," Lady Sybilla said loftily.

"Did I hear my name being mentioned?" Lisa oiled her way into the room, and leered at Alden. "What's that you need me to do, Lady Sybilla? You know it's my pleasure to give help whenever it's needed."

She might have been addressing Lady Sybilla, but her eyes were on Alden. I decided that I was a big enough person to ignore her continued attempts to entice him away from me.

"Mercy here has undertaken to sort my personal papers, and those of my husband, but she seems unable to find the time to do so."

"I told you that I intend to work on them in the evenings. It's just that . . . well . . ." I looked at Alden, who was not in the least bit flustered, as I had expected he'd be with the arrival of Lisa. In fact, he didn't even look like he was paying attention to her (or me) at all. He was frowning at the crude floor plan of the house that he'd drawn, complete with notes on dimensions of rooms, and in red ink what I assumed was his guess of the route the passageway from his room had taken. "I've been busy," I finished lamely.

"I will be happy to help you with the papers, Mercy," Lisa offered. "I've been told I'm ever so good with organizing things. We could work together on the project, don't you think?"

"Sure," I said glumly, aware of Lady Sybilla's pale eyes on me. She might be old, but she had a gaze like a basilisk. "That would be helpful."

"There, now, isn't that nice? We have solved that problem. And I hear you're solving one of your own," she said, putting her hand on Alden's arm.

He looked up, startled. "Eh?"

"I'm told that you found a secret passageway in the house, one that someone has been using to spy on all of us, but that you've come up with a brilliant idea on how to catch the culprit by putting some sort of chemical on the light switches that the person uses. I have to say, that's the cleverest idea I've heard in a very long time."

Alden stared at her for a few seconds, then transferred his gaze to me. Only by then, it was a glare. A furious glare. "Mercy, might I have a word in your ear?"

"Uh . . . sure." I followed him when he marched over to the far side of the room, where a marble fireplace that probably hadn't been used in at least fifty years lurked with an oddly menacing air. Lady Sybilla and Fenice left the room, leaving me alone with Alden. "What's up?"

He whirled around to face me, his eyes narrowed, and his nostrils flaring. "You told Lisa about our plan to catch whoever is sneaking around in my house?"

"No, of course not." I cleared my throat. "I did tell Fenice, but I figured that was OK. I mean, she was all freaked out about the idea of someone being in the house able to watch her, so that means she couldn't be doing it. Not that I ever thought it was her. Or Vandal, for that matter."

"Oh?" He stiffened. "Why are you so quick to exclude Vandal?"

I whapped him on the arm. "Silly, your jealousy is showing."

"I'm not jealous," he replied with great dignity, which was immediately blown when he added, "You're not falling for him, are you?"

"Of course not." It was on the tip of my tongue to tell him that the only man I was falling for was standing right in front of me, but I decided that not even I was ready to investigate that thought, and I certainly wasn't up to talking about it with the man who expected me to be leaving in a week. "I simply meant that he isn't the sort of man who would go skulking around the innards of a house spying on people. For one thing, I have it on the best authority that he's spending most of his free time wooing the local ladies, and for another, he hardly ever comes up to the house for meals, let alone anything else."

"That doesn't prove anything."

"No," I said, leaning in to give his lower lip a little nibble. "But neither does your unwarranted suspicion based on jealousy."

"I told you that I'm not jealous."

"Of course you're not, darling," Lisa said, oozing over to us, her hips swaying with exaggerated movements. "A man like you would never have cause to be jealous."

"Dude," I told her, shaking my head. "Do you spend all your free time watching old Falcon Crest reruns? Because you're sure doing the same sort of scene-eating overacting that they used to have on that show."

"Scene-eating!" she snarled, her hands fisting. "Overacting?"

"In spades," I told her, at the end of my tether. "Since the day you came here, Alden has made it perfectly clear that he was not interested in a sexual or romantic relationship with you. And yet you continue to slink around and cast innuendos at him, and make sly little digs at me, and butter him up one side and down the other. Well, I've had it with your shenanigans. Just knock it off already, and we'll get along fine."

She gawked at me for a moment, then turned to Alden with her hands spread wide. "You see? I try to be nice, but she's forever insulting me, and trying to belittle me in front of others."

"What do you mean, you see?" I asked suspiciously. "Have you been complaining to Alden about me? Oh! You have, haven't you?"

She smiled.

Alden looked incredibly uncomfortable, and began fidgeting, a sure warning he was about to run off.

"Don't you dare," I told him, poking him in the chest with my finger. "If I'm going to have a dramatic scene with Lisa, the least you can do is stand there and be supportive! So get with the program!"

He thought for a moment, then applauded politely. "Brava, Mercy."

Lisa tched, and with a last lingering look at Alden (my rant clearly had no effect on her), she hustled her hips out of the room, murmuring something about attending to Lady Sybilla's latest literary output.

"That's your idea of support?" I asked Alden, my lips thinned.

He shrugged. "It was the best I could do on the spur of the moment. If you give me ten minutes, I could write you a supportive note."

"All right, but later." I couldn't help but smile at him. "I like your notes."

He smiled back. "I like yours, too. I particularly like the one you slipped into my pocket yesterday, with the drawing of—"

He evidently remembered there was someone else in the room, and stopped.

Fenice, busy with her phone, paid us no attention.

"Yeah, that's not for public discussion," I said, my cheeks warming a little at the memory of the drawing I'd done of a depiction of him and me engaged in one of the more athletic positions from the Kama Sutra. "So! You were chastising me. Are you done with that, or should I explain more why I told Fenice what was going on?"

"I'm done," he said with a mock sigh, but his lips were warm when I leaned in to kiss him. "But please do not tell anyone else."

"I won't. And I'll tell Fenice not to tell anyone else, too, since I assume she is the one who told Lisa about our plans. What are you going to do this afternoon?"

"I have to run into town to pick up the things we need," he said with a sidelong look at Fenice, who had finished with her phone, and was in the act of packing up several icy bottles of water for the refreshment of the afternoon students. "A friend of the chemist who ordered the . . . erm . . . objects, and who was with a criminal investigation branch for several years, is going to meet me here later to show me how best to apply the substance."

"Awesome! I'll see you later, then. Here, Fenice, I'll take some of those down to the garden with me once I grab a quick sandwich."

"Thanks, Mercy. The caterer didn't bring nearly enough water for a day this hot." Fenice staggered out with a box filled with water bottles. I followed a short while later, hastily eating a chicken sandwich as I made my way down to where the students of the day were reclined in whatever shady spots they could find, enjoying their tongue sandwiches.

The next two hours passed with speed while I ran three more students through their archery paces. Just as I was putting everything away, a huge hand reached out to tap me on the shoulder.

"Your name is Mercy, isn't it?"

I turned to find the big red-faced man named Barry Butcher smiling at me. "Hello. Yes, I'm Mercy. You're Mr. Butcher, aren't you?"

"That's right. Barry to my friends. I've seen you with Alden Ainslie, haven't I?"

"Well . . . yes, I know Alden."

His smile grew. "Our Mr. Ainslie knows what he's about all right. He's quite the man, although I will admit to being somewhat frustrated with him right now."

"Oh? In what way?" I was a bit wary, not quite comfortable talking about Alden to a man I didn't know well.

"It's his stubbornness in holding out for a better offer." His smile changed to a frown. "The Hairy Tit Conservancy has made him a generous offer for the house and lands—a quite generous offer—but he simply refuses to listen to it. I don't suppose you are a twitcher?"

"Twitcher being bird-watcher?" I made a noncommittal gesture. "I like birds, but I don't go out of the way to study them, although I did think of becoming a zoologist once. But I was more interested in mammals, particularly African mammals. I want to save all those lions and elephants and rhinos that are being hunted into extinction."

"Now, that's just exactly what we at the conservancy are doing," he said, his frown melting away. "We want to preserve and protect our friend the Hairy Tit, and we have a prime opportunity to do that, but Alden is being stubborn, very stubborn." He shook his head. "Perhaps you could talk to him for me? Point out just how many birds he'll be saving if he allows us to take over conservatorship of the precious breeding grounds?"

"I'm sure you're eloquent enough for both of us," I said, smiling a wholly false smile, but determined not to get into whatever business Barry was trying to conduct.

His smile slipped a notch, but he nodded, and murmured something about being grateful for anything I could do.

I edged around him. "If you'll excuse me, I have to go see if there's a student waiting for me."

"Ah, there I can help you." He gestured toward the archery butts. "Or rather, you can help me. I was hoping you could find time to teach me some practical uses of a bow and arrow."

"Practical?" I rubbed my nose. "I'm not sure what you mean."

"Rabbits," he said, nodding toward the line of woods that stretched beyond the far pasture. "I've got a little garden, you see, and it's overrun with rabbits. I'd take a shotgun to them, but the missus, she doesn't like that. Plus, it's the devil's job to clean buckshot out of a rabbit carcass."

I kept my lips from curling in disgust. I might be an occasional meat eater, but I'd never eaten a bunny, and didn't intend to change that fact. However, it didn't mean I could hold others to my standards. "I'm afraid I've never done any bow hunting, Mr. Butch—Barry."

"But a target is a target, isn't it?" he said, giving me a little prod in the ribs that sent me staggering a couple of feet. "If I paid, oh, say, double the fee, do you think you could take me out to the field and teach me to shoot at a few things?"

"I don't want any part of shooting animals," I said firmly.

His eyes, an uncanny pale grayish brown, narrowed. "You one of those vegans?"

"No, but I am an animal lover, and I don't like hunting in any guise. I'm a bit surprised that you are into it, frankly, since you are with the bird conservancy group."

"Rabbits that eat your garden are not the same as endangered birds," he retorted.

"I'm not going to debate you on the point, since I realize that you choosing to thin the rabbit herd on your land is your own business."

"That's the ticket," he said, totally ignoring my comments to clap his giant hand on my shoulder. "I knew you'd be up for the job. I'll just go pay the lady with her arm in a sling, and then you can take me out to the fields, and we'll do a little shooting."

"I just said I wasn't going to shoot any animals—" I called after him as he strode away.

He raised a hand to show he heard me, and a few minutes later, over my continued protests that all I would do was teach him how to shoot stationary objects, he carried two of the student bows, a stack of paper targets, and two quivers full of arrows. I had my borrowed bow, and spent the time it took walking out to the far pasture quizzing him about his experience with archery.

"Did it as a child, of course," he said, tacking one of the targets onto a tree stump that sat just outside the pasture, on the fringe of a small wood that divided Alden's land from the next fields. "Da used to say I had a right eye for it, but of course, a shotgun is more efficient, so once I learned to shoot a proper weapon, I didn't go back to this."

I said nothing other than to give him basic instruction on how to hold the bow, notch the arrow, and aim at the target.

"You certainly didn't lie about your eye," I told him a half hour later, collecting the remains of seven paper targets. We'd scattered them around the edge of the small wood, taping them to a fallen tree, a couple of low-hanging branches, and a small clump of shrubs. "You have the makings of a very good archer."

"Aye, but these are just static targets," he said, waving one of the bows toward the woods. "It's a world of difference hitting a moving one."

"Very true, and that, as I explained numerous times, is not something I'm prepared to teach you."

He eyed me speculatively. "I bet you could do it."

"Yes, but I've had training in moving targets. My college used to have competitions where we had to do all sorts of crazy shots, including through small objects like oranges and grapefruit, and hitting the bull's-eye painted on a dummy on a pulley that was jerked across our line of vision. The best, though, was what we used to call our spy missions. Our instructor would go out into a local forest, and hang a shirt with a heart painted on it from high up in a tree. We had to hunt down the target, and then hit it in the heart, if we could. It was great fun, and I won that particular contest three months in a row."

"Now, then," he said in a warm, approving voice. "That must have been something to see."

"It was kind of fun," I admitted, glancing around to make sure we'd picked up all the bits of paper.

"What say we have a wee competition ourselves?" Barry suggested.

"For what?" I asked, taking a peek at my watch. Barry had paid double the normal fee to do this spontaneous shooting, so I felt obligated to give him his full hour, but at the same time, I very much wanted to get back to the others. It wasn't that he made me feel uncomfortable ... I simply did not enjoy being alone with him.

"Well, if you want a prize of some sort," he said slowly.

"No, no, I meant what sort of competition did you have in mind?"

He thought for a moment, then gestured at a group of somewhat stunted fir trees. They were about twelve feet tall, and clustered together tightly, too tightly to allow any one of them to grow to its proper size. Beyond them, I knew from rambles with Alden, was a rocky outcropping that dropped down into a small ravine ending in the pasture of a sheep farmer who was his neighbor. "What say we each take a turn playing your spy game? I'll hide a target for you, and you can hide one for me, and whoever wins will buy the other a pint at the local."

"All right," I said, willing to do just about anything to finish up our hour and get back to the Hard Day's Knights area. "What do you want to use for a target? I'm afraid we're out of paper ones."

"Anything wrong with my shirt?"

He was wearing a blue checked short-sleeved shirt.

"You'll ruin it," I said, eyeing him warily as he started to unbutton his shirt. To my relief, he had a tank top under it.

"I'll tell you a secret," he said, pulling the shirt off, and giving me a big wink. "I never liked this shirt. My wife bought it for me at a jumble sale. Now, then, you take half, and I'll take half."

With a loud ripping noise, he tore the shirt in half as easily as I'd have torn a piece of toast. "We don't have anything to paint a heart on it," I said, holding his shirt with the very tips of my fingers.

"Let's just say we have to hit the center of the target. Now, you go that way—" He pointed to the right, where the clump of firs gently swayed in a light afternoon breeze. "And I'll go through to the other side of the copse. Shall we meet back here in five minutes?"

"All right." I trotted off in the direction he pointed, choosing what I thought would be a difficult spot for him to shoot (into the sun), and tied the shirt around the trunk of the spindliest of the trees.

"I set you a right challenge, I did," Barry said as we rendezvoused. "I'm thinking you won't be claiming this win."

I smiled politely, not really giving a damn whether I did or not. "Good luck with yours."

"Aye, same to you, same to you."

I wandered around the area from which I'd seen him emerge, but didn't see any blue cloth hanging anywhere. The sun was lower in the sky now, stretching long shadows, and dappling through the copse with long, golden streamers. Birds chattered overhead, with flies buzzing around in an intensity that warned I was close to the boundary of the sheep farmer. Five more minutes passed and I was just about to call it quits and go back to Barry when out of the corner of my eye I saw a blue flutter. I headed toward it, pulling out an arrow to set onto the bow, frowning at the devious way Barry had hidden the target. The cloth was barely recognizable as such through a clump of broad-leaved shrubs, with fleeting glimpses of it visible as the branches moved gently in the breeze. I took aim, held my breath, and was just about to release the arrow when something struck me as odd.

A faint noise sounded to the left of me, followed almost immediately by a startled yell.

"What the hell?" I jumped forward, aware of the noise of someone moving through the trees to the left, and Barry calling out to ask if I was all right.

I pushed through the shrubs, tangling my hair and dress on them in the process, which is why it took me longer than normal to emerge from the other side. When I did, I stopped in horror. Before me, Alden stood, one hand braced against a tree trunk as he yanked an arrow from it.

"Holy crap, Alden!" I hurried forward at the same time Barry crashed his way through the shrubs. "Are you OK? Are you hurt? Who shot at you?"

"I'm not hurt," he said, glaring at the arrow before looking up at me. His frown deepened as his eyes went to the bow I held, and the quiver slung over my back. "As to who shot me, I believe you could answer that better than me. What the hell do you think you're doing shooting out here? There are any number of people who come through this copse—it's part of the right of way that leads to the coast. That was an extremely dangerous thing to do, Mercy."

"I didn't shoot you!" I said quickly, showing him the arrow in my hand. "I was going to, thinking you were Barry's target, but something didn't feel right, so I stopped. But I did hear someone else shooting." I spun around to pin Barry back with a mean look.

"It wasn't me," he said quickly, glancing around. "I was over there, to the south. I heard Mercy cry out and came to see what was the matter."

"Well, someone shot at me," Alden said irritably. "And I don't see anyone else out here with a bow."

I felt his accusation was pointed at me, and got a bit irritated, myself. "I may not be a master archer, but I do know the difference between shooting a person and a piece of torn cloth," I said brusquely.

"And that's not my type of arrow," Barry said, holding out his quiver. His were all fletched with bright orange feathers. "That's red, that is."

"Red . . ." I swallowed hard, suddenly feeling my palms sweat. I looked down at the arrow in my hand. It bore red feathers. "I . . . this isn't Fenice's quiver. This is what we use for the intermediate students."

I looked up to Alden, unable to say more. I knew I hadn't shot an arrow, but would he believe me?

He took the arrow from my hand, and held it up to compare with the one he'd extracted from the tree. They were identical.

"Well," Barry said with a soft whistle. "I believe my missus is expecting me home, so I'll be saying good-bye, and thank you for the lesson."

"Bye," I said absently, shaking my head at the two arrows. "I didn't shoot at you, Alden."

"I know you wouldn't intentionally shoot me," he said, watching as Barry plowed his way through the shrubs. "But perhaps it was a mistake. What are you doing out here?"

"I was about to ask you the same thing. Barry wanted some practice shooting in the real world, as he called it. We were having a little contest." Briefly, I explained about the lesson, finishing with, "But I didn't let go of the arrow, Alden. I would know if I did. Someone else did this."

"Barry?" he asked. "He had orange arrows."

"That doesn't mean he didn't have a red one," I said quickly.

"You said he's been shooting the last hour—did he have any red arrows earlier?"

"No," I admitted, knowing full well I would have noticed if he'd been using arrows of a different color. "They were all orange."

"Ah."

That was all he said, but it was the way he said it that made me both frightened and annoyed. "It's nice to know you trust me so much," I said, taking my arrow from his hand and stuffing it back into the quiver. "Nice to know you have my back when the going gets rough."

"You're not the one who was almost gulleted by an arrow!" he pointed out.

"And speaking of that, just what are you doing out here lurking around the bushes?" I asked, my hands on my hips.

"I told you I was meeting with the ex-CID man. We were out here trying out the powder where we wouldn't be seen." Alden collected a small squat jar with a black lid, and stuffed it into a backpack. "He just left, and I was seeing if I could lift my fingerprints from a rock, in case we happen to get the opportunity to take everyone's prints and compare them to the lanterns."

"You picked a hell of a place to be covert," I said, stung at the fact that he didn't seem to believe me. "Also, Alden!"

"What?"

I slapped my thighs with my hands. "How can you believe I'd shoot at you!"

"If you didn't know I was there—"

"I didn't shoot! Why won't you believe me? Do you think I'm lying?"

"No," he said slowly, his frown darkening, but I was relieved to see it was aimed at the arrow, not at me. "But if you didn't shoot it, and Barry didn't—"

"Then someone else did," I finished for him.

We both glanced around the area.

There was no one else to be seen. I shivered despite the heat of the afternoon, a cold, clammy feeling gripping my stomach.

Who had shot the arrow if it hadn't been Barry or me? And more important, who was trying to harm Alden?

THIRTEEN

My very dear Mercy,
There is no need to snap at Lisa. Despite the shooting inci-
dent earlier, you and you alone hold my interest.

Alden slipped the note under Mercy's door, wincing
with pain as he returned to his room to take a quick shower.
He'd been so distracted by the fact that he'd almost been
gored by an arrow that he hadn't been paying attention at
afternoon melee training, a fact that Vandal and the other
two men training soon realized, and which they took what
Alden felt was undue advantage of.

His mind returned to Mercy, and a little smile curled his
lips while he turned on the water as hot as he could stand it.
She clearly was smitten with him, else why would she get so
irate over Lisa's attempts to flirt?

"She's in love with me, that's what it is," he told the
empty bathroom, ignoring the pain of the bruises that lined
his back, ribs, and upper arms. "She's fallen hard for me, but
doesn't yet realize it."

While he showered, he mulled over how he felt about
Mercy being more than just a delightful summer interlude.
It occurred to him that if he was wrong, if she wasn't head-
over-heels in love with him, then by rights she could be leav-
ing the following week when the Hard Day's Knights left
Bestwood.

He stared sightlessly at the shower wall, a sudden chill sweeping over him despite the hot water.

"No," he said aloud, just as if speaking the words would give them validity. "No, she has to love me. That's all there is to it. If she doesn't love me, then she'll leave me, and that's just . . . no. She's just going to have to fall in love with me by next week."

He would not consider the fact that it was of vital importance to him not only that Mercy stay on at Bestwood after the combat troupe had left, but that she also be in love with him. He told himself it was just that she provided such excellent therapy that he couldn't afford to have her go, and blithely refused to acknowledge the warm well of feelings that made him feel aglow with happiness every time she was near.

A square of white on the dark, hideous carpet of his bedroom caught his eye when he emerged from the bathroom to dress.

"Ah, another love note," he said, unfolding the sheet of paper with much anticipation. Would Mercy have done another of her erotic drawings? Would she include a smutty limerick, as she had a few days past? Or perhaps a slightly pornographic haiku, which she had been promising to do for almost a week?

Alden, the note read. *I did not shoot you! DID. NOT. SHOOT. Got that?*

Mercy.

He frowned at the note. This was not the writing of a woman in love. This was the work of a woman who was annoyed because she knew there was no one else who could have shot the arrow at him, and yet insisted that she hadn't been the one who had done it.

He stared at the note, indecisive for a moment as to how to deal with it. He wanted to believe her—everything in him told him to believe her—and yet, the evidence told a different tale.

My lovely, adorable Mercy, he wrote, sitting down naked at his desk. *If you will glance again at my note with those beau-*

tiful eyes of yours, you will notice that nowhere in it do I state that you shot me. Or attempted to. Or even did not intend to, but accidentally did. I simply said how much you fill my thoughts. Which you do.

I look forward to kissing your delectable body, all of it, every last inch of it, tonight.

With a towel around his waist, he slid the note under Mercy's door, and returned to his own room to dress.

A rustling sound alerted him to the arrival of a new note. He paused in the act of tying a shoelace, squinting at the white sheet of paper. Was it something good, or was she still annoyed? No, she was in love with him (or soon would be)—it had to be good.

He tied his shoe and went to fetch the note.

Look, buster! I can read between the lines as well as the next girl. I did not shoot you, and you know, I'm actually fairly annoyed that you refuse to believe me. Do you think I'm lying? Huh? Is that it? You think I'm a big ole liar?

God, Alden! I'd never think that about you!

Mercy

"Well, hell," he said, contemplating going to her room to set things right. But the thought of facing an angry Mercy had him hesitating, and eventually, he sat down at the desk.

Mercy, goddess of all things bright and beautiful,

You fill my every waking thought, and many of my sleeping thoughts. I know you didn't shoot me. And even if it happened without you being aware, it wouldn't matter to me. I'd relish the pain simply because it was you who had done the shooting.

I am yours, my adorable one.

Nodding with satisfaction at his adroit handling of a difficult situation, he slipped the note under her door, and ran upstairs to the attic space to make sure the doors were all closed. He then made a quick survey of the house to see if any new damage had occurred, told the house it was doing well coping with the fact that he was going to update it, and returned to his room to check the window seat.

A note was waiting for him, not under his door, but

stabbed into the wood of the door itself with a wickedly sharp letter opener that he had found in the attic and left on his desk.

Mr. Emanuel Alden Ainslie,

This is a cease and desist notice. Cease referencing the shooting incident THAT I WAS NOT RESPONSIBLE FOR, and desist in sending me notes I no longer want or desire. I will not be coming by your room later tonight for romping between the sheets, and on top of them, and possibly on the rug by the fireplace assuming you found some firewood, and a rug to go in front of it.

Good day, sirrah.

Ms. M. Starling (single woman with no handsome English boyfriend)

"Hell," Alden said aloud, and setting the letter opener back in his room, he did a quick check of the window seat to make sure the way was still blocked to anyone hoping to climb into his room, and with the letter in hand went to find Mercy.

The library was empty, but when he entered the kitchen, he found Lisa at the sink, washing a mug.

"Good evening, Alden," she drawled in that slow, honey-sweet voice she liked to exaggerate whenever he was around. "My, don't you look charming, and so delicious I could just eat you up."

Alden fought his usual reaction to run away, and instead forced a polite smile to his lips. "Good evening, Lisa. Thank you. My mother bought me this shirt for my last birthday. Have you seen Mercy?"

"Why, yes, I have. She went with Fenice and that yummy brother of hers into town to have supper at the local pub." Her eyes glittered, but Alden wasn't sure if it was due to emotions or the overhead lights. "Why, did you need something?"

"No, no, I just thought we could . . . that is, Mercy wanted to check out a couple of rooms, and I thought now would be a good time to inspect them—"

"A tour!" Lisa clapped her hands together. "I hope you will give me a full tour this time, not two rooms like you did that first day I arrived here. I can't tell you how long I've been waiting for the grand tour of the hall. And how thrilling that it'll be by the master of Bestwood himself."

"No, I—"

"Let's see, I'm supposed to be doing some work for Lady Sybilla tonight, but I'm sure I can get it done early." She blinked eyes with impossibly long eyelashes, and slid her arm into his, tugging him a step toward the door. "Why don't we go ahead with the tour now, and later, we can have dinner together?"

"Oh. Er . . ." He thought wildly of an excuse, but his mind, fascinated as it was with Mercy, was not offering up any help with Lisa. "Erm . . . Lady Sybilla . . . won't she want you?"

Lisa's eyebrows waggled. "She might, but that doesn't mean she'll get me, sugar. Now, let's have that tour, and then after, I'll take you to a marvelous Italian restaurant that is run by one of Adams's nephews. Did you know she has eight nephews? She might look like a dried-up old piece of carpet, but evidently she has sisters and brothers coming out of her ears. . . ."

He was trapped in hell, but these last few weeks with Mercy had taught him that he could survive such encounters. He didn't resist as Lisa pulled him down the narrow hallway out to the entrance hall proper; he figured he'd get the tour she wanted over with as quickly as possible, and then would go to the pub in search of Mercy.

"This is the great hall, as you probably know," he said, dredging up facts he'd learned about the house from the sale prospectus. "The oldest part of the house was built in 1518, and the hall dates back to then. The floor is marble, although it needs a good deal of work. The paneling is not original, however—I'm told it was refinished during the Georgian period, when there was a call for wooden panels. The staircase was added in the early nineteenth century, although we don't know the maker. And upstairs, we have the gallery."

"It's all so very authentic," Lisa said, her hand firmly on Alden's arm as they made their way up the stairs to the long open gallery that ran the width of that section of the house. "It just makes me feel like I'm standin' right in a Pride or Prejudice movie, that's what it does!"

"It's quite a bit older than Jane Austen's Pride and Prejudice," Alden said, and felt an overwhelming relief when Lisa released his arm to go over to one of the long windows that ran down one side of the gallery.

"And this view! Why, I could drink this in forever. The drive up here in a carriage must have been glorious."

"The road would have been in much better repair," he said, glancing out of the window, and feeling a sense of pride in the stretch of trees that lined the now rutted and potholed drive. "But that's an easy fix."

"These bars remind me of New Orleans," she commented, opening one of the big windows to touch the wrought iron fretwork that had been added sometime in the early twentieth century. It consisted of intricate spikes and curlicues, and ran the length of all the windows in the gallery, and was badly cemented to the stone of the building, a fact Alden knew well, since one of the pieces had nearly crushed his head when it came loose and tumbled down right in front of him. "They're so ornate."

"Be careful, those are loose," he warned. "Whoever put them on the house didn't use the proper mortar, and it's crumbling to dust."

"Well, it's still very pretty," Lisa said, gazing out along the front expanse of the house. "You must have a party here someday, you really must."

Alden drifted down a couple of windows just in case she had ideas about latching on to his arm again. He glanced around the gallery, wondering what he could tell Lisa about it, when he noticed that one of the faded and threadbare rugs that dotted the floor was slightly rumpled at a corner. "I've thought of renting out the space to wedding parties and the like, which is something my brother does with great success, but obviously, I'll need to get the work done first." He headed for the rumpled carpet, intent on smoothing it out so no one would stumble over it in the dark, but as soon as his foot hit the carpet, the world slipped and went askew.

His feet seemed to fail just at the moment he realized that the floor had given away from underneath him, his entire body plummeting forward. A hoarse cry erupted from him as he flailed arms and legs, managing to catch the edge of the dangling rug with one hand.

For two seconds, he hung in midair, tied by one hand around a century-old rug from who-knew-where, his heart pounding as he looked up from the dark abyss into which he'd fallen. He had a moment to wonder at the way the golden early-evening light streamed into the window before the rug started moving toward him, sliding with him into whatever pit he'd fallen into.

With a loud slithering sound, the rug tumbled in after him. Pain burst hot and bright in his head and shoulder, and the last thing he heard before he was consumed by darkness was his name on Lisa's lips.

Slowly, an awareness returned to him. He had an idea that time had passed, but he wasn't sure how long it had been since . . . since what? He frowned, and opened his eyes, remembering with a sudden jolt the fall he'd taken.

"Bloody floor giving way underneath me," he croaked, his voice as dry and dusty as he felt. "You really don't have to try to kill me, you damned house. I just want to make things nice again."

He coughed a couple of times, and pushed himself upward, taking stock of his limbs as he did so. His legs felt fine, but there was a slight pain in his right shoulder, as well as a dull throb above his right ear. He touched it with tentative fingers, and found the lump he expected.

"Hello?" he called, looking upward. He'd been with Lisa; that much he remembered. But where was she? "Lisa? Hello? Anyone?"

There was no answer.

"Bloody, bloody hell," he groaned as he got to his feet, squinting in the light that drifted downward from the gallery. All he could see was broken wood, bits of plaster, and large, head-sized pieces of what looked like mortared brick and stone.

Dammit, there wasn't enough light to see the dimensions of the space he was in. He shuffled forward, hands outstretched, moving aside bits of wood and stone for three steps until he felt the rough surface of a wall. "There's one." He turned his back to it, and repeated the process, this time taking five steps before he reached the second wall. He glanced upward at the hole, noting the jagged edges of wood that stabbed across the hole like accusing fingers. "Anyone there?" he called, although he hadn't heard any sounds of people.

Five minutes passed while he located a third wall, this one made of rough stone, fist-sized chunks of which were missing at various spots. But when he tried to find the fourth wall, he nearly came to grief, the boards under his feet cracking and popping ominously a few feet past where he'd fallen. Hastily, he scrambled backward, not wanting to fall through yet more rotten floorboards.

Distantly, he heard the sound of footsteps, and hurried back to stand under the hole that was located about six feet over his head. "Hello?" he called again. "I'm here, if anyone is looking for me."

"Alden? Sugar, are you all right? Merciful heavens, I just about died when you went through the floor like that." Lisa's voice drifted down to him. "I swear to you, I just about died!"

"Don't get too close," he warned. "The floor is weak."

"It's all right, I brought you a rope. I just need to tie it to something. . . . Oh, this'll do nicely. Alden, I'm throwing you the rope. Now, you climb it carefully, you hear?"

"Stay well back from the hole," he called, ducking when a rough bit of rope spilled over the edge onto his head.

"I'm being careful, but you do the same," she answered.

He took a firm grip on the rope, and tugged. It seemed sturdy enough. He started to climb, Lisa's continued admonitions to be careful and not hurt himself following his painful progress upward, inch by inch, as he awkwardly hoisted himself up the rope.

He was a few feet from the hole, when he heard a commotion from above, resolving itself into Mercy's voice demanding to know what was going on.

"It's Alden. He's fallen into the floor below. I thought I would die when he disappeared like that, I can tell you."

"Alden? Are you OK?" Mercy's voice came clearly down to him. He gritted his teeth against the pain in his hands, and inched upward again.

"I'm fine," he grunted.

He heard Fenice asking what was going on, and Lisa repeating how she could have died, she really could have died, when he'd disappeared from sight.

"You're not hurt? Are you—holy shit! What did you do? Alden! Let go of the rope! Let go right now!"

"No, he'll fall and hurt himself," Lisa answered, her voice losing some of its sweetness in her annoyance with Mercy.

"Let go, Alden!" Mercy demanded. He saw a shadow flicker near the edge of the hole, and, gritting his teeth, reached upward to catch the edge of the floor above him.

"I'm almost . . . there . . . ," he said in between pants.

"Let go now!" Mercy all but screamed, and with a swift glance downward, he hesitated.

"Why—"

A horrible grating noised reached his ears, followed by a shriek from one of the women, and the sound of glass and wood breaking. He released the rope, landing heavily on one leg, biting back an oath that soon turned to a shout of surprise when a loud grating sound was followed almost immediately by dirt, dust, and a large piece of black wrought iron crashing down next to him.

Dust stirred from the floor, surrounding him in a cloud that blinded him for a moment, but after a few seconds of coughing and waving his arms, he managed to get a look at what had happened.

"Alden!" Mercy was shrieking his name over and over again. "Alden! Holy shit, he's—"

"I'm all right," he said, coughing and spitting out bits of dust and dirt. "It didn't hit me."

"Thank god for that." He was pleased to hear just how much worry there had been in Mercy's voice, which had turned soft when she realized he was unharmed. That quickly changed when she lit into Lisa. "What the hell do you think you were doing? You could have killed him! Those railings are totally unsafe, and having him pull one of them in on top of him could have ended up with him impaled by it, at the very least."

"I did the best I could," Lisa said, her voice as sharp as a knife. "After all, I was here all by myself while you were out having dinner with your friends."

"I do not have time for you right now," Mercy said in a voice that shook with anger. "Alden! Tell me where you are."

He explained his circumstances, ending with a suggestion that he might be in some hitherto undiscovered hidden room. "It's a small one if it's that, although I can't get to one end of it."

"Stay where you are," Mercy ordered without a shred of irony over that statement. "I'll go down a floor and find you. Do you have something you can tap the wall with?"

He gave a grim little smile at the debris piled around him. "Any number of things, yes."

Forty minutes later, after much tapping and calling to each other, Mercy finally located a panel in a linen cupboard that opened into the small, stunted room where Alden had slumped to the floor.

"Mercy!" He got to his feet painfully when light streamed in through the narrow opening, motes of dust dancing as the air was stirred by her entrance.

"At last!" She entered the passage, bringing with her a flood of emotions.

Pleasure at the sight of her filled him . . . pleasure and something else, something warm and serious, too serious to think of at the moment. Later, when he had time to do nothing but reflect, then he'd examine the emotions her presence triggered in him.

But for now . . . "That was smart thinking on your part."

"Eh," she said with a little twist of her lips. "It's nothing Nancy Drew wouldn't do. Come on, Ned, let's get you out of here."

FOURTEEN

Alden took a step and winced at the pain.

"You're hurt," Mercy said, hurriedly picking her way over the debris. She paused to glare for a moment at the piece of railing that had fallen into the room, holding out her hands to help him. "You said you weren't, but you are. Dammit, Alden!"

"I'm not injured badly. My knee is a bit sore, but to be honest, it was that way after my session with Vandal today."

"Go ahead and lean on me," Mercy told him, and almost an hour after falling into the passage, Alden stumbled out of it, sweating, covered in dirt, dust, and minute shards of the glass that had come down with the railing, and more grateful for being alive and able to kiss Mercy than he ever recalled.

"You know what this means," he said a short while later, sitting in the kitchen and allowing Mercy to dab at the various cuts, scrapes, and bruises from the fall.

"You're not a superhero?" she asked, spreading a little antiseptic ointment on a bandage and applying it to one of his injured fingers.

"That's a given. No, what my experience means is that the house is unsafe. I'm going to have to insist that everyone move out of it to the gatekeeper's lodge, which is perfectly habitable since it has been renovated."

"I don't think you have to lock down the entire house," Mercy said, tucking away the bandages into the first aid box. She was still kneeling at his feet, her eyes grave as she looked up at him. "With the exception of the furry four-legged invaders, I like the house. I like being in it, and since you had the exterminator guys upstairs, I haven't seen so much as a mousey whisker. And now you want us to leave?"

"It's not safe," he said stubbornly, admitting to himself that he really would hate to see everyone leave the house. He'd stay, naturally, since it was his home and his responsibility, but he wouldn't risk anyone else's well-being. "If the floor can go like that at any time—"

"Yeah, but what if it didn't—" She stopped, and got to her feet when Lisa and Lady Sybilla entered the kitchen.

"I understand that you have been injured," Lady Sybilla said in her slow, precise voice. She pursed her lips and made a show of examining Alden. "You do not look seriously harmed to me."

"He's not, but he could have been," Lisa said, giving him what he thought of as her come-hither look. "I declare, he's just the luckiest person alive. No one else would have walked out of that horrible situation with just a couple of scratches."

He felt Mercy start behind him, but she said nothing.

"I'm fine," he said, addressing Lady Sybilla. "As you see, I have just a few minor injuries. However, the accident has made it clear that until I can complete the renovations, the house is not safe for habitation. I must insist that you and everyone else move to the gatekeeper's lodge."

"That sounds like a very smart idea," Lisa said, nodding vigorously. "Very smart."

"Nonsense," Lady Sybilla said with a ladylike snort. "There is nothing at Bestwood Hall to fear, certainly not the floors. Adams and I will remain."

"No," Alden said, stiffly getting to his feet. He didn't want to upset Lady Sybilla, but he'd be damned if anyone else was harmed in the house. "I'm sorry, but I'm adamant about this. Take what you need for the evening, and tomorrow, we'll get the rest of your things."

"Young man—"

"You are going to the gatekeeper's lodge," Alden said firmly, pinning the old woman back with a look to let her know that this time he wasn't going to accede to her wishes. "You can either do it voluntarily or I can carry you, but you are going there. Go pack up a few things that you will need for the night, and I will drive you to the lodge."

Lady Sybilla sniffed loudly, and tried to go all lady-of-the-manor on him, but he was having none of it. "Do it on your own, or I'll carry you," he repeated, then turned to Lisa. "The same goes for you. Pack up and meet me by the car in twenty minutes."

"Oooh," she said with a little fake shiver. "You're so forceful. I like that in a man."

He heard a snort of disgust from behind him, but didn't bother to give Mercy a stern look.

"I will not be spoken to in this manner," Lady Sybilla said, making a show of sweeping by him to the door. "I shall retire to my chambers, where I will stay perfectly safe."

Alden held out his wrist, displaying his watch to her. "You're down to eighteen minutes."

Her lip curled. "Good night, Mercy. Lisa, please be so kind as to stop by later to take dictation of a few thoughts I've had regarding the war years."

With another sniff at Alden, she creaked her way out of the room.

Lisa hesitated a few seconds, giving him a sympathetic look.

"Pack," he told her. "Help Lady Sybilla if you have the time, but we leave in eighteen minutes."

Lisa left without saying anything more.

"The urge to say 'good riddance to bad rubbish' is almost overwhelming," Mercy said, strolling over to his side. "But I wouldn't want you to think I was that catty, so I'll keep it to myself."

His lips quivered as he looked at her. She was as beautiful as ever, but it was the memory of her eyes shining with emotion when she reached for him in the hellhole that stayed with him. No one had ever looked at him the way she'd done.

"You love me," he found himself saying without realizing it, and when he did, he didn't know whether he should stammer out an apology, blush hot enough to fry an egg, or wish the earth would open up at his feet and let him fall in.

On second thought, he'd already experienced the last one, and it left a lot to be desired. In the end, he simply stood and watched her, waiting for her outraged response.

She blinked a couple of times. "You must have hit your head when you fell."

"I did, but that's not why I said that. You love me. It's a fact. I saw it in your eyes when you climbed into that passageway to rescue me."

"You didn't need rescuing," she said, her gaze dropping from his. "You'd have found a way out once you had caught your breath again."

"You don't love me?" he asked, his stomach feeling as if it had fallen without him.

She chewed on her delicious lower lip, instantly causing him to want to be doing that. "Do you want me to be in love with you? I thought we didn't have a thing. We were just . . . you know . . . enjoying each other's company."

"Ah." He cleared his throat, feeling bereft for some absurd reason. Stupid, stupid, stupid, he chastised himself. Now you've gone and made her think you're in love with her, and want her to feel likewise, when clearly she just wanted a summer fling. "Just so. You'd better get your things for the evening."

"Things?" she asked, tipping her head so her hair swung down. He loved her hair. He loved letting it run through his fingers, like cool, silky water. "What sort of things? Are you going to let me tie you down with scarves tonight?"

Instantly, his penis was on board with that idea. He told his nether parts to calm down, and shook his head. "I meant things you'll need to sleep over at the gatehouse."

"Why would I do that?"

"Because it's not safe for you here." Just the thought of Mercy being hurt made his guts tighten painfully.

"Oh, that." She pursed her lips for a minute, then smiled. "I'm not going. There's no need."

"Mercy," he said with a sigh, "I'm not feeling up to yet another verbal battle."

"Good," she said, taking his hand in hers, and gently rubbing his hurt fingers with her thumb. "Then don't argue. Also, can we leave the relationship talk for another time? Later tonight, maybe? Because I have something important to show you, first."

"What?" he asked, following her when she headed toward the main staircase.

"I want to show you that floor you fell through."

He stopped her before she could get to the second floor. "No. It's not safe. I meant what I said, Mercy—I don't want anyone else getting hurt."

She squeezed his hand on the part that wasn't grazed, and gave him a fleeting smile. "Don't worry, no one is going to be hurt. I want to show you what I barely had time to see before I realized the railing was about to come loose."

"The floor is dangerous—"

"Not anymore, it isn't," she said grimly.

"Don't let the hole fool you into thinking that was the only weak spot," he warned, following her up the second flight of stairs. He wanted badly to get her out of the house, to tuck her away somewhere safe and sound, preferably a place that had a nice bed, and a shower big enough for two. "If the floor is weak in one location, it will be weak in others."

"I doubt that," Mercy said, the words drifting over her shoulder as she leaped up the last couple of stairs, and started down the long gallery. "She didn't have time to do the whole thing."

"She? She who? Mercy!" He caught at her arm when she continued forward, shaking it a little. "What the hell are you talking about?"

"I'll show you," she said, gesturing down the hall. The hole gaped rough and black in the twilight, and even the lights that Mercy flipped on didn't do much to illuminate the damage to the floor. She walked toward it, keeping to the wall, with one hand in his. "It's OK, it's safe over here. This is where Lisa was standing."

They stopped a few feet from the broken floorboards.

"Am I supposed to see something that will make me change my mind about how dangerous the house is?" he asked, nodding toward the gaping blackness. "Because from where I stand, all I see is weak floorboards and a drop that could have been quite harmful, if not downright deadly."

"Knees," she said, kneeling. "You have to get down close to see it. Look. See that?"

He knelt next to her, and cautiously leaned forward to where the hole began. He didn't see much but broken hardwood, crumbled underflooring, and the wooden ribs that held up the floor. Except two of the ribs were missing. "All I see is broken floor."

"Then you're not looking close enough. I saw it as soon as I realized what had happened—and for that, I thank the University of Strathclyde Forensic Detection class, because they taught us to look closely at all the bits surrounding an accident site."

He looked where Mercy was pointing, frowned, and edged forward to touch the broken piece of hardwood floor.

It wasn't broken. The edges were too neat. And a closer look at the underflooring and ribs showed that they, too, did not display the edges of wood that had simply rotted away. He looked back at Mercy, his mind struggling to process this information. "Someone did this deliberately? Someone deliberately sabotaged it?"

"Cut the floor, you mean? I don't think so. Look at the wood underneath the top layer. That stuff is old, really old, and it doesn't show signs of any fresh cuts. I think what you have here is basically a trapdoor that led down to the little passageway."

"Hmm." He examined it more closely, carefully testing the floor before he put his full weight onto it. "I believe you're right. There are no signs that the wood was sawn. That simply means that it gave way, and is, as I said, dangerous."

"I don't think it did it on its own," Mercy said slowly, sitting with her back to the wall. "If you look at the edge nearest me, you'll see some scratches. They do look fresh, although someone has tried to cover them up with a wood crayon. What I think happened is that someone found out about the trapdoor, took a look at it, peeked into the passage, saw a lot of wood and stone debris in there, and decided it would make a grand booby trap. They just kind of helped it along by loosening the trapdoor so that it wasn't resting on the supports the way it was supposed to—and voilà. The second you stepped on it, down you went."

"You think this is deliberate?" he asked, appalled at the thought that someone would dislike him so much as to want to seriously harm him.

"I do." She pulled her knees up and wrapped her arms around them. "And I know how they did it, too. The only person other than me who has access to papers about the house."

"Lisa?" He shook his head. "I can't believe that she'd want to hurt me. And if she did—why? What purpose does that serve?"

"I don't know, but I'm sure as hell going to find out." She patted his knee when he sat next to her. "Look, I know it's hard to try to process the fact that someone wants you out of the way, but when you go through the evidence like I've been doing while I patched you up, you'll see that it's clear that the culprit is Lisa."

"For some unknown reason," he said skeptically.

"Yeah, well, I'm still working on that," she admitted. "But think about it, Alden—ever since she got here, you've had more and more accidents."

"That's the house falling apart around me."

"A couple of the accidents can be accounted for as just an old house, but not all of them."

"Don't you think it's a bit melodramatic to credit simple accidents to a murderous plot?"

"Not really, no. Especially if you think about the so-called accidents that happened during the last week. Every single one of those could have been engineered to happen to you."

He pursed his lips. "The shooting incident."

"Exactly. Because as I've said numerous times, I did not shoot you."

He took note of her narrowed eyes, and decided to move on. "I know you don't like Lisa, but I believe that's taking animosity a bit too far." He wondered how he could appease Mercy, and yet dissuade her from this line of thinking. He might not be overly fond of Lisa, but that didn't mean he was going to accuse her of trying to do him in.

"How do you explain this, then?" she asked, waving at the floor.

He thought for a few minutes. "Coincidence."

"Nuh-uh."

"It's an old house. Things shift in it."

"Not trapdoors from their bases. No more than lights in hidden passageways."

"Are you implying that Lisa is the one who has been going through the passages?"

She shrugged. "Possibly. Probably. But I'm not sure about that. I mean, it makes sense if she's looking for something."

"For what?"

She bit her lip again, distracting Alden from the seriousness of their conversation. He wanted her in bed, his bed, all warm and pliant, and offering up her lips for him to nibble on. "That's a good question. I'm willing to bet you that she found something in the house papers that says there's something in the passages. Or in the smugglers' tunnel. Maybe an old treasure, or an old master painting, or an important historical document worth a fortune, or ... oh, I don't know. Something worth a ton of money."

"Unfortunately, I don't think that's very likely. According to the documents given to me at the sale, the Baskerville family fortune has declined since the day the house was first built. If later generations knew there was something valuable hidden by earlier ancestors, they surely would have found it and used it to fund the estate."

"Well, it has to be something," Mercy insisted, waving her hand toward the hole. "Why else would Lisa be doing this?"

"We don't know it's Lisa."

"Fine, whoever is doing it." She took a deep breath, which again distracted him. He did so enjoy watching her breasts. And touching them. And tasting them. "All of this leads to the fact that I don't think the house is as dangerous as you say it is. Although I think it's a good idea to get Lisa out of here, since that'll limit her reasons for being in the house."

He stretched out on his belly, and told Mercy to get back. "Just in case more of the floor goes," he said, slowly inching his way forward toward the gaping hole. It took him almost forty minutes, but by the time he'd completed first one circuit of the damage on his belly, then another on his feet jumping up and down to test the floor, he had to admit that Mercy's idea about a trapdoor had merit. "Although who would place a trapdoor right in the middle of the gallery is beyond me."

"Dunno, but I bet there's something about it in Lady Sybilla's papers. Dammit, why did Lisa have to show up and take that job away from me?"

Alden said nothing other than telling Mercy he'd put a temporary patch over the floor. She helped him haul some two-by-four boards he'd remembered seeing tucked away in one of the basements, and with a few nails, he made the hole safe from anyone else stepping through it.

By the time they returned to his room, he was tired, sore, covered in dirt, dust, and cobwebs from the basement, and very much desirous of giving Mercy the attention she so obviously deserved. But first, the last comment she'd made about Lisa reminded him that he'd been keeping a secret from her, one that he was no longer comfortable hiding.

"So . . . about Lisa," he said, opening the door to his bedroom, and gesturing her in.

"Yes? What about her?"

"There's something I haven't been forthright about. That is to say, I did tell you about it, but I didn't go into detail." He coughed, suddenly self-conscious, a fact that made him swear to himself. He'd been getting better the last few days, so much better.

"Oh?" Mercy crossed her arms over her chest, her body language unmistakable. "And just what is this deep, dark secret concerning Lisa that you've held from me, the woman with whom you like to play Nancy Drew Visiting Ned in a Sleazy Motel?"

Alden would have laughed except he was now a bit concerned about the ire visible in Mercy's eyes. "Lisa coming here wasn't happenstance."

"I gathered not. You said she was a blind date."

"Yes, well . . ." He cleared his throat and wished desperately he could dash to the shower, where he'd have privacy to hide. "It's kind of like that. You see, I have a sister-in-law."

"So?"

She wasn't making it any easier. For some reason, that fact eased some of his strain. It was because she loved him that she was so irate over the subject of Lisa. "She fancies herself a matchmaker. She's not that I know of, but that's what she believes, and my brother humors her because she's pregnant. A few weeks ago, she promised she had the perfect woman for me, and would send her down to help at Bestwood."

Mercy didn't say anything. Her expression hadn't budged, either.

"And that's who Lisa is," he finished lamely. "She's the woman my sister-in-law thought would be perfect for me.

That is why Lisa has been so ... aggressive ... in her attentions toward me. She assumed from what Alice—my sister-in-law—told her that I'd be just as interested in her. But I'm not."

Mercy shifted her weight, her eyes losing some of their sparkly ire, turning more watchful than angry. "And that is because ...?"

"Because you love me," he said matter-of-factly. He felt that the sooner Mercy faced up to that, the sooner they'd be in bed doing all those wonderful things to please each other. "Well, that's part of it. There's also the fact that you are enticing, and intriguing, and sexy as hell, and I can't think straight when I'm around you. So why don't you get into bed, and after I have a quick shower to wash off the worst of the dirt and dust, I'll join you and we can let Nancy have her way with Ned."

She pursed her lips, thought for a moment or two, and then said brusquely, "I think I'll pass on that offer. Nancy isn't so desperate for Ned's attentions that she has to put up with him being an asshat."

Alden gawked at her. "But—"

"No thanks, Alden. Seriously, if I wasn't pissed enough about that whole shooting thing and the fact that you think I'm lying about it—no, don't say you're not, because you keep bringing it up—then I'd be more than a little miffed that you'd jump into bed with me when you thought your potential match was on her way here. Yeah, yeah, I know when we first met, you had said that there was a blind date coming out, but you acted like you didn't want to see her. At least you did until Lisa got here, and now you're all shades of defensive about her."

"Are you ... jealous?" Alden couldn't think of any other reason Mercy was acting so unreasonably.

"No, of course not! Maybe. Just a little, but that's certainly understandable, given the situation. I mean, what were you going to do if it turned out you liked Lisa better than me? Just dump me? Tell me I was a warm-up for the main action? Send me back to my mousey room without so much as a backward look?"

"Your room, and indeed this entire floor, have been de-moused—"

"Faugh!" Mercy said, evidently having read one too many historical novels in her day, and marched out of his room, making sure to slam the door behind her.

"She loves me," he told the still-vibrating door. "She's jealous, and angry because deep down she knows it's her love for me making her that. She's just a little resistant to that fact. But she'll figure it out in the end." He strode to the bathroom, purpose filling him with every step. "And if she doesn't, I'll make sure she gets the help she needs to realize just how much she wants me. And needs me. And can't live without me."

Pot, kettle, black, a distant part of his mind said softly.

He ignored it. He had more important things to do than sit around and be introspective.

FIFTEEN

I was of half a mind to go to the gatekeeper's lodge with the others, but decided after helping them haul all of Lady Sybilla's belongings to her new quarters that close confines with Lady S. and the others was the last thing I needed. It took Fenice, Lisa, Vandal, Alden, and me combined a total of three hours to get all of Lady Sybilla's things moved.

"Tell me again why she's not just taking an overnight bag like the rest of us," Fenice groaned when we lifted an upholstered recliner onto Vandal's truck.

"Alden said she wouldn't leave without everything. Thank god Adams got the loose stuff into boxes."

"I can think of about a million other things I'd rather do tonight," Vandal said, passing with two cardboard boxes, which he loaded beside the chair.

"I think that goes for all of us." I stretched and thought about telling Lady Sybilla just how unreasonable she was being, but decided it wasn't worth it.

We struggled on. The others took their things (which were easily packed) as well, but they didn't need help with that.

"You're sure you and lover boy don't want to stay with us?" Fenice asked, having picked one of the bedrooms at the lodge for her own. "If the house isn't safe—"

"It's safe enough," I snapped, instantly feeling bad because it wasn't Fenice's fault I was such an idiot. "Sorry, I'm just cranky tonight. I think the house is perfectly safe, but thanks for thinking of me. Us. Oh, hell, just ignore me, I'm being an idiot." I left with a quick wave.

"The whole issue with Alden aside," I said to myself as I marched up the drive to the house, a flashlight picking out the potholes along the way, "if I had to be that close to Lisa, I'd be sure to punch her somewhere impolite. The murderous she-devil. Hussy she-devil. Murderous, hussified, obnoxious she-devil."

I passed Alden, hauling a flat-screen TV on a dolly, as I entered the house, but said nothing. He had a confused air about him, as if he couldn't understand why I was upset. I paused at the door to the house, half wanting to run back after him and explain my feelings, but since I didn't even understand them, I figured it was better if I just kept to myself. "Especially if he thinks I'm crazy in love with him. Ha. I scoff."

I held on to that and assorted other dismal thoughts while I undressed, and got into the bed in my room, now thankfully sans rodents of any sort.

"Boy, it's lonely in here," I said aloud a half hour later. I'd been lying in the dark, staring up at the ceiling, dimly aware of noises coming from Alden's room next door, half hoping to hear the silent swoosh of a letter being pushed under my door, but nothing appeared. Not even Alden at my door begging me to come to bed with him. "Lonely and quiet. So quiet I can hear house noises. Like that. That sounded like a footstep in the hall, but I know everyone but Alden and me are gone, and he's sure to have locked up."

Although there were the secret tunnels. I sat up in bed at that thought, straining to listen, but the noise wasn't repeated. Surely if it was footsteps, I'd hear more. After ten more minutes of intense listening, I lay back and stared up at the ceiling again. "Lonely, lonely lonely. And it's all Alden's fault."

I thought about how at fault he was, and decided to write him a note to let him know just what it was I found so objectionable about his actions. I pulled out a sheet of his notepaper that I'd filched and, with a book underneath it, sat on the edge of my bed and wrote.

Dear Alden,

You are probably feeling pretty sorry for yourself right now, telling yourself that you've done nothing wrong, and that I'm overreacting. So I thought, in the interest of Anglo-Canadian-American relations, to detail your wrongdoings.

"Yes," I said, looking with approval at the letter. "It's a good start. My English Comp professor would be pleased."

You insist that I shot you when I've told you repeatedly that I didn't.

You . . .

I stopped, frowning at the first item. Come to think of it, Alden hadn't recently accused me of shooting him. He'd agreed that I hadn't, and wondered who could have, since it hadn't been me and most likely wasn't Barry, unless the latter had smuggled a differently colored arrow upon his person. I struck out the first item, and restarted the list.

You didn't tell me that your potential girlfriend was coming to visit.

Dammit. That wasn't true, either. He had told me that a woman was coming to stay with him, although I had gotten the idea that it was a blind date, an unwanted one at that. But never had he actually said that. I bit my lip and, after a soft oath to myself, struck out the item and started again.

You allow Lisa to fawn all over you when you and I have a thing. OK, I know I said that we don't have a thing, but . . .

"Well, that's just balls, too," I snapped, scratching out that item with unnecessary force.

You told me that I loved you. Ha! Double ha with bells on it! For one thing, you don't know my feelings, and for another thing, I don't in any way, shape, or form love . . .

I said an extremely rude word, and sat staring at the paper. The word love seemed to grow and throb, like an engorged penis, dancing around the page trying to attract my attention.

"Love," I scoffed. "Just who does Alden think he is that he can tell me what I feel? Pfft. He wishes it was love."

I kept on that vein for another two minutes, then eventually worked enough scoffing out of my system that I could face facts.

What I felt for Alden was more than just a casual hookup. Was it love? It certainly wasn't the crushes I'd had in college when I was a young thing. No, the emotions that Alden generated in me were more . . . deep. Profound. Unshakable. Oh, sure, I'd been angry with him earlier, but that didn't mean that I didn't at that exact moment want to be with him, touching him, kissing him, talking to him. I just wanted to be with him, to be a part of his life, to know I mattered to him.

"Well, hell, I am in love with the great big toad," I said, somewhat at a loss. "When did that happen? When I saw him swinging the sword the first time? When he sent me that first note? When I thought he'd fallen into a hole and killed himself? And why the hell am I sitting here asking silly questions and describing why I'm angry with him over things that have no merit or basis in fact? Get up and go molest that man, Mercy! Seduce him like he's never been seduced before!"

I suited action to word, throwing away my note and donning my sexy nightie, figuring that if I had to make an apology for my behavior—and I definitely needed to do that—then I was going to do it in a garment that would give me the best chance of distracting him once the apologizing was over. I grabbed a shawl I'd bought when I was in Scotland, and padded my way barefoot to Alden's door. I tried to open it, intending on slipping in to surprise him, but the door was locked.

"Crap. He must be pissed at me because I was so bitchy earlier. Guess he's really going to earn this apology." I tapped on the door, and waited, mentally practicing my explanation of why I was there, and all the ways I'd been wrong in accusing him of bad behavior.

I frowned at the door after a couple of minutes. Maybe he was in the bathroom? I knocked again, this time putting my ear to the door to listen for sounds that he was willfully ignoring me.

There was no sound, but a scent wafted out from the doorjamb.

I sniffed a couple of times, then froze in horror. I knew that smell—it was natural gas, the stuff Bestwood used to heat up the ancient radiators that lurked in every room. What on earth was Alden doing turning on the heat when it had to be at least eighty during the day?

"Alden?" I banged loudly on the door, putting my face right up to it to yell. "Alden, what are you doing in there? Alden?"

There was still no answer, but as I gave a couple more sniffs, the smell of gas was still present.

What if he'd fallen down in the bathroom, and somehow turned on the gas while doing so? What if a gas pipe had broken and was expelling deadly fumes into his room at that very moment?

What if someone was trying to murder him in his sleep?

I spun around, and raced back into my room, running to the windowsill, where I flung open the curtains, jerked up the window, and stuck a leg out while feeling for the six-inch-wide decorative stone ledge that ran under all the windows on that floor. I eased myself out, refusing to look down, clutching the smooth stone of the building as I got to my feet.

"Don't look down, don't look down," I repeated in a desperate sort of mantra, edging my way along the building to the window of Alden's bathroom, which was between our two rooms. The mantra changed to, "Don't be dead, don't be dead," when I (breathlessly) arrived at the window.

The urge to look down was almost overwhelming, but I kept my attention focused on staying balanced on the narrow ledge while bending down to pull up the window sash. Luckily, the heat of the day meant that Alden had left the bathroom window partially open, so all I had to do was grasp it with the hand not holding on to a decorative stone rose that dotted a line above the windows, and yank upward.

The smell of gas was strong—not overwhelming—in the bathroom, but the door to Alden's room was firmly shut. I hopped down and, clutching the doorknob, jerked it open, staggering back almost immediately from the smell of gas. It made me cough, and almost retch. I ran for the bedroom window, pulling it open and sticking my upper half out, drawing in long, gasping breaths of untainted air. The second my head cleared, I spun around and stumbled over to where the radiator sat along the wall near the bed. I twisted the knob that turned on the flow of gas, gratified to hear the sibilant hissing die down to nothing before turning to Alden.

He was lying half on the bed, his legs on the floor, while his upper body had apparently melted onto the bed itself. No doubt he had tried to get up but was overcome by gas. I grabbed his arms, intending on carrying him out of the bedroom, but he was too big and heavy for me. Plus, I was holding my breath, and about to run out of air. I bolted to the window, took several painful gulps of air, and jerked the belt off Alden's bathrobe that hung from the bathroom door.

Two more quick breaths of nondeadly air, and I was back at his side, tying the belt around his chest and under his arms. I wrapped both hands around the belt and started pulling him backward to the door to the hall, having to breathe about halfway there. By the time I got his body to the door, and turned the old-fashioned key that was sticking out of the lock, I was giddy, my throat burned, and I was close to vomiting. Fumbling with the door, I managed to get it open, and hauled Alden the last few feet until we hit the cool wood of the hallway. I kicked the door shut, sliding down it onto the floor next to him.

"Alden," I said hoarsely, crawling over to him. "You have to wake up. I can't carry you, and I doubt if I can drag you the entire way outdoors. You have to get up so we can get out of the house. Alden. Wake up."

He lay still as death. Instantly, my brain rejected that thought, and I put a hand on his bare chest to make sure that its rising and falling weren't just my imagination. Beneath my hand, his heart beat steadily, if a little slowly.

I had to get him some medical help. I ran back into his room to grab his cell phone, dialed the emergency number once I was back in the hall, and spent eight minutes of frustration describing to the call center where we were, why Alden needed help, and why the gas would be turned on during a summer heat wave.

"Look," I finally said, uncaring if I was being rude, "I don't know why the gas was on, but I'm sure it wasn't a suicide attempt, and I don't know why you insist on arguing with me about how and why gas was turned on so that it almost killed Alden, when you should be sending medical aid!"

"Madam," the woman on the other end said with cool indifference. "The paramedics were sent five minutes ago. I am merely trying to get additional information for the council. They like us to document regional emergencies so that they know better how to allocate funds designated for such events. You say this was not a suicide attempt, but how are you certain of that? Are you a family member?"

"No, I'm . . . I suppose you could say I'm his girlfriend. And what does that have to do with—"

"Would you say that this emergency is one that could be avoided with proper in-home safety measures?"

"No! Someone tried to kill Alden—"

"Would you agree that the city council has an obligation to investigate homes to ensure they are up to code, and that every protection is in place to eliminate the possibility of future emergencies?"

I hung up the phone, and stood staring down at Alden. I wanted desperately to go wait at the entrance of the house for the medics, but I didn't want to leave him alone, lest the murderous Lisa be lurking somewhere.

I ran back to my bedroom, leaving the door open so I'd see if she tried to creep past in order to get to Alden, and hurried into the nearest thing I could find—my blue archery dress. After a moment's thought, I snatched the duvet off the bed and laid it down next to Alden, rolling him over onto it with a murmured apology. "Sorry, I know I probably shouldn't move you, but I can't leave you here for Lisa to find, and I have to be downstairs to let the paramedics in, so you have to come with me. Ready?"

Grasping the edge of the duvet firmly, I backed my way down the hallway, dragging Alden with me. It wasn't easy getting him down the stairs (at one point, he slid off the duvet and rolled down a couple of steps), but fifteen minutes later I triumphantly opened the front door to the two women waiting, and said in between gasps, "Hi . . . so glad . . . you're here. . . . He's over there. . . . Got a few bumps . . . on stairs . . . whew!"

The paramedics said nothing, just pushed past me and knelt next to where Alden was crumpled up on the now somewhat torn and dirty duvet. A zigzagging line of little white feathers led across the hall to the stairs, ending at the spot where a hitherto unknown carpet tack had snagged the duvet and torn it, releasing its guts in a snowy trail.

"You'd think it was easy pulling a man on a blanket, but it's not," I said while the women worked on Alden, slapping an oxygen mask over his mouth, and listening to his heart. One of them peered closely at a lump over his left eye. "Oh, yeah, that. It has nothing to do with the gas thing, I'm afraid. He rolled off the blanket and hit the banister when I was dragging him downstairs. You can see that the bump isn't bleeding, so I figured he'll just have a black eye. It's his brain I'm worried about. Gas poisoning can mess with that, can't it? Is he going to be OK?"

Alden started coming to while I was speaking, his arms and legs doing an odd swimming motion for a few seconds before he reached up and tried to take the oxygen mask off. "Sir, please do not move," one of the women told him, while the other leaned over him and asked, "Do you remember your name?"

"Of course I remember my name," Alden said, his voice muffled by the oxygen mask. He winced as he spoke, reaching up to touch his bruised brow. "What happened to me?"

"It's OK, Alden," I said, peering over the shoulder of one of the paramedics, who was taking his blood pressure. "You're all right now. Sorry about your head, but I didn't want to leave you where Lisa could get you. These are paramedics. They're here to help you."

"Why are you . . . ow . . . talking to me like I'm an imbecile?" he asked, touching his nose.

"Sorry about that, too. You and the duvet slid down part of the stairs, and your nose kind of kerthumped on each step. Oh, good, you're going to take him to the hospital?" This last was in response to one of the medics, who had fetched a wheeled gurney.

"The patient appears to be somewhat disoriented," one of the medics said. The two of them lifted the blanket, and hauled Alden onto the gurney. "He needs to be checked over thoroughly."

"I like that—yes, he should be checked over thoroughly," I said, following as they wheeled him out to the aid unit. "I'll come with you."

"I'm sorry, family only," one of the medics said, locking the wheels of the gurney inside the truck.

"Oh. Crap. OK, I'll take his car. Alden! They're going to take you to the hospital! To see a doctor! But you're OK. Don't worry about anything—just breathe nice clear oxygen."

"I don't know why she's speaking to me as if I'm three years old," Alden complained to one of the medics. "I seem to have a second lump on the back of my head now."

"Sorry! That was the big heavy chair just at the bottom of the stairs. I lost control of the duvet and you, so you kind of swung into it," I yelled just as the second medic closed the door.

I stood wringing my hands for a few seconds, watching as the truck zoomed off, then realized I needed to get to the hospital to make sure he was all right.

Once back in his room, I grabbed his laptop case, and stuffed into it a change of clothes (since he had been clad in nothing but his underwear when I dragged him downstairs), a pair of shoes, his phone, car keys, and wallet, and, after a moment's thought, crammed in his laptop, so that I'd have something to do while I waited for the doctors to run their tests. I wanted to document the event, and since I knew Alden was keeping a journal of all the various repairs he was having to make—along with the parts of the house that fell off, crumbled away, or, in the case of the gallery floor, were sabotaged—I decided to add my own notes about Lisa's attempt on Alden's life to his house document.

The night crawled into morning, an ugly, gray morning that accurately reflected my state of mind while I sat in the hospital waiting room, typing away everything that had happened since I'd come back from dinner with Fenice and Vandal. I made a particular point to list every possible opportunity that Lisa had to facilitate the "accidents," and even went so far as to pose a few speculations as to what reasons I thought she would have to want Alden dead.

An hour before dawn, I was allowed to visit him.

"Alden!" I hurried past the other patient in his room, who was half-hidden by a privacy curtain, and threw myself onto Alden where he sat on the edge of the bed, pulling his clothing out of the laptop bag. "Tell me you're all right! The doctor said you were, but I want to hear it from you, too. Holy crapballs, Alden! You look like hell!"

"Thanks," he said, touching the bump over his eye, which was bright red due to an ice pack that lay discarded next to him. "I feel like hell, although I guess that's good, since it means I'm alive. No, don't stop kissing me. I'm not that bad."

I continued kissing every spot on his face that wasn't bruised or scratched, ending at his lips. He groaned into my mouth, causing me to jerk back. "Did I hurt you? Is your mouth sore? I checked your teeth and they were all there, so I assumed nothing had been hurt, but if I'm hurting you, tell me."

"You didn't hurt me," he said with a rusty chuckle. "I was just enjoying the kiss."

"Oh, good." I gave him one more quick peck, then stood back, eyeing him. His color was much better than when I'd rescued him, and although the bump over his eye was red, and he was starting to show a darkish halo that foretold at least a partial black eye, he looked relatively hale and hearty. "I was so worried."

"So I gather." He reached for his jeans, carefully putting them on. "I still don't understand exactly what happened. All the doctor would tell me was that there was some sort of incident with the radiator, and that you'd pulled me out and then thrown me down a flight of stairs. He asked if I wanted to talk to the police, in order to file charges against you."

"Well, I like that!" I handed him his shirt. "Here I go to all the trouble of saving you from certain death by asphyxiation, or gas poisoning, or whatever it is that too much gas does to you, and he asks you if you want to call the cops on me."

"What did happen?" he asked, grimacing when he bent to put on a shoe.

I went over the events, apologizing numerous times when I explained how he came to have the various bumps and bruises. "You're not the easiest person in the world to move when you're unconscious," I ended, gently brushing back his curls. They didn't need moving, but I liked touching his hair, and it just made me feel better to fuss over him.

"I imagine not." He stood, wobbled a little, but steadied almost immediately. "I guess I'd better call a plumber about the faulty gas line."

"Faulty, my ass. That was no accident," I said, frowning when he pulled his phone out of the bag. "Oh, I turned that off. Your battery was almost dead."

"Thank you." He turned on the phone and did an experimental stretch. "I know you think the worst about Lisa, but you have to admit that it's highly unlikely that she would be so spurned by the fact that I have picked you over her that she'd try to gas me. Good lord. I have twelve messages. I wonder what—"

He held the phone up to his ear as he hit his voice mail button.

"I don't think it's because you spurned her," I told him. I put the laptop back into its bag. "In fact, I have a list of items that I think explain her actions. . . . What's wrong?"

I could hear the faint tinny sound of a voice talking on the voice mail, and as it stopped and another, more urgent started up, Alden's face changed from one of mild bemusement to outright horror. "Alden?"

"The house," he said, his eyes huge. "The house is on fire."

"What? Holy hellballs!" I leaned in to listen to the phone with him, and heard snatches of first Vandal, and then Fenice, yelling into the phone that Alden needed to let them know he was all right, and that the house was fully engulfed.

If there was a record for two people to run out of a third-floor hospital room, down to the parking lot, and into a car, then we broke it, because I swear we didn't even have time to blink before I was struggling to unlock the car.

"I'll drive," I told him, sliding into the driver's seat.

"Do you have a license?"

"Not for the UK, but I know how to drive."

"Mercy—" he started to protest, but I leaned across and opened the passenger door.

"You just got released from the hospital. Now get in the car and let me drive you home!"

"If there's any home left," he said grimly, but did as I ordered, and got into the passenger seat.

I said nothing, but sent up a prayer to every deity I could think of to preserve Bestwood Hall.

SIXTEEN

It was worse than we could have imagined.

I watched Alden as he stumbled away from speaking with the fire chief, his face gilded red and gold by the light of the fire as it consumed his house. The fire trucks had given up trying to stop the blaze in the house—it was fully engulfed, thick oily black clouds rolling upward into what otherwise appeared to be a flawless morning sky. Instead, they sprayed the nearby trees, the garden, and the outbuildings, soaking them so that stray embers wouldn't spread the fire.

"I didn't think a stone building could burn like that," I said in an undertone to Fenice, who stood huddled with Lisa, Vandal, and Alec (the last of whom had arrived once he heard about the fire).

"The stone was only on the outside, I guess," Fenice said, casting a worried look at the outbuildings near the garden. "I feel terrible for Alden. What's he going to do?"

"I have no idea." I rubbed my arms against the chill of the early morning air. What should have been a crisp, clean morning had turned into one filled with the scent of smoke, small bits of ash drifting to the ground, and a profound sense of sadness at watching such a historic building be destroyed.

"I'd better go check on the gear to make sure none of the water the firemen are using is getting inside our buildings."

Fenice patted me on the arm. "Give Alden our sympathy, will you? I can't imagine how devastated he's feeling right now."

"He is, but he's also grateful that no one was hurt." I shook my head, marveling at how things had turned out. "At the time, I thought he was way off base kicking everyone out of the house, but now I'm intensely thankful he did."

"Likewise," she said, giving me another pat before hurrying off to remind the firemen that the buildings nearest the garden were being used.

While Fenice and I had been talking, Lisa had moved over to where Alden stood, leaning in close to him while she spoke. He didn't react to her, or what she was saying, so I gathered he was so stunned by the fire that he simply could not cope with her.

One look at his face as I approached told me I was correct.

"—know it's hard to find the good in something bad, but really, there is some good to this. You're insured, naturally, which means you'll get just oodles of money. Enough to let you buy a house somewhere else. Maybe even another historic house, one you could do little fixes to, you know? Just so you have the satisfaction of making it your own."

I ignored Lisa and wrapped my arms around Alden, kissing the side of his neck before saying into his ear, "It's going to be all right, my dumpling."

His arms tightened around me, his gaze never leaving the shifting pattern of light and smoke as the fire consumed the guts of the house, leaving only a broken, blackened shell. We were far enough back that we had escaped the heat of the flames, but the roar of the fire as it consumed the house was soul-shattering.

"I was just telling Alden that things are not as black as they seem. There are so many things he can do with the insurance money—" Lisa would have continued, but I cut her off with one venomous glance.

"This isn't about the insurance money," I told her. "It's

about a lovely old house being destroyed, something that you don't seem to care about."

"Of course I care," she said, exasperation evident in her voice. "I care a great deal. This was Lady Sybilla's home, if nothing else, and she is devastated, absolutely devastated! But as my mama always told me, there's no use in crying over spilt kitty litter. You just have to clean it up and move on."

"Oh . . . go away," I said, too tired to worry that I was being rude. I tightened my arms around Alden, and breathed in his scent, but it was barely discernible over the smoke.

"There's no need to be rude, Mercedes Starling," she said with an exaggerated sniff. "I'm sure Alden understands what I'm saying. Oh dear, there's Lady Sybilla. I thought Adams was going to keep her in the lodge."

Alden said nothing during the conversation, just rested his chin on my shoulder, his arms warm and solid around me, and continued to watch the fire.

"Alden?" I whispered near his ear. "Did you have insurance on the house?"

"No." His voice was flat and emotionless. "I was waiting for the last of my trust money to be released."

I sighed, and wanted badly to be anywhere but at that spot at that moment. "I kind of figured that must be the case. What do you want me to do?"

At last he glanced away from the fire, a question in his eyes, but one that was tinged with pain. "About what?"

"Your house."

"I don't have a house anymore." His gaze slipped back to the fire. "I have nothing but a bunch of land that is mostly leased out, and the broken remains of my dreams."

"You have me," I said softly, stroking my hands up his back. "It turns out you were right, you know."

"About what?" He looked back to me, and I took the opportunity to move him slightly, so he couldn't see the fire over my shoulder.

"I am in love with you. I don't how or why or when that happened, but it did, and now you're stuck with me, you great big boob, because if you try to dump me, I'm going to be miserable and heartbroken. And you don't want that on your conscience. You're too sensitive for that, and I can assure you that the idea that you'd destroyed my one chance at happiness would make you a neurotic mess. More of a neurotic mess than you were when I first met you."

One side of his mouth twitched. "Are you trying to distract me from the hellish nightmare that is now my life?"

"Yes. Is it working?"

"Yes," he said, sighing heavily before kissing me. "I'm glad you admit that you love me. Would it make you think less of me if I sat down and cried?"

"Not in the least. Men have just as many emotions as women do—you simply process them a bit differently. Let's go find somewhere private where you can cry to your heart's content, and I will hold you and tell you it'll be all right and that we'll get through this, and then afterward I will tie your hands to a bed frame and have my way with you in such a manner that you'll forget about this horrible day for at least a little bit."

"I accept your offer," he said gravely, and made no protest when I took his hand and started to lead him down the drive to the gatehouse, our temporary new home.

Lady Sybilla was being assisted into a camping chair by the redoubtable Adams. Both women were dressed, their matching white hair tidy as ever, their faces equally dour.

Alden stopped in front of Lady Sybilla, his fingers tightening on mine as he obviously tried to think of something to say.

Lady Sybilla wasn't about to wait around for that, however. "Young man," she said dispassionately, her gaze running over first him, then me, before turning back to the house. "Bestwood Hall has been destroyed."

"Yes," Alden said, his shoulders slumping. "I'm sorry. I was in the hospital when it started."

She was silent for a moment, then made a tching noise. "It always was an abomination. That gatehouse is much more desirable."

Both Alden and I gawked at her, outright, full-fledged, gob-stopped gawked.

"The hell?" I asked, finally able to speak. "What on earth are you saying? You loved Bestwood Hall!"

"Whatever gave you that idea?" she asked with a sniff.

"You did! In the many times that you refused to leave because you told Alden that it was your late husband's beloved home."

She gave a ladylike shrug. "It never was very comfortable to live in. Drafty, very drafty, and inconvenient in the layout. Many is the time I told Adams the whole thing should be pulled down and rebuilt, is that not so, Adams?"

"It is, your ladyship." Adams's pinched face grew even more pinchy, a thing I didn't think was possible. "I've always told her ladyship that whoever laid out the house should be hung by his toes, and so I say now. It was a sprawling confusion of a house, and we are much happier at the gatehouse."

"No," I told them both, pointing a finger at Lady Sybilla, who opened her eyes wide at both my words and action. "No, you cannot simply do an about-face now. I refuse to let you. You made Alden's life a nightmare for the last two weeks, and now you're trying to pretend you wanted to leave all along, and I'm not going to let that pass. Here's Alden all torn up—his house is destroyed, along with the last few bits of your furniture that were too heavy for us to move—and I know he's the sort of man who feels responsible for that, despite the fact that he tried for weeks to get you out of there, and had to resort to threats of physically removing you before you finally did."

"You make no point with that statement," Lady Sybilla said, dismissing me altogether. "Young man, I will wish to speak to you at your earliest convenience about the rent due to me for the people you have housed in my domicile."

I did a little more gawking at the apparent balls she had in charging rent for Fenice and Lisa. "The nerve—" I started to say, but shut up when Alden answered her.

"There is no rent owed to you," he said firmly. I wanted to applaud him. "The gatehouse is still mine—you only have tenancy in it for your life. If I wish to house guests in it, I will naturally consult you, but in this instance, I consider the situation an emergency, and as such, I will proceed without consulting you."

Lady Sybilla didn't like that, but didn't get a chance to say more, because Alden started forward, taking me with him.

"I still can't believe this place is called a lodge," I said five minutes later when we arrived at the gatehouse. It was a red stone building, sitting back off the drive, but near enough that in centuries past, a gatekeeper would dash out and open the gates whenever a carriage (or, later, motorcar) wished to arrive or depart. "This has a tower! A square tower, stuck right there on one end. And gables! Lots of gables. Not to mention the fact that I personally saw four bedrooms when we were moving Lady Sybilla's stuff in."

"There are six bedrooms, actually."

"Six bedrooms is not a lodge. Not even remotely." I stared up at the pointed gables, and counted the windows. "Lodges are supposed to be small, primitive buildings that men go to in order to get away from their women, drink a lot of booze, and go out and shoot innocent animals. This is a freaking mansion."

"Not quite, although I was told it was used as a dower house for many decades." Alden's shoulders were definitely slumped as he escorted me into the house and up a lovely oak staircase that split into two arches midway up. We took the right arch, and proceeded down a hallway, with Alden opening doors as he came to them. At last he found a room that wasn't occupied. He lay down on top of the naked mattress, and covered his eyes with his forearm. "Christ, what a day. And it's only just started."

I sat next to him on the bed, one hand on his chest. "It's been awful, hasn't it? I meant what I said, you know."

He moved his arm to look at me. "That you love me? I should hope so."

"Not that, you toad." I pinched his side. "I meant that I would do whatever you needed done. To help. Is there someone I can call for you? Insurance agent? Banker?"

"No, but I appreciate the offer." He rubbed his face, and I thought seriously about molesting him, but decided he might not be in the mood.

"I'll go find us some sheets and blankets," I said, getting slowly to my feet.

Now that the adrenaline rush of the hospital and the fire was wearing off, I felt like I was a hundred years old and my feet were made of cement. It took me only five minutes to find the linen closet and gather up the necessary items, but when I returned, Alden was sound asleep on the bare mattress.

I stood next to him with my arms full of pillows and sheets, and looked down on his face, at that lovely square chin, and the cheek indents that weren't quite dimples, and the long, long eyelashes.

"You're mine," I told Alden, and covered him up with a soft blanket. "Whether you want it or not. But I'd prefer you want it, which means you need to get down to the business of falling madly in love with me, so we can live together happily, and I won't have to go back to the U.S. a sad and morbidly depressed person."

"All right," Alden mumbled, and rolled over onto his stomach.

I laid a blanket down next to him, and curled myself into it, deciding that although I had about two hours before I was due to start my teaching duties, I couldn't face the public— assuming the firemen let them into the garden—without a little sleep.

It turned out I was able to sleep five hours before Fenice came to find me.

"Are you awake—oh, lord, you're at it again?"

"Hrn?" I woke up at the sound of a voice to find that Alden had rolled over until he was halfway on top of me, one leg thrown over mine.

Alden jerked back at the same time, blinking wildly and trying to focus his gaze on the door.

"Oh, it's you, Fenice. We weren't doing anything but sleeping," I told her, stretching and yawning. "What time is it?"

"It's gone half after eleven. We're finally being allowed to hold classes, although obviously the remains of the house are off-limits." She peered at us. "You look like hell, both of you. When did Alden get a black eye?"

"When I dragged him away from certain death." I yawned again, and swung my legs over the edge of the bed. "How many people do I have today, do you know?"

"Just three, but if you are too tired to cope—"

"No, I'll be fine." I stretched again. "I just need a little coffee and some food, and I'll be good to go."

"I'm glad to hear that, because I was worried you weren't going to be up to it, and since the Fight Knight is only six days away, we need every man and woman on board. So to speak."

"You think you can still hold that?" I asked her, unsure of whether it was wise, given the disaster. "Won't people be put off by the fire?"

"Are you kidding? They'll think it's great—can't you just imagine the pictures? Melee combat in front of the ruins of an Elizabethan house will be pure camera fodder." She eyed Alden worriedly. "You . . . er . . . you won't mind us having the event, will you, Alden? It means the world to Vandal and me, and we promise to give you all the proceeds if you're taking funds for rebuilding. It's the least we can do."

"You can hold it," Alden said tiredly. "It makes no difference to me."

"We'll take care of everything, don't you worry." She flashed me a low-wattage smile, and beckoned me.

With a glance back at Alden, I followed her out to the hallway.

"I didn't want to say this in front of Alden, but I heard there was going to be an arson inspector out to look through the ruins once they are cool enough."

"Arson!" I rubbed my arms. "No, not even Lisa would be crazy enough to burn down an entire house."

"You think Lisa is responsible for the fire?" Fenice asked, looking askance. "Do you have any proof?"

"No, but I'm positive she's behind the fall he took in the gallery." Quickly I explained my theory, adding, "It makes sense when you think of her being up to something in the secret passageways."

"I thought you didn't find anything there but lights hung all over?"

"We didn't, except a chemistry bottle and some trash."

Fenice looked confused, so I gave her a brief rundown of our sole finds in the secret passageways.

"How very odd. Why would Lisa leave that?"

"I don't think she did. At least, not intentionally." I glanced back through the open door to Alden. He hadn't moved. "To be honest, I think she has a crush on Alden, and is pissed because he chose me over her, and the murder attempt in the gallery was her way of getting back. She must have found the way into the secret passages from Lady Sybilla's documents, and done some poking around there, even discovering the smugglers' cave. But there wasn't anything she could do there. Unless that's where she started the fire . . . if she did do it. I admit that it might also be a faulty gas line that started the fire, although it's damned highly suspicious that it started in Alden's room."

"Could be. Both the plumbing and wiring are quite old." Fenice glanced at her watch. "I'd best get a move on. See you in half an hour?"

I nodded, and she left, allowing me to return to Alden. He lay on his back, his face shadowed by beard and sorrow.

"I didn't dream it, did I?" he asked, staring up at the ceiling. "The house is really gone."

"I'm afraid so." I leaned forward to kiss him. "What can I do to make things better?"

"Nothing, unless you have a magical ability to reverse time." He rubbed at his whiskery chin. "All our things were lost. Your clothes, and whatever else you brought with you. My clothes. My books. All my plans and papers."

"You still have your laptop, though," I pointed out. "And I didn't lose anything but clothes and a few paperbacks. Nothing that can't be replaced. Oh, Alden, I feel so horrible for you. You have to give me something to do, something that will help you and make you feel better."

He smiled a faint, sad smile. "I know how you feel. I want to be doing something to fix the situation, too, but there's nothing I can do. It's all useless now. I might as well sell the land to the Hairy Tit people, since they, at least, would have some use for it."

"That's defeatist talk, right there. I think the first thing to do is to look at the remains—when you can, since I assume it's probably still unsafe to poke around now—and see if there's anything to be salvaged. And then maybe talk to the bank about getting a loan to rebuild."

"Rebuild?" He frowned. "Why would I want to do that?"

"Because it's your home, and I like it here, and dammit, you made me fall in love with you, and that means the least you can do is provide me with a gorgeous country home on the coast of Cornwall where we can live in peace and raise children and horses and possibly sheep. I like sheep. You can use them in place of lawn mowers. Did I tell you that I did a year of agricultural management?"

He laughed, and pulled me over his chest, kissing me in a way that lit up all my insides. "No, but I'm not surprised. You'd better get to your waiting pupils before I decide that the best thing for me is incredibly steamy morning sex."

"Hey, there's nothing that says I can't get in a quickie before class."

He waggled his eyebrows. "Who says it will be quick?"

"Oooh." I leaned down to kiss him, murmuring, "I do love you, you know," against his lips.

"I know," he said.

I thought of pinching him and telling him that now was the perfect moment for him to reciprocate, but decided he'd had enough for the last twenty-four hours, and instead took myself off for a fast shower, and a faster breakfast.

Things would get better, I promised myself as I ran down the drive to the blackened burning wreck of what used to be the house. It certainly couldn't get worse.

SEVENTEEN

Alden was beginning to feel hunted. Barry Butcher seemed to dog his footsteps for four straight days. No matter where he was, he'd turn around and there was Barry, trying to force on him a sheaf of papers and an offer for the land.

Alden tried hard not to think about Barry's offer, or the future of the house and land. Not after the bank refused to give him a loan, and his insurance agent regretfully told him that there was nothing they could do without a policy in place.

To be sure, there was the time two days after the fire when Mercy found him sitting on a fallen bit of the north wall, a notebook in hand, idly drawing an outline of what the house used to be, unmanly tears staining his cheeks.

"Do you want to talk about it?" Mercy had asked, putting both of her arms around him, and distracting him from the depressing contemplation of the house. Her warmth and love surrounded him, cocooning him in a way that left him breathless with want.

"No," he said, turning and kissing her. "I don't want to even think about it."

Despite that statement, he found himself obsessed with the house. He thought about it when he woke up, his limbs pleasantly entangled with Mercy's, taking quiet pleasure in her soft snores against his shoulder. He thought about it during the day, when he threw himself wholly into the Hard Day's Knights' gearing up for Fight Knight, as well as several additional training sessions with Vandal.

"You're a natural at this," Vandal told him, pulling off his helm. "You have the balance to remain on your feet—most of the time—and the sword arm to take down even the biggest competitor. If you stay focused, which you don't far too often for my liking."

Alden unhooked his helm and peeled off his arming cap, using it to wipe the sweat from his face. "I said I was sorry."

"You don't have to apologize to me," Vandal replied, taking a towel and soaking it with water before wiping it over his face. "You're the one who took a mace to the back because you weren't paying attention."

Alden wiggled his shoulders inside the armor, wincing at the ache in his back as he did so. He'd definitely feel that in the morning. "I'll try to be more focused, although I really don't belong competing in the Fight Knight event. I'm just an amateur."

"We're all amateurs. And you have just as much talent as any of the other competitors, or you would if you'd not let your mind wander." Vandal tossed the towel into a bucket.

During his time away from the fighting ring, Alden drew plans, made lists, and brainstormed ways he could raise the funds to build something—anything—on the land that he owned, so that he could live there with Mercy and her horses and sheep and children. For a man who was determined not to think about it, he certainly spent a vast amount of time doing just that.

"What are you doing?" Mercy asked the day before the big event, stopping where he sat on a bale of hay. She had bunting in her hand, and was helping Fenice decorate the garden. "Thinking about the house?"

"Of course not," he said resolutely, closing the notebook in which he'd been making sketches of a modified version of the old hall. "I haven't thought about it in days."

"Right. And how's that working out for you?"

He glared at her.

She blew him a kiss. "You keep at it, Alden. I have faith in you, even if it means you have to sell off that tit part of the land so we can build our dream Bestwood Hall II: The Next Generation."

"It's your unconditional love for me that is making you so optimistic," he called after her. "I don't think there's any chance I can rebuild."

She waved her hand to show she heard, but hurried off to put up the bunting.

Alden slumped on his seat of hay until Vandal approached, a clipboard in hand. "Alden, I know you aren't crazy to do a one-on-one battle, but according to the schedule the committee gave me, there's room for you if you wanted to do the triathlon duel, or the professional fight."

"What are those?" he asked, pulling his attention from the miserable circumstances of his life. Although he wasn't particularly thrilled to be in Vandal's event, he had agreed to be a part of the big all-in melee battle.

"Triathlon is one versus one, three rounds, each round a minute and a half. First round you use long sword, second you use sword and buckler shield, and third you use your regular shield and sword."

"That sounds painful," Alden said.

"The professional fight might be more to your style. It's three rounds also, but three minutes per round, and each contestant uses the same randomly picked weapon. Points are given for blows by your weapon, shield, fist, leg, and knee. You're damned good with your fists, and I can show you a few leg moves this afternoon."

"I'll do that one," Alden said after a moment's thought. "But just so we're clear that I'm doing this as a complete novice, and won't be bringing your company any glory."

"You don't know until you try," Vandal said, making a note on his schedule. "I'll see you this evening, after the regular class is over, all right? Your friend Butcher has decided to form his own team, by the way."

Alden made a noncommittal noise. "He's hardly my friend, although I'm surprised he's not fighting for you."

"I asked him to, but he said I had enough people with you and the other students, and that he'd bring his own group." Vandal shrugged. "So long as they pay the entrance fee, I don't care."

Alden found it difficult to be very interested in much of anything other than Mercy. He went through the motions for the rest of the day, helping with the decorations, moving equipment, and fashioning a temporary list where the melee fights would be held. By the time night had come upon them, he was tired, but strangely distant from everyone.

Everyone but Mercy, that is. She seemed to thaw out his frozen heart like nothing else could, the warm, happy glow about her making him feel alive again.

"Aren't you excited about tomorrow?" Mercy asked that evening when she was changing from her now somewhat ragged blue—but much beloved—archery dress into a new pair of jeans and shirt that she'd bought the day after the fire. "I am. Actually, I'm nervous as hell, especially since I'm the only archer for Fenice and Vandal. You're doing two things, aren't you? Fenice said Vandal sweet-talked you into doing another one, which will make Team Hard Day's Knights look good. Oh lord, I hope I can hit the target. That's all I ask—just hit the target and not shame myself."

"You won't shame anyone," he told her, relishing the aura of light and love she brought into his life. Being near Mercy made him feel like he was bathed in golden sunshine, warm and happy and contented with life. It was only when she'd gone that he returned to an icy state of indifference. "I have just as much confidence in you as you claim to have in me."

Mercy stopped trying to examine herself in the small hand mirror she'd set on a wardrobe shelf, and turned back to him. "Are you OK, Alden?"

He looked puzzled. "I've healed up quite nicely, a fact you should know, since you've examined me each night to make sure I was lovemaking-worthy."

Slowly she approached, sitting next to him on the bed. "I meant that in more a metaphysical way. You seem . . . depressed."

"I am depressed. My house and sole form of livelihood has just burned down," he said, far more acid audible in his voice than made him comfortable. He cleared his throat and added, "There's not a lot to be ecstatically happy about in my life, present company excepted."

She watched him silently for a moment. "Is there anything I can do?"

He smiled. "Just love me."

"That's a given. I don't suppose you're in love with me, yet?"

He pursed his lips, and looked thoughtful.

"Honest to god, Alden, if I was as slow as you are, we'd never have gotten together." She threw a hand towel at him, and stomped out of the room.

He caught it, his smile fading as she left, and a familiar sense of despair returned. She loved him—of that he was dead certain—but how on earth could he ask her to share his life now that he had nothing? How could he even admit to her that sometime over the past twenty days, he'd fallen as deeply in love as she had, when their life together would be fraught with stress and financial unhappiness?

What sort of a man would he be to expect her to bind her life to his only to end up sharing his poverty?

"Dammit," he swore to himself. "I'm going to have to take Barry's offer."

You can start anew, he told himself, washing his face and hands. *You can use the money to buy a smaller house, one that isn't so historical, and renovate that and then flip it. Mercy would like that.*

Mercy liked Bestwood Hall. For that matter, so had he. If only there was a way he could rebuild without having to sell off any more land.

Dinner that evening was a lively affair, made more so because the gatehouse was playing host to not just its regulars but also a handful of people present for the battle on the following day.

"This is Tamarind," Fenice said, introducing a tall, elegant black woman who had bright red hair. "She's a workmate who was in the area, so she thought she'd stop by to watch the proceedings tomorrow."

"Too bad you're not a fighter," Vandal said, strolling up and giving Tamarind a clearly lascivious once-over. "If I told you that you have the body for it, would you hold it against me?"

Alden almost groaned at the blatant way Vandal was flirting, but Tamarind needed no help in taking her swain down a peg or two.

"Not likely, mate. Didn't your sister tell you? I prefer the other side." Tamarind smiled at everyone before turning to Alden, who was seated next to her. Her voice dropped to an intimate level. "I heard about your house. I'm so sorry."

"Thank you," Alden said, experience having taught him how to politely escape the well-wishers. "That's very kind of you. The house is mostly destroyed, although there is one wall still standing."

"Do you know the cause of the fire?"

"No. I assume there will be an investigation at some point."

"No doubt," Tamarind said. "Fenice told me—I hope this isn't a painful subject, given the fire, but I am very interested in caves and such—Fenice told me about your smugglers' cave. Evidently it leads up to the house proper?"

"It did." Alden, distracted for a few minutes by the obvious interest in Tamarind's face, told her about the discovery of the secret passageways. "I'm sure one of the previous Baskervilles used the passages to transport wine and rum, although we found no signs of any hidden cache, more's the pity."

She laughed. "I can imagine that such a thing would be quite valuable today. It's interesting about those lights you said were strung along the passageways. That can't have been a product of the free-traders."

"No, I gather Sir James Baskerville had them installed." He glanced down the long table in the dining room, where Lady Sybilla sat next to her maid, both of them picking at their spaghetti dinner. "Although Lady Sybilla claimed that the passages hadn't been used for at least a century or two."

"How very curious. Do you think she was hiding something?"

"Possibly." He gave Tamarind a long look. "Then again, I think it's possible you're doing the same."

She blinked at him, a half smile on her lips. "Me? What would I have to hide?"

"Fenice said you were a workmate, but given that she is with the police, that could mean a great many things, couldn't it? It might even stretch to someone who was responsible for looking into house fires."

Tamarind's smile grew. "You're a perceptive man, Mr. Ainslie."

"Alden, please."

She glanced around the table before saying quietly, "As a matter of fact, I'm with a different branch altogether. But I can assure you that the fire is being looked into. Would you mind if I had a peek into your cave?"

"I beg your pardon!" Mercy, in the middle of a lively conversation with one of Vandal's Swedish friends who had shown up with his team for the competition, evidently caught just the tail end of the conversation with Tamarind. "You want to do what to his what?"

Alden couldn't help but smile at the outrage in her voice, and was tempted to tell her right then and there just how much he loved her, but he couldn't do that to her. He had to find a way to provide some sort of a life for them both before he could ask her to join him. "You misheard, Mercy. She was asking to look into the smugglers' cave."

"Oh. Sorry." Mercy looked mollified for a few seconds, then frowned. "Why would you want to do that?"

Tamarind gave an enigmatic smile. "Perhaps I'm a big fan of caves."

Mercy said nothing, but Alden noticed that she glanced at the other woman several times during the rest of the dinner.

"To bed, to bed!" Vandal called after another hour. By then, Lady Sybilla and Adams had retired, and the rest of the group—including the Berserkers, as the Swedish combat team were known, and a handful of Vandal's British friends—were scattered around the ground floor of the gatehouse, singing, drinking, and generally having a good time. "I want all of Team Hard Day's Knights in bed!"

"You can't have us," one of the local students answered. "Not while there are ale wenches to be amused!"

"I'll wench your ale," Mercy said, having reentered the dining room after a visit to the loo.

"Promise?" the local asked, to the cheers of the Berserkers.

"I will if you all don't keep it down. Lady Sybilla is trying to sleep, and you lot are making enough noise to drown out a bull elephant in full trumpet."

"Aw, you know how to take the poop out of every party," Lisa said, her words slurring a little. She was seated on the lap of one of the Swedes, and leaned out to the side, almost falling off him.

"That doesn't even make sense," Mercy replied, scowling. "Not that I'm surprised, since nothing you've said since Alden was almost impaled on the window railings has made sense."

Alden moved over next to Mercy, wrapping an arm around her waist, the better to whisper in her ear not to make a scene with Lisa.

"Oh!" Clearly, Lisa was outraged by Mercy's comment. "You are so mean to me! I've tried to be as nice as I can, and you're just mean in return. I told my husband about you, and he said you're just jealous of me. So you can just put that in your jealous pipe and smoke it."

"What on earth are you talking—wait, husband? You're married?" Mercy stopped scowling and shot Alden a questioning look. "You never mentioned you were married."

"Of course not. It's a secret." Lisa was speaking in a singsong manner now, her words sloppy with extra sibilants. The Swede in whose lap she was sitting was also clearly well past sober, because he gave Lisa a smacking kiss on the cheek and told her he didn't care if she was married to a hundred men—she was still welcome to sleep in his tent.

"An' what's more, I think he's right. You are jealous," Lisa added, jabbing a finger toward Mercy. "And you're bossy, too."

"Did you know she's married?" Mercy asked Alden.

He shook his head. "I'm just as surprised as you. I can't imagine why my sister-in-law would send her to me if she was already married. Perhaps Alice didn't know."

"Yeah," Mercy said slowly, and was about to add something to that when a shout went up, almost deafening them. The Berserkers declared it was time to dance, and someone brought out a set of speakers for his phone.

"And this is where the party ends," Alden said.

"Things do look like they are getting out of hand," Mercy agreed.

With Vandal's assistance, and Mercy's blatant shoving of men outdoors, they managed to get everyone who wasn't currently residing at the gatehouse outside and returned to the various tents that now dotted the front lawns of Bestwood.

"I'll put the diva to bed," Mercy said as Vandal carried Lisa, now well plastered, upstairs to her room.

"You sure? I don't mind doing it," Vandal said with a waggle of his eyebrows.

"Are you sleeping in the stables?" Alden asked. "If you are, I'd rather you stay out there and keep an eye on the outbuildings. We don't need any more fires or other incidents."

"That was my thought as well," Vandal said, reluctantly dumping Lisa onto her bed. With quick precision, Mercy removed her shoes, skirt, and blouse, leaving Lisa in her underwear and a tank top.

"We're going to have a little talk, you and I, in the morning," Mercy warned, throwing a blanket on top of the prone woman.

Lisa gurgled something, and curled into a fetal ball.

"I hope she has a hangover to end all hangovers tomorrow," Mercy said when they returned to their own room. "Which reminds me—you haven't commented on the fact that I have not pestered you about getting the police to talk to her."

"I may not have commented, but I did notice that fact," Alden said, sitting on the edge of the bed and wondering when he had last felt this exhausted.

"Good. I decided that I wouldn't pursue it until after the shindig tomorrow, since the evidence has been destroyed anyway."

"What evidence? The house?"

"Yeah. It's just too bad that we couldn't get back to those light switches to dust them with the stain. I'm sure Lisa's hands would have proved that she was the guilty party."

"But guilty of what?" He watched with interest as Mercy disrobed, neatly folding each garment she took off and placing it tidily away in the wardrobe. He wondered if his habit of just dumping his clothes on the nearest chair annoyed her, and if so, whether it would cause strain in their marriage in years ahead.

His brain stumbled to a halt. Marriage? Since when was he thinking of marrying Mercy? He narrowed his eyes on her as she tidied his things up, noting how graceful she was, how intuitive to his desires—both carnal and otherwise—and, most of all, how her lovely shining self seemed to light up all the dark corners of his soul. Of course he would marry her! He didn't want her looking at another man the way she looked at him. The matter was settled.

"Obviously, of trying to do you in with the trapdoor in the gallery. But as to what she could be doing under the house . . ." Mercy stood still, his newly purchased shirt in her hands. "You know, a thought occurred to me."

"Oh?"

"It's kind of an out-there thought, so feel free to tell me I'm crazy."

"I would never do that," he said nobly. "At the worst, I might tell you that you were a bit mad, but never barking so."

"Hee-hee. Barking mad is such an English phrase." She set down his shirt, now neatly folded, and slipped into bed next to him. Unfortunately, her deliciously wicked night-gown had been lost in the fire, but he made a mental note to buy her a suitable replacement as soon as possible. "It's that stuff we found the other day. The wash bottle and the bit from an OTC package."

He smiled to himself. Ever since his conversation with Tamarind, he'd been having some very startling thoughts, and now it appeared that Mercy was on the same track. "You think they are important?"

"I do." She eyed him. "What if . . . what if rather than some homeless person hiding out in the passages who was allergic to dust, or old homes, or whatever, what if it was someone doing something specific in the passage?"

"Something specific like making drugs?"

Her eyes widened. "You think so, too?"

"I didn't until this evening, but now . . . aren't antihista-mines and decongestants used in making methamphetamines?"

"I believe so. Now I wish I'd done some medical courses. Should we tell the police?"

"I think," he said slowly, sliding a hand down her arm. She was clad in a tank top and a pair of knit shorts, and he desperately wanted her naked, and in his arms. Or sitting astride him, telling him just how wonderful he felt. Or be-neath him, moaning and writhing. "I think that they might already be thinking along those lines."

"Good. If Lisa was cooking meth under the hall as well as tried to murder you, then she definitely needs to go to jail."

He laughed, and pulled her down over his chest so he could kiss her properly. "She's been here less time than you have, sweetheart. I doubt if she could set up and dismantle a meth lab in that time without us knowing it."

"Dammit, I hate it when you're right. Oh well. I guess I'm just going to have to make mad, passionate, wild bunny love to you so that you totally forget I even mentioned that. Oh!"

She slipped out of his embrace, much to his dismay.

He watched her kneel next to a new duffel bag. "And here I was enjoying the idea of mad bunny love. Why have you forsaken me for the charms of a bag, madam?"

She looked up, grinning. "I love it when you talk all ye olde English. I bought something for you in town the last time I was there, and what with all the stuff going on, I forgot to give it to you."

"What is it?" he asked suspiciously when she did a seductive walk back to the bed, her hands behind her back. "It's not handcuffs, is it?"

"Of course not," she said with a little snort of disgust before whipping her hands around to the front. "It's furry cuffs!"

"That is the same thing as a handcuff."

"Nope." She knelt on the bed, and wrapped the leather and bright pink faux-fur restraint around his wrist. "This is a leather cuff. Handcuffs are made of metal and are hurty. This is nice and soft. And look, I bought yarn to use as a tie, so if you get panicky and freak out, you can break it and be free, although I really hope you don't, because I think you'll like this if you give it a chance."

And that is how Alden found himself, some five minutes later, lying on his back, naked, his hands tied to the headboard, nervously watching Mercy shimmy her way out of her sleeping apparel.

"And just to make sure that you enjoy this . . ." She reached over the edge of the bed to a nightstand, pulling out a small bottle. "A little love potion of the slick type. I thought we would start the proceedings by me oiling you up and licking you off."

Just like that, he was hard. It was an instantaneous event. . . . One moment he was his normal quiescent—although interested—self, and the next, he had a full-on erection.

"Do I need a condom?" he asked, his breath coming a bit short as she poured a little reddish oil into her hands, swishing it around on them.

"I don't think so. I'm on birth control, and now that we know each other better, it's not so vital, is it?"

"No. Definitely not. Absolutely not. We're good there."

She grinned, and leaned over to kiss him. "You're babbling, my love."

"I know. I can't help it. Are you going to use that oil, or just sit there holding it all night?"

"Anticipatory? That's part of the fun of having your hands tied. Now, let's see if you like this. . . ."

He liked it. He liked it very much, something he told her repeatedly as she rubbed the oil into his penis, her hands like fire, leaving little oily streaks that warmed on his flesh. She used her hands and mouth on him, causing him to thrash around on the bed, his entire body now an erogenous zone.

"This is exquisite torture," he gasped at one point, when she was rubbing her breasts across his penis. "I want to make you stop, but at the same time, I never want it to end."

"I told you it would be good," she said, looking up. "It's the feeling of being helpless. Normally, I don't like that in sexual play, because, as a woman, we're almost always in the submissive role, but I have to say that the idea of having you run amok on me is enough that I want to ride you like a two-bit camel."

"Ride me," he begged, his hips thrusting upward when her hands did a slippery dance along his length. "Please god, if you have any mercy in your soul, ride me hard and ride me long."

"Well, as you begged . . ."

"I did! I begged! I'll do it again if you want!"

"Then I guess I can give in to both our desires." She positioned herself with her knees around his hips, rubbing the very tip of him against her womanly parts. He bucked upward, making her eyes widen when he entered her just a little bit. Without another word, she sank down on him, causing them both to moan in pleasure.

It didn't take long for either of them. Just as Alden was gritting his teeth, thinking of horrible things like boils and pustules in order to not leave Mercy behind, she arched back, her muscles gripping him in rippling waves that ensured that even the most repulsive thoughts couldn't stop his orgasm. He jerked his hands down, snapping the yarn, and holding on to her hips as he pistoned, his mind and body one with the effort to pour himself into her.

When she collapsed down onto him, slick with perspiration and the body oil, he peeled off the wrist restraints, and wrapped his arms around her, capturing the wild beating of her heart against his chest, where his own raced madly.

"You are mine forever," he murmured, kissing her forehead and eyes and cheeks and that adorable little chin. "I love you, and I'm never letting you go."

"That's fine with me—wait, what?" She pushed herself back just enough to see him. "Did you say what I thought you said?"

"Yes." He pulled her back down to where she belonged, next to his heart. "Go to sleep. I plan on waking you up in the middle of the night and tying your hands to the headboard."

She giggled against him as he rolled onto his side, wiggling until she was comfortably smooshed up against him. "I don't suppose you'd like to repeat that?"

"Certainly. Go to sleep."

She disengaged one hand and pinched him on the nipple. He swatted her behind, immediately followed by a caress. "That isn't what I meant, and you know it."

"I know, but I'm a man. We have to sleep after sex."

"That's the biggest cop-out in the world. Say it."

He sighed, ruffling the hair on the top of her head. "Fine, but this is cutting into the time I will need to make you squirm with utter delight. I love you, my sweet Mercy. You make me feel like a different man, a better man. You make me happy. You delight me on every level. Now go to sleep so I can show you later just how much I love you. You do have more yarn, yes?"

"Lots."

"Good. We're going to need it." He kissed the top of her head, allowing exhaustion to claim him.

EIGHTEEN

Fight Knight was in full swing by the time I made it out to Bestwood's garden.

Yellow police tape had been placed ten feet beyond the perimeter of the ruins, bolstered by hay bales, and tall orange traffic cones. Periodically along the yellow tape, signs that Alden and I had written warned visitors that they were straying into off-limits territory.

I turned my back to the black shell of the house, feeling that was something I couldn't cope with when the world lay out before me like a glittering, wonderful map of everything good and happy and sexy.

Approximately a hundred and twenty people milled around the garden, a good number of them in plate armor, while the others (mostly women) trotted around with various bits of plate and weaponry in their hands. The main list had been set up where Vandal's lesson ring had been, with an assortment of lawn chairs, blankets, and coolers set up three rows deep around the edges. There were some children running around, but not as many as I'd expected. I speculated that they were left at home because of the potential injuries that might result from the fighting.

I waved at Alec when he passed by carrying two tubs of armor, smiled and greeted people who'd taken my classes and who were competing, and dodged my way around various men and women who were getting geared up for the various melee fights.

"Morning, Mercy. You look . . . good."

I stopped when Fenice called to me from the stables.

"Thanks. I feel good." I tried not to beam my happy "Alden loves me! Alden loves me!" vibes to everyone, feeling it would come across as unbearably smug.

But I hugged myself with the knowledge nonetheless. I was loved, really and truly loved. Not by a geeky kid in university, but well and properly loved by a man.

I loved Alden, and he loved me, and everything was going to be jim-dandy fine.

"Is something going on?" Fenice asked, giving me an odd look as I did a happy little twirl in my now somewhat ratty blue dress. I'd cleaned it up as best I could for the big event, since I felt it was my lucky dress. At least it felt lucky to me, and that's what luck was all about. "Is something . . . you're not . . . are you pregnant? I swear you're glowing."

"Not pregnant," I said with a laugh, and did another twirl before giving Fenice a big hug. "Just in love."

"Oh, that." She rolled her eyes, and handed me the heavy canvas bag that held her backup bow, the one I'd be using in my classes. "I'm glad you and Alden are happy, but are you going to be able to focus? The team competition is in twenty minutes, and since you're the only one on our team, it's vital you're ready to go. You can be spacey this afternoon, for the individual competition."

"I'll focus, I'll focus. Promise. Just one more twirl, and then I'll go warm up."

"No twirls. Twirls are forbidden at Fight Knight unless you are a ninja. Go warm up." She pointed to the two archery butts that were designated for practice.

"Can I skip there, humming 'Zip-a-Dee-Doo-Dah'?"

Her lips thinned. "No skipping, no twirling. You are a professional."

"I'm not."

"You could be one if you applied yourself. You are an adult."

"An adult who is in looove," I all but sang.

"And you represent Hard Day's Knights, so no skipping, twirling, or any actions that a five-year-old girl might make."

"Well, hell, now I can't even stick my tongue out at you," I said, slinging the case's strap over my shoulder, and making a point of stomping my feet when I left.

"I hear that!" she called after me, which just had me giggling.

I lined up for the practice butts (the British are very serious about their queues), and managed to get five minutes of warm-up in before my group of four was called to do our best.

Alden, I knew, was getting geared up and receiving any last-minute instruction and advice from Vandal before his one-on-one battle, so I didn't expect to have any supporters other than Fenice when I took up my borrowed bow.

"Competing for Hard Day's Knights," the ring announcer yelled, holding up a clipboard with the schedule and contestants. "Mercedes Starling."

There was a brief commotion at the edge of the ring, a metallic sort of commotion. As I lined my toes up on the official mark, I glanced over to see Alden clanking his way to the ring, fully armed, carrying his helm.

He held out a mail hand and gave me a thumbs-up. I grinned, and blew him a kiss.

Beside him, Fenice did a little jig of anger, and stabbed her finger toward the archery butt. The glare she sent my way could have taken paint off a barn door. I spread my grin to her, just barely refrained from blowing her a kiss, too (I didn't want her to have a fit right there in front of everyone), and instead turned to face the target.

The judge blew her whistle, alerting me that I had two minutes to shoot six arrows.

Breathe, I remembered my old archery coach telling me before a competition. Feel the air coming into your lungs, and exiting. Forget everything else but your breathing, and the target.

I lifted the bow, trying to push out all the jubilant feelings that rolled around inside of me, making me want to dance and sing and shout with happiness.

I breathed. As I drew air into my lungs, I lifted the bow upward until it was over my head, exhaling as I brought it back down, my other arm pulling the string back to my jaw as I did so.

For a split second, I didn't breathe. The whole world seemed to stop, my gaze narrowing on the center point of the gold bull's-eye, exactly where I wanted to put the arrow. As I let my fingers relax, the string slipped past them, and I knew by the sound of the twang that the arrow was true.

Polite applause met my bull's-eye, along with some metallic clanging that I took to be Alden clapping. I locked another arrow into place, deciding where I wanted it to go in the bull's-eye (neatly alongside the first arrow), and I breathed.

I left the archery ring with a score of four bull's-eyes, and two in the next ring down, or a total of fifty-eight. I knew that wasn't good enough to win the competition (since the other archers had a lot more experience than me), but I was pleased with my result nonetheless.

And so was Fenice.

"Nicely done," she said, buffeting me on the shoulder. "You did us proud. I'm almost tempted to let you keep that bow."

"Oooh," I said, clutching it hopefully to my chest.

"Almost," she said, smiling as she walked away to help Vandal.

I looked for Alden, but he wasn't there. I tucked the bow away in the stable, made sure the doors were locked, and did a quick patrol of the area as suggested by Fenice. Most people had enough sense to avoid the outbuildings, but I did rumble a couple of kids and one couple who were old enough to know better.

"Seriously, people," I told the shamefaced couple, shooing them toward the door of the shed. "You wouldn't do this in your own garden, would you?"

"Every Sunday!" the man said, making the woman give a nervous giggle.

"Well, it's not Sunday now, and if I catch you in there again, I'm going to tell Vandal."

They left with only minor grumbling.

The crowd outside the melee ring was large, since most people came for that, and I had a hard time working my way around the various bodies to where the men were being readied to fight. As I rounded the far side, I realized that the reason I couldn't find Alden was that he was already in the ring.

Alden staggered back when the man—a veritable giant of a guy—slammed his shield across Alden's arm and chest. I ran for the other side, one eye on Alden while he took a hell of a beating, the other scanning the crowd for Vandal or Fenice. I found them both assisting one of Vandal's students into his armor.

"Who is Alden fighting?" I asked, knowing the lots weren't drawn for the matches until the last minute. "I missed the start. How is he doing—ow. Oh, that had to be unfair! Why aren't the judges stopping that huge man!"

"That's Dan Jacobs. He used to be regional champion five or six years ago, and that backhand to Alden's helm was a perfectly legal move," Vandal said, shouting encouragement to Alden when the latter staggered forward and almost fell on his face. "Stay on your feet, man!"

"Is it legal to have a champion fighting a newbie?" I asked, clutching my hands together and wincing when the huge man kicked out, catching Alden on the knee. Alden swung around and slammed his shield into the man, sending him staggering to the side. "That seems wrong to me."

"It would be if he was still a champion, but he's been out of competition for a few years due to back surgery, so he's considered a beginner just like Alden. Shield up, Alden! Keep the damned shield up!"

I left Vandal and Fenice, and scurried along the crowds until I found a spot where I could push up to the edge of the hay bales that marked the ring.

"Beat the tar out of him!" I yelled over the sounds of the crowd shouting their own encouragement. "Knock him to the ground and stomp all over him! Kick him in the balls! Hack him to bits with your sword and dance a jig on the bloody remains!"

A hush fell over the crowd nearest me as I bellowed out the last sentence. I was caught by surprise when I noticed that everyone was staring at me.

"Um. Too far?" I asked the sea of startled faces turned my way.

"Newbies," one woman said, shaking her head and turning back to the action.

"Sorry. I just wanted to give Alden some encouragement—oh, hell, it's over?"

The giant, who had knocked Alden to the ground right at the end of their allotted time, held out a hand and hauled him to his feet, the two men leaving the ring together in apparent accord.

I excused myself out of the crowd, and headed for the staging area where the combatants were armed and disarmed, almost stepping on Lisa, who popped up suddenly in front of me.

"Sugar! Just the person I've been wanting to see." She looked a little worse for wear, her hair gathered up in a very messy bun, her clothes a bit wrinkled, and the scarf she wore knotted around her neck had a coffee stain on the end, no doubt from the latte she clutched in her hand. She also wore sunglasses, which I suspected covered bloodshot eyes. "Have you seen Alden?"

"Yes, yes, I have," I said obnoxiously, and put my hands on my hips, fighting hard to keep from outright accusing her of trying to murder him.

She clicked her tongue. "Honestly, Mercy, I don't know why you have to be such a bitch to me. All I want is to tell Alden that there are some people trespassing over there."

I turned to look where she pointed. Two silver vans were parked on the far side of the remains of the house, with a group of four people standing together in a cluster evidently consulting.

"I know Alden doesn't want anyone to go poking around in the bits and pieces of the house. If you won't tell me where he is, then you can at least tell him that there are trespassers doing who-knows-what."

"They aren't trespassers," I said shortly, wanting to get past her to Alden to see how he was after his fight. "They're probably the fire investigators, or the police."

"Police?" Her voice went a bit shrill, and she took a sip of her coffee to cover it. "Whatever are the police doing looking at a burned-up house?"

It cost me a lot, but I kept from telling her they were probably looking for signs she had been cooking meth in the walls. "I know they were waiting for it to be safe to investigate the cause of the fire. No doubt they're doing that."

"Ah, that makes sense." I swear she relaxed at the news, which troubled me. I had been trying to work out a reason why she would want to burn down the house, but couldn't come up with one, and now here she was relaxing when it came to the idea that people were going to investigate the fire, just as if it had nothing to do with her.

"Well, dammit," I murmured to myself when she left me without another word. "If it turns out I can't blame her for any of the evil things that have befallen Alden, I'm going to be very pissed."

The next few hours slipped by without me being aware. There was Alden to see and beam loving looks to (and receive a few in return, which made me want to dance and sing all over again), and my former pupils to cheer on when they went into the archery ring. Alden and I helped out wherever possible, mostly with squire duties arming and disarming the various combatants, or pointing out where the portable toilets had been arranged (behind the stable, thank heavens), where drinking water was available, and where the catering company needed to set up their long tables of food, which the participants and their helpers alike descended upon like voracious wolves.

By early afternoon, I'd forgotten the people who were poking around the ruins of the house. I sat next to Lady Sybilla and Adams for a half hour, watching the various forms of melee fighting.

"I have to tell you that I'm a bit surprised you are enjoying such a bloody sport," I told Lady Sybilla when one of the combatants had to be assisted out of the list, and was having the doctor attend to what appeared to be a broken arm.

She tilted her parasol so that she could pin me back with her pale blue gaze. "Why would I not enjoy medieval combat? It is, of course, upon the backs of knights just like these that our country was created. It is a noble sport, after all."

"I guess so, but it's a bit . . ." I waved a hand around while I thought of the word I wanted. ". . . gory."

"It is invigorating," she said, turning her eyes back to the ring as the next two combatants—two women, this time—were announced. "I am very pleased that I had the foresight to bring these people here, and look forward to seeing them next year."

"I don't know that there's going to be a next year," I said slowly, my gaze searching the crowd for Alden. He'd told me at lunch that he had decided to accept Barry's offer for the land, assuming I had no objections to him using the profits to buy a house elsewhere.

"Nonsense. Why wouldn't there be?"

"Well . . . I should let Alden tell you, since he's the owner of the house, and I'm just his . . . er . . ."

"Mistress?"

"Girlfriend," I corrected. "Permanent girlfriend. I think you should know that Alden has been offered a nice chunk of money for the land by the bird conservancy people. It wouldn't affect you, because you were given the use of the gatehouse for life, and of course, that would be included in the deal."

"Poppycock," she said dismissively. "Your young man would not sell Bestwood. He is going to rebuild the hall into one that is not so drafty, and once he has finished, Adams and I will move back into it."

"Ah. Gotcha," I said, not wanting to upset her, or ruin the fun she was having watching people fight.

My individual competition in the late afternoon was pretty anticlimactic. I stood in position, Fenice's bow now feeling like a familiar friend, and loosed twelve arrows, not overly stressed about where they landed. I was getting tired, to be honest, and just wanted to curl up with Alden and have him tell me again how much he loved me, all of which contributed to the fact that I came in sixth in the team competition and fourth in individual.

"Well done," Fenice said, appearing to be pleased despite my lackluster performance. I slid the bow into its bag, zipped it up, and handed it to her for what I realized would be the last time. "I'm proud of you, Mercy. You had a lot of competition, but you shone despite not competing for a few years."

"Well, I did have three weeks of practice," I said, accepting her praise nonetheless. "But thank you. I couldn't have done it without your awesome bow. I don't suppose you'd be willing—"

"No," she said firmly, hoisting the bag a little higher. "But if I ever do want to get rid of it, you'll be the first person I tell."

"That's a deal," I said with a grin. We strolled back toward the melee list, chatting with people who'd come to the classes over the course of the last few weeks. There was a general sense of excitement as everyone began to gear up for the big all-in melee battle.

"Have you heard the good news?"

I jumped at the booming voice that came from behind me, spinning around to see Barry Butcher in armor, his hands and head bare as he strode toward me like he wasn't wearing at least fifty pounds of plate metal strapped to his person. "Uh . . . no?"

"Alden has agreed to sell the estate to the conservancy." Barry beamed, his red hair standing on end.

I still hadn't forgiven him for shooting at Alden during our lesson—because I was fully convinced it had been him, although I couldn't work out how he had hidden that red arrow without me seeing it—but now was not the time to raise that particular fuss.

"Yes, he told me. I hope the birds will be very happy."

"Oh, they will be, they will be indeed." He actually rubbed his hands together. "The board is just thrilled at the thought of designating not just the breeding ground but the whole estate as a sanctuary and learning center. In fact, I am having some plans drawn up—"

"Barry, you've got to get your helm on." A smaller man, dressed in what I imagined was a squire's garb, trotted up to Barry, a metal helm and mail gloves in his hands. "The all-in is about to start."

"Wouldn't want to miss that," Barry said with a grin at me. "Last man standing gets five hundred quid."

"I know. And Alden's going to get it," I said, filled with bravado on the love of my life's behalf. "Speaking of him, I should go wish him luck, and give him a favor or something. . . ."

I started to drift away as Barry stuffed the helm on his head, allowing the squire to pull on the mail gloves.

"Mercy!" Lisa raced up, stopping me with her shriek.

"Jeezumcrow, Lisa," I said, turning to give her a glare. She'd removed her sunglasses, and had, as I'd suspected, red, bloodshot eyes. "What's the matter now?"

"It's the men!" she said, waving a hand behind her.

"What men?"

"The investigators!" She grabbed my arm, all but yelling her words. I wondered if she'd been hitting the bottle a bit in an attempt to hair-of-the-dog her hangover. "They're going down into the cave you said you found."

"Can you turn down the volume a little?" I asked, frowning.

"They're going into the cave!" she repeated at an even louder volume.

I shook off her hand, not wanting to deal with a drunken, loud Lisa when there was a sweet, adorable Alden to see off to battle. "So? Look, that's their job. And if you don't mind, Alden is about to go—"

"The men," she bellowed, trailing after me as I dodged the stream of men and women who were entering the list. "The men are going into the cave!"

"Get an effing grip on yourself," I hissed, spinning around to fire a really first-class glare at her. "Go sleep it off if you have to, but stop making a scene. Oh, great, now Alden's in the ring and I didn't have time to give him a good-luck kiss, even. Thanks a lot, Lisa."

"But the men are in the cave!" screeched Lisa, her voice carrying across the sound of the armor clanking, and the crowd chatting and getting ready to cheer their favorites on.

At that moment, something odd happened.

The men in the list had been arranged loosely in groups of five, and were just taking up their positions. Vandal had created a group with himself, Alden, and a couple of his other top students, while some of the other students formed up their own group. The rest of the groups consisted of the combatants who had come just for the event, leaving about ten distinct clusters of men dotted around the list.

Suddenly, the group of five that consisted of Barry and his buddies took off at a run. A slow run, a shambling run, one that kind of reminded me of zombies lumbering after fresh meat, but still, a run.

Away from the melee.

"Well, that's odd," I said to Lisa, but she was gone.

A whistle blew, and some of the men in the list shouted at the group that had run off. I hustled around to where Fenice was standing, shading her eyes with her good hand as she stared after Barry's group.

"What's going on?" I asked, coming to a stop next to her. "Why are they leaving? That's not part of the combat, is it?"

"No, and I don't know what they're up to. Looks like Patrick is talking to one of the judges about it."

Alden had been standing with Vandal as the latter spoke to the three judges that monitored the fighting, but after a minute's conversation, he suddenly pulled off his helm, and ran after Barry's group.

"Now Alden's left!" Fenice said, swearing under her breath. "What is going on out there? Patrick!"

"The cave," I said, thinking over what Lisa had said.

"What?" Fenice didn't even look at me. She was waving her good arm, trying to catch Patrick's attention.

"Lisa was bent out of shape about the investigators going into the cave. She was . . . it was like she was warning me."

"Why would she do that?" Fenice froze as the words left her lips.

"But she wasn't warning me," I said, sorting through pieces that were slowly sliding into place. "She was warning someone else."

"Bloody hell." Fenice jumped over one of the bales of hay, and ran out to where Patrick was still talking to the judges.

I stood watching the scene for a few seconds; then I was running, racing through the crowd, dodging people and chairs and bales of hay as I gained speed, breaking free of the garden and hitting the gravel drive. Alden was about a hundred yards ahead of me, and beyond him, I could see the five figures who were heading straight for the wooden staircase that descended to the beach.

"She wasn't warning me," I yelled to Alden as I caught up to him. "She was warning Barry. Her husband! Barry is her husband!"

"They're in it together," Alden said, puffing, his face red with exertion. "You were right all along—they were manufacturing drugs in the passages."

"Or in the cave. You want me to help you take off some of that armor?"

"No," he puffed, charging forward. We could see the wooden structure that was the top of the zigzagging stairs that led down to the beach proper. "Need it for fight."

"What fight? You're not going to fight Barry, are you? Alden, you are not a medieval knight! There are cops here!"

"Just in case," he said, gasping as we reached the top of the stairs.

The cliff was such that the stairs had four flights to get down to the beach, and since I wasn't carrying around one hundred extra pounds of metal strapped to my body, I dashed ahead of Alden, leaping down the steps with the speed—although not the grace—of a gazelle in full flight.

Down the beach thirty or so yards, Barry disappeared into the cave, his men at his heels.

"If the cops are already there, they'll arrest Barry," I yelled back over my shoulder at Alden.

"Possibly. But they might not be there yet," he answered.

"Lisa seemed to think they were," I said, jumping the last five feet to the rocky beach, and immediately turning my ankle. "Oh, bloody effing hell, this is the last thing I need."

"Are you all right?" Alden asked, pausing beside me, his breath as rough and ragged as when we made love.

"Yes," I said, taking his hand and getting to my feet. "Just stupid."

Alden took my arm, slowing his pace to match my hobble. We reached the cave entrance in what seemed like an excruciatingly long amount of time. Alden entered first, pausing so we could listen. There was no sound other than the gurgle of the stream.

"Where do you think they are?" I asked in a whisper, following him when he led the way into the dark cave. The lights weren't on, no doubt their connection having been destroyed in the fire, which made the going rather treacherous. "I don't hear anything."

"I don't know, but they have to be in here. The passages must have collapsed when the house burned."

We crept our way down the wet rocky ledge, the curve of

the cave blocking the sunlight from the entrance.

"Look," I said, pointing. "Someone has a lantern."

We hurried forward as best we could, emerging into the cave proper, where the makeshift dock was slowly rotting away. Someone had set a camping lamp there, its blue-white glow illuminating the cave. Behind us was the entrance to the passageways leading into the house. Alden started into it, but stopped almost immediately.

"Blocked," he said. "As I thought."

"Then where did they go?" I asked, lifting the lamp to look around. The cave stretched back into blackness, ending with the same wall we'd seen when we first examined it. "It's empty."

"It can't be."

"But it is." I walked to the far end of the cave, and swung the lamp around to show him. "See? Nothing. Maybe the passage into the house just looks blocked."

Alden was frowning, his brows pulled together as he slowly clanked his way down to me. "Do that again."

"Do what?"

"Hold up the lantern."

I swung it up in an arc, and then turned in a full circle to illuminate the area.

Alden's eyes narrowed. "Get behind me," he whispered, leaping across the stream. At that point, it was only about a yard wide, evidently emerging from under the wall.

"What—"

I stopped when he held his finger up to his lips, gesturing for me to follow him.

With my ankle throbbing and complaining, I jumped over the stream, and trailed him when he headed for the back wall of the cave.

Only it wasn't a wall. Not a complete one, anyway. There was a narrow slit right where the back of the cave met the side wall. The opening hidden by the shadows of the cave, there was just enough room for a person to squeeze through it.

Alden went first, then stopped suddenly, blocking the opening.

I gave him a little nudge, but he didn't move. Pressing myself against him, I got him to take a step forward, giving me enough space to enter behind him.

Five men faced us, each armed with a sword.

"Crap," I said softly.

"So. You finally figured it out, did you?" Barry asked, shaking his head. He, like the other men, had pulled off his helm, and as he shifted, I saw the prone form of a woman behind him, crumpled up like a discarded bit of clothing.

"What have you done to that woman who lusted after Alden!" I demanded to know, trying to come around beside him, but he held me back. "You bastard! You killed Tamarind, didn't you!"

"Of course not," Barry said, exasperation rife in his voice. "We just knocked her on the head. She was in our way, and we don't have long to get this equipment out. She'll be fine, and when she comes to, we'll be long gone."

"The meth lab!" I said, peering over Alden's shoulder. Visible behind the group of men were several white plastic tubs, clearly packed with all sorts of drug-making paraphernalia. Included were a couple of wooden tables loaded with high-tech scales, what looked like distilling tubes encased in glass, various metal pots, beakers, and wash bottles. "Holy crap, we were right! Alden, we were right!"

"So we were." Alden hefted his sword. "Although I'm still a bit confused as to why you chose my house to serve as your drug lab."

Barry sneered. "If you think I'm going to explain anything to you, you're more stupid than I thought. Now, you have two choices: you can either turn around and walk away from this, forgetting you saw anything, and in the morning, you'll receive a nice check from the conservancy, or you and Mercy can join the cop here."

"Over my dead body," Alden said.

"Full points for dramatic elements, sweetie, but I think

the less we mention dead bodies, the happier I'll be," I whispered to him.

"You can't expect to fight us all," Barry said, laughing. "You're not that good."

"Perhaps not, but I can try," Alden said, the manly personification of everything brave if somewhat unrealistic.

"You are so sexy right now," I told him. "I can't tell you how awesome you look fending off the bad drug lords with just a shield and a sword, and I'm going to remember this moment for a long, long time. But you know, the odds aren't terribly in our favor."

He winked at me, actually winked at me. "Aren't they?"

"No, they aren't," Barry said, and, lifting his sword, was about to charge.

And that's when I realized that the dull murmuring that I'd assumed was the sound of the stream echoing around the chamber had grown louder. I recognized that sound; it was the murmuring of a crowd.

Alden gave a battle cry at that moment, shouting, "For the shire!" as he rushed forward, taking Barry and gang by surprise. At the same time, answering cries, muffled and somewhat dulled, sounded, as well as excited voices calling out questions.

"My kingdom for a bow!" I yelled, looking around desperately for something to use as a weapon as the five men all leaped on Alden.

I ended up grabbing one of the plastic tubs, and smashed it down on the head of one of the men, then used a wooden stool to beat at the back of the one who was banging Alden on the head with his shield. Bodies poured in through the narrow opening, first Vandal, then one of his students, and then three more men who weren't in armor.

"The cavalry is here!" I shouted gleefully, doing a dance of happiness before using the stool to bash Barry on the head.

"Drug enforcement, actually," one of the uniformed men said.

"Same difference, really." Now that Barry was not blocking the way, I pushed past the men to where Tamarind lay, quickly checking her for injuries. One of the uniformed guys joined me. "I think she's just been knocked out. There's blood on the back of her head, but she's breathing, and her pulse seems to be fairly OK. I've done a CPR course, if that's needed."

The cop nodded, and pulled out a radio, speaking into it to ask for medical aid. I left Tamarind in his charge, and returned to the pile of men. One of the guys was on his belly, his hands tied with zip ties, while the other three were in a pile, struggling with the police and the melee combatants.

Barry, swearing up a blue streak, was fighting with two of Vandal's students.

"Alden? Where are you, my darling? Vandal, do you see him in that pile of plate? They all jumped him."

"I'm here." Alden's voice came from beneath everyone. He sounded pained, his voice thick. "Just a bit winded. Can you get them off me?"

It took a few minutes, but in the end, there were five men lying prone, their hands shackled behind them. Alden sat on the stool I'd used to brain Barry, while Vandal and I disarmed him. There wasn't enough room for more people than were already present, so one of the Scandinavian fighters stood at the entrance and recounted everything that was going on.

"The woman is all right. She just came to," he said through the crack in the wall. A muffled cheer followed.

"The owner of the place has two black eyes, and a split lip, but now there's a woman in a dirty blue dress who's kissing his face and crying and dabbing at the split lip. I think she must be his partner."

A group "aww" could be heard.

"Girlfriend," I told the narrator.

"Fiancée," Alden said, his voice getting thicker by the minute as his nose swelled up. It was broken, and I thought briefly of trying to set it myself, but decided to wait for the medics that had been called for Tamarind.

I blinked at him. "Oh, really?"

"Yes, really," he said, trying to grin, but flinching when his hurt lip protested.

"They're engaged, evidently," the man called to the crowd through the crack.

"No, we aren't," I told him, still dabbing at Alden's lip while Vandal unhooked his chest plate.

"We are."

"You haven't asked me to marry you. Until you do that, and I accept, we aren't engaged."

Alden looked at me with his now two black eyes. "You don't think I'd marry you after everything we've been through?"

"Of course I do."

"Then you don't want to marry me." Instantly, his body language changed. He went into full awkward mode.

"Trouble in paradise," the narrator yelled. "He wants to marry her, but she doesn't want him."

The boos that met that statement were so loud, they echoed in our chamber.

"I do want to marry him," I told the guy at the wall. "But I want a proper proposal."

"My bad," he called out to the crowd. "She does want him."

Alden sighed and, with a groan, tried to go down on one knee. He ended up just kneeling in front of me, taking my hand in his. "Mercedes whatever-your-middle-name-is Starling, will you save me from being an inarticulate lump of social anxiety, and marry me?"

Love filled every last inch of me. "Yes, Emanuel Alden Ainslie, I will."

"He just proposed," the narrator yelled. "She accepted."

Another cheer could be heard.

"Now he's trying to get up. Oh, he's down, flat on his face. She's helping him up. So is Vandal. They have him on the stool, and she's kissing him. He's giving me the thumbs-up. I think it's all good."

Another cheer could be heard, this one including what I assumed were some ribald suggestions, if the laughter that followed was anything to go by.

"He's got his hand on her arse now, and she's stroking his thigh—"

I stopped kissing Alden, and glared at the man.

He grinned and turned back to the crack. "My work here is done! Let us go celebrate with ale and wenches!"

A cheer so loud it made bits of dust flake off the wall shook the entire cave.

We waited until the medics arrived to check Tamarind, and take her away, saying she'd suffered a slight concussion. Several more police arrived, but by then, we were out in the cave proper, where there was room for everyone who was tramping back and forth while they led out Barry and his cohorts, and dismantled the meth lab.

"We will want a full statement," one of the cops told us, but, after seeing Alden's face, added, "You can do that tomorrow."

"Thank you," I said, leading my tired warrior out of the cave. He was limping, his face was battered, he had numerous bruises, swellings, and a few scratches, but otherwise, he was relatively unhurt.

"Just get me home and into a hot tub," he said when I suggested driving him to the hospital. The medics had said there was nothing they could do for him, but I thought they were being a bit callous. "Then I'll be able to reciprocate."

I paused as we started up the many stairs to the top of the cliff. "Reciprocate a bath?"

"No." His cracked and split lips moved in a stiff smile. "It's my turn to use the leather cuffs on you."

"You have remarkable staying power," I told him as I slid my arm around his waist, helping him up the steps. "But I'm not sure if even you could survive the sort of attentions I want to give you tonight."

"Just you wait and see, Nancy Drew. I'll surprise you yet."

I smiled, and decided that although he probably wouldn't

be up to romping with the restraints, there was no reason I couldn't show him how much fun a bath for two could be. "You're on, my darling Ned. You are so very on."

EPILOGUE

"And this is, of course, the famed verandah of the famed Ainslie Castle, with the famed west view of the Roman dig site."

"Famous!" I said, giggling a little as Alice, Lady Ainslie, led me out of the house onto a stone verandah that was dotted with a couple of round glass tables. At one, a woman who had been introduced to me as Alden's sister-in-law Lorina sat with her stepdaughter, a charming, if talkative, girl in her late teens.

"It is, isn't it? Well, perhaps just to us." Alice sank down at one of the unoccupied tables, sighing with relief, and propping her feet up on another chair. "But the tourist numbers are increasing, thanks in part to Gunner and Lorina doing that archaeology show."

"I think I heard about that. There was some trouble about it. . . ." I tried to remember the gossip I'd seen going around at the time.

"Yes, but that's all over with. Everyone is fine and well and receiving medical treatment."

I stared at her, aghast.

She laughed. "There was an issue with one of the men being HIV positive, and he didn't know, but Lorina tells me he's doing quite well on the medications." She stretched her back, and settled into the white wrought iron chair.

I eyed her large belly. "You must be tired of hauling that baby around."

"You have no idea." She patted her stomach fondly. "Just another month to go, and then the alien life-form will be out, and I'll be able to do things like bend. And get out of a chair by myself. I won't need to call Elliott every time I want to get up."

"Where's the fun in that?" the Elliott in question said, strolling out of the building with Alden and their brother Gunner in tow. Gunner immediately went to sit with his wife and daughter, bending over the former to give her a swift kiss, and ruffling the hair of the latter. "I happen to like you needing me to do things. It makes me feel like I have a part in this whole baby process."

"Oh, you had a part," she said, poking him in the side. "But that's best not mentioned in front of others."

Alden smiled down at me, and said softly, "How are you getting on with Alice?"

"Just fine."

"Good. I told you she'd like you." He gave me an awkward pat on the shoulder. I took his hand and bit the tip of his finger, enjoying the brief look of surprise that flashed through his eyes, followed by smoldering heat.

"I never doubted she would," I said, giving him back his hand.

"Alden, I want you to see the progress we've made on the tower since you were last here. We're thinking of using it as a special honeymoon suite for visitors. . . ."

"Affluent visitors," Alice called after them. "The affluent part is important."

The men waved at us, and proceeded down the steps and off to the other side of the castle to inspect the latest renovation work.

"I'm glad to see Alden excited about rebuilding," Alice said, wiggling in her seat to get more comfortable. "Things sounded pretty dire there for a bit, what with the fire and all."

"Yes, well, they were dire. Luckily, the Hairy Tit people still wanted that north pasture despite the underhanded business that Barry was pulling, and Alden decided that selling off just a small amount of the land was better than selling it all."

"Will the money be enough to rebuild Bestwood Hall?"

"No, but Tamarind—she's the cop who fancied Alden, although he claims she didn't—she said we might be in for some reward money if the conviction for drug manufacture and trafficking sticks to Barry and Lisa."

"I don't think I understand exactly how they were related," Alice said, slipping on a pair of shades against the afternoon sun. "Was she working with him, or not?"

"Kind of both, actually, although she's not saying a word other than she was not hired by Lady Sybilla before she arrived at the hall."

"Then why did she go there? And why was she trying to seduce him if she was married?"

"I suspect it was just her way to get Alden in a position where she could blackmail him into selling the house to Barry, although who knows why she assumed Alden would be that foolish." I made a face, then grinned. "As for the other, Alden thinks you sent her."

"He does?" She looked startled. "That's odd of him."

"He's a bit confused about that whole thing."

Alice looked at me for a few seconds. "You didn't tell him, then?"

"That it was me you wanted to match up with him? No, I think that would ruin his idea of the serendipity that brought us together."

"But you didn't agree to be matched with him," she protested. "I deliberately didn't tell Alden about the Hard Day's Knights people just so he wouldn't spend time fretting about meeting the woman I'd picked out for him."

I shrugged.

"And then you insisted on taking that job with the horrible children, while Vandal found someone else for your job, and . . . oh, I suppose it doesn't matter, since you ended up with both the job and the man I had planned for you anyway."

"To be fair, I didn't know that job I took over from Janna was the same one you talked to me about. All you'd told me was that it was a unique opportunity, and that your brother-in-law desperately needed a woman just like me. I didn't figure it out until he told me his name."

"Well, you were obviously meant to be together," she said, patting her belly happily.

"I know we were, but I think I'll wait a bit before I tell Alden that you had planned for us to meet."

She snorted. "Men just don't know what's good for them."

"Amen to that."

Alden and Elliott, evidently done looking at the renovation, headed across the lush grass toward the verandah.

"Returning to the previous subject—why did Lisa show up at the house?"

"Her husband's aunt asked her there."

Alice's face scrunched up in confusion. "Her what? Who is that? Not—you're not going to tell me that Lady Sybilla was involved with the drugs!"

"Not directly, no," Alden answered, taking a chair next to me. "It was her husband who installed all the grow lights in the secret passages."

"Grow lights? Like for pot?" Alice asked, her eyes big.

"That's what the cops tell us," I answered, nodding and scooting over so I could put my hand on Alden's leg. "They figured that, by the date of them, Sir James Baskerville was running a grow operation in the seventies and eighties. Lady Sybilla maintains she knew nothing about it, but Alden thinks she's not so innocent."

"It's one reason why she didn't want to leave the house until it was destroyed," Alden said. "She was afraid we'd find the passages, and guess how her husband had funded the estate decades ago."

"So if she's not the aunt, then who is?" Alice asked.

"Her maid, Adams," Alden answered, laying his hand on mine, and squeezing my fingers. "Evidently she was hired by Sir James to help him with the plants, and she just stayed on, morphing into a companion."

"So . . ." Alice looked thoughtful. "So this Barry character, the one who was making meth under the house, he was Adams's nephew."

"Yup. That's how he learned about the passages. The best the police can guess is that they'd been making it down there for about seven or eight years," I answered, feeling about as happy as a person could feel without actually breaking into a Disney song.

"They used the cave to get the stuff out onto a waiting boat," Alden added. "It was a perfect plan—no one knew they were down there except Adams, and she got a cut of the proceeds. Lady Sybilla was in her own little world, and didn't have the slightest idea of what was going on. Adams made sure of that."

Alice tapped her fingers on the table, and frowned.

Elliott, who had been looking into the distance (Alden told me he wrote espionage books, so I assumed he was mulling our recent events over as book fodder), asked, "Why did Lisa try to kill Alden?"

Alden and I exchanged looks. "We don't know," he admitted.

"We know—we just have no proof until Lisa spills the beans," I corrected. "She wanted Alden out of the house in case he found the drug lab, and since he wasn't taking Barry up on any of the lucrative offers he forced the board of the tits to make, she took matters into her own hands. I figure at least half of the accidents Alden had were caused by her trying to scare him off. Or injure him so gravely that he'd have to sell out."

"We have no proof," Alden said gently, and rubbed his thumb over my hand.

"Perhaps not, but it's the only thing that makes sense." I sighed. "Part of the problem is that the police aren't finding much to charge Lisa with. She says she had no idea there was a meth lab beneath the house—which they moved out of the secret passage and into the cave after Alden arrived—and Barry, her husband, isn't saying she did."

"So she'll get off without any repercussions?" Alice asked.

"Possibly. I'm going to work on the cops to third-degree her and get her to admit she tried to kill Alden with the trapdoor and the loose railing outside the window."

"You're going to do no such thing," he said, lifting my hand and kissing my fingers, much to my delight. "You're going to be too busy helping me rebuild Bestwood Hall."

"Planning, surely," Elliott said.

"Not just planning. We're going to do as much of the work as possible by ourselves," I told Alice and Elliott. "To save money, because the Hairy Tit funds will only go so far. And we've already signed up for a home builders' course so we can learn how to hang Sheetrock and build joists and do roofing. Alden says he knows enough architecture stuff to do the design work, and we're going to take the elements of the old hall that we liked and incorporate them. It's going to be awesome."

"I'm sure the new Bestwood will be delightful," Elliott said, making googly eyes at Alice.

She giggled at him and blew him a kiss.

"But not as delightful as the new mistress," Alden said, waggling his eyebrows.

"Are you flirting with me, Alden? Right out here in the open, in front of your family and everything?" I teased.

"I am, I am, and I will," he said, standing up, pulling me to my feet and into his arms.

"You will what?" I asked, wiggling against him.

"That you won't find out until we get to my room. We'll be down for dinner. Maybe," he told his brother, scooping me up in his arms and marching into the house. "Don't count on it, though."

"You've turned into a brazen, brazen man," I said with a happy sigh, and kissed the side of his neck as he carried me up the stairs and into the room that had always been his. "Luckily, I like brazen. You brought the cuffs? Really? Alden! Not my feet, too! Oooh!"

We didn't make it down for dinner, but neither of us minded.

A NOTE FROM KATIE

My lovely one! I hope you enjoyed reading this book, which I handcrafted from the finest artisanal words just for you. If you are one of the folks who likes to review books, I'd love it if you posted a review for it on your favorite book spot. If you aren't a reviewing type, fear not, I will cherish you regardless.

I'd also like to encourage you to sign up for the exclusive readers' group newsletter wherein I share behind-the-scenes info about my books (and dogs, and love of dishy guys, and pretty much anything else that I think people would enjoy), sneak peeks of upcoming books, news of readers' group only contests, etc. You can join the fun by clicking on the SUBSCRIBE TO KATIE'S NEWSLETTER link on my website at

www.katiemacalister.com

ABOUT THE AUTHOR

For as long as she can remember, Katie MacAlister has loved reading. Growing up in a family where a weekly visit to the library was a given, Katie spent much of her time with her nose buried in a book.

Two years after she started writing novels, Katie sold her first romance, *Noble Intentions*. More than fifty books later, her novels have been translated into numerous languages, been recorded as audiobooks, received several awards, and have been regulars on the *New York Times, USA Today*, and *Publishers Weekly* bestseller lists. Katie lives in the Pacific Northwest with two dogs, and can often be found lurking around online.

You are welcome to join Katie's official discussion group on Facebook, as well as connect with her via Twitter, Goodreads, and Instagram. For more information, visit her website at www.katiemacalister.com

DONT MISS:

The Importance of Being Alice
A Midsummer Night's Romp
and *The Perils of Paulie,*
the other books in the Matchmaker in Wonderland
series featuring the Ainsley brothers.